KU-388-927

Blur

Blur

MICHELLE BERRY

Weidenfeld & Nicolson
LONDON

First published in Great Britain in 2002
by Weidenfeld & Nicolson

A CIP catalogue record for this book is available
from the British Library.

ISBN 0 297 60787 1

Printed in Great Britain by Clays Ltd,
St Ives plc

Weidenfeld & Nicolson

The Orion Publishing Group Ltd
Orion House
5 Upper Saint Martin's Lane
London, WC2H 9EA

As always, for Stu

Acknowledgements

For financial support, thank you to the Ontario Arts Council's Writers Reserve Program, and through them, *The New Quarterly* and Insomniac Press.

For help with research, thanks to Bruce Moran, criminalist at Sacramento County District Attorney Laboratory of Forensic Services; Professor Nicole D. Anderson, Ph.D., C. Psych; Nicholas Tabborak at Darius Films; Justice David Fairgrieve; and Clayton Ruby and Heather Pringle at Ruby & Edwardh Barristers.

I'm extremely grateful to Agnes Vago, M.D., F.R.C.P.C., pathologist.

Thank you to Michele Hutchison at Weidenfeld & Nicolson for her wonderfully thoughtful and precise editing, and for answering e-mail queries so quickly. Special thanks to Sarah Davies at Random House Canada for her excellent and insightful editing (again!), strong friendship, and lovely lunch dates. And much gratitude to Christine Kidney in the U.K. Thanks also to Bernice Eisenstein, my copyeditor, and to Pamela Murray and Scott Sellers at Random House Canada.

My agents, Hilary McMahon and Nicole Winstanley, thank you. Such hard work and such enthusiasm for books is hard to find.

Thanks to all my friends who have been supportive, each in their own way, especially Shawna Destin, Barb Tyler and Allison Sekuler.

And, of course, all the love in the world to my family: Stu, Dad, Mom, Dave (my first editors), Abby and Zoe (my best creations).

Part One

In her bedroom there is an eight-by-ten photo in an antique silver frame. In it she is sitting on the front porch of her house, her long legs touching at the knees, her feet angled in, toes together. She is barefoot. She is wearing a blue summer sundress and her shoulders are tanned and naked. Her long hair is ringed around her head, lit up in the sunshine. A halo. She is looking directly towards the camera, holding her head in slender hands, her bony elbows resting on white knees. Awkward and thin, but with a type of gangly beauty that radiates. The stairs below her are dirty white, in need of a coat of paint, chipped and weathered. There are two huge, ornate pillars holding up the front porch roof. She is sitting smack dab in the middle, precisely between both pillars. She is laughing, her mouth open wide, her lips stretched tight across white, straight teeth. She is seventeen years old.

Chapter One

He has spent the last seven years looking for the big scoop.

Seven years of sitting by his phone waiting for it to ring, biding time, writing articles for *Entertainment Magazine*, meeting with has-been movie stars in cheap hotels and trying to make it sound complicated. Seven years. Nothing interesting, nothing hot, nothing so different it would knock his socks off. Just the same old. Just lame movies and silly TV sitcoms, porn queens and rock stars, who's dating who, who's leaving who, who's on drugs and who isn't, whose breasts are real.

When Bruce quit his job at Realty Plus, quit selling houses and condos and country retreats and the occasional mansion to the stars, when he quit to pursue journalism, hoping to have more time for himself, more money, more independence, more of everything life had to offer, he couldn't have known how godawful boring the job would be. He thought by now he would be somewhat famous. He thought that he, Bruce Dermott, would be sitting in a sunken hot tub in the living room of his own mansion, sipping cognac and smoking cigars. He'd be looking at the plaques lining his walls, awards for his fine writing style, his honed investigative ability. That's all he wanted, really, a little appreciation for his hard work. Some money. Some fame. He wanted to be noticed on the street, maybe, questioned on CNN, an expert journalist, because, although every day he's getting older, he certainly still has the hair for publicity.

Instead, it's been seven years of quietly typing. Seven years in his two-storey townhouse, sitting at his desk in his small office next to the kitchen which connects to the dining room which meets with his bathroom — no hot tub, no sunken living room — often dreaming of the thrill of closing a housing deal, the thrill of showing a young couple around a mid-sized condo. He dreams of the pleasure he used to get taking his shoes off at the front door and wading through plush carpet around a skylit, balconied, many-windowed mansion. Sometimes, if he was lucky, he showed clients a movie star's house — Freddie Valentine's ranch, Susanna Hurster's condo. He dreams of sitting on a treed terrace while prospective buyers roam the house, flushing toilets, looking in closets, measuring space. But Bruce made a choice and he has to stick with it. The wrong choice, maybe. He didn't realize the drain, the loneliness, the sheer pain of sitting on his ass for days on end waiting for his editor to call, waiting for the next story to unfold around him. He didn't believe the other journalists when they told him how crappy the money was and he didn't realize how much the support payments to his kids would damage his bank account. He's never met anyone who knows his byline and he's certainly never seen anyone reading his articles. The occasional person holding an *Entertainment Magazine* is always scanning the pictures, never reading the words. Lined up at the grocery store, staring at the front page. And, although Bruce's choice seemed obvious seven years ago, seemed to be the right thing to do to put his life back on track, now he's pretty sure he should have stayed where he was. Toed the line. Settled in comfortably. But Realty Plus isn't taking anyone back — he checked last week, walking in off the street, pretending he was just coming in to say hello — and now he has another deadline to meet. He has an interview to write about the teen pop-group sensation, Trash.

What Bruce wants to know is how these underage, blond boys could rise up to be so famous with only one CD out, only one dance song, only one hip-gyrating video. How he can work half his life away and get nowhere and some blond boys can lip-synch a song they didn't even write and make millions. Bruce often wonders why anything is worth the time and effort any more. He often wonders why life is worth living. It's not as if he's ever thought of doing himself in, he wouldn't even know where to begin, but he does sometimes notice when he steps on the ants littering his sidewalk and he equates them with his measly existence. One small bug, what difference does it make? When he had the children living with him he felt there was a reason for being, he was a father, a husband, but now there is no one and the kids are probably better off without him.

Bruce swallows a large, flat gulp of cream soda, warm now, which has been sitting by his computer for over two hours. He looks at the empty screen, the flashing cursor. He looks at the blank phone. Bruce pulls up the file with the transcript of the interview he did and he scans the lines searching for anything that is intelligible, anything interesting.

Bruce runs his fingers through his thick hair and stares down at his phone. He has two lines, call-waiting, an answering service, but not a single voice to pull him away from what he is doing. Except for the nattering presence of his editor threatening him, the phone hasn't rung for days.

Bruce knows that if he doesn't finish this article by the evening, he might as well say goodbye to his paycheque, what little bit of it he actually sees. His editor has given him one last deadline, has extended it twice already, and Bruce knows that this is it. This was Will's final warning.

Seven years looking for a big news story, something so crazy it would knock out all the newspapers in the world. That was his goal. Something that would put his name up there in lights, show all the magazine publishers who he really is. Show his ex-wife and kids, prove something to himself. Because Bruce wanted to make himself believe that he could easily be part of something bigger in life, that he could wallow in wealth and fame just like the next guy in L.A. Sure, he should have chosen acting, but he's met one too many would-be actors serving him Greek salads in the local restaurants around here. He's never met a would-be entertainment reporter. But that should have told him something about the profession.

He'd love a story like that one — what was it? — that famous actress who disappeared after they found a body in her pool. Ten years ago. That's what he'd really like. He would have been rich. Rolling in money. He would have found a fancy angle and sucked the world into the story. He is sure he would have sold book rights, film rights, made television deals.

Bruce types, "Tingly and tantalizing, Trash takes teenagers by storm." Then he deletes it and walks to the kitchen where he opens another can of cream soda, sips it, and puts it beside the first can on his desk. He looks at the phone again. He burps. He picks up the receiver and listens to the dial tone. He places it back in its cradle. Bruce runs his fingers through his hair again and he looks at the palm of his hand to check for dandruff, to check for hair falling out. Bruce likes to pretend he's able to manage the signs of aging.

Once you hit forty, Bruce muses, you tend to fall apart. Bruce is forty-two years old now and his body is giving him more problems than he would expect. At least he still has his hair, Bruce thinks, and he touches his head over and over as if reassuring himself. Will told him once that the more he touched his hair, the more his hair would fall out. Nervously, Bruce looks again at his hands.

It is times like this, with the overwhelming feelings of inadequacy, with the rising hatred of what he is doing in life pounding down on his brain, with deadlines he's supposed to meet and nothing tangible to distract him, that he misses his wife and kids the most. Not the marriage, but the activity of marriage, of being a father. He misses having errands to run, someone to pick up at school, someone to drive to dance lessons or guitar or piano. He misses his wife's voice on the phone from her office telling him that the Smiths are coming for dinner, that he has to pick up chicken at the grocery store, that Amy needs a new pair of ballet slippers. He misses the busyness of a life fully lived, the mind-numbing responsibility of taking care of others.

Ten years ago his wife and kids moved up to Canada with a man named Michael, an archaeologist who, twice a year, packs them up and takes them to Jerusalem and Mexico. Now the kids phone him only on his birthday and Christmas Eve and Bruce can hear his thirteen-year-old daughter Amy and his sixteen-year-old son Tyler in the background whispering, "Do I have to talk to him?" His ex-wife Shelley has a new look, all perfumed and stiff, her hair dyed red, styled so the wind can't muss it, false eyelashes, and freckles that Bruce can't remember ever having seen before. He thinks of the times he would lean up on his elbow at night and study her sleeping face, he would look at her every crease and wrinkle, her every line, and now, for the life of him, he can't remember that she had freckles. At the end of their marriage, when the days were a series of missed connections, incomplete eye contact, tight mouths and necks and chins, he would lie there and stare and then stare at the ceiling dreaming of something better, something that made life worth living. Because no matter how much money he made at Realty Plus then, Bruce knew that the thrill Michael had finding old bones communicated to Shelley the thrill of life.

And Bruce had no thrill, no nothing.

Hence his stupid decision, three years after she left, to become an entertainment reporter, to apply for and receive a job at *Entertainment Magazine,* hoping his byline would become a household name. And what did that amount to? Nothing. Did Shelley care? No.

It must be the bright Canadian sunlight that is giving Shelley freckles. Or the fresh, unpolluted air.

Bruce sighs. He scratches his crotch. He looks out the

window. The day is brilliant and cool. The humidity is at a low and the pollution, for once, seems to be hovering somewhere else. The windows are closed and he has his air conditioning on out of habit. Bruce sees his neighbour two doors down get into his car and drive off, sunroof open, radio loud enough to blast through his walls, his closed windows. He sees a woman walk past the townhouse with her poodle and the poodle stops to piss on Bruce's lawn. A palm tree waves in the breeze. A garbage truck stops at the corner, the brakes squealing.

Bruce leans on the windowsill. He presses his face against the glass. He sits down again at his desk and writes, "Trash is trash is trash is trash." Then he deletes this too and turns off the computer. He sips at his cream soda.

Often, when everything is crashing into place, when Shelley and the kids come haunting, when he knows that Will is going to call and demand some sort of instantaneous magic from his computer, Bruce leaves the house. He walks away from the inevitable. And he knows that this time, while Will screeches into the phone (as he always does, a little huffing and puffing), Bruce will not have a reason or a convincing argument to give Will, to force this man, the editor of *Entertainment Magazine*, to keep Bruce on the payroll. There is nothing he can do. Bruce can see his future looming over him. It's not on the horizon any more. It's right in front of him. Unemployed, single man. Child support payments.

Shit.

So Bruce pulls on his running shoes at the front door, checks his hair in the mirror over the hall table, takes his keys off the hook, fingers his wallet in the back pocket of his shorts, and leaves the house. A nice walk to the new office-supply store. It opened recently about four miles away. He's been getting flyers in his mailbox all month: "Computer Sales Galore," "Fax Machines 50% off." He decides to pick up some toner for his printer, a package of tapes for his tape recorder. He's running low on things that convince him he runs a business, things that make him think he's really a journalist, that he has something worthwhile to do — paper clips, sticky notepads, red pens. Even though he thinks his career will be over in a matter of hours, Bruce feels compelled to buy things that make him feel good. Besides, he could use the exercise.

Bruce tries to bounce down the front stairs, he tries to feel purposeful, but he hasn't got it in him. Even the thought of the new office-supply store that he's never been in, the thought of the bright fluorescent lights and new computers, the rows full of binders and briefcases, doesn't interest him. Instead, probably because he knows full well he may be fired in an hour or so, Bruce drags his feet and heads down the block squinting in the sunlight, struggling in all his pockets to find his sunglasses, and hoping like hell he doesn't have to go back to the house to get them.

Chapter Two

The maid is running down the long front driveway, her hands waving in the air, her apron snapping against her thick legs. She is running towards the car, she is limping slightly, and she is calling out. The plainclothes police in the car cannot hear her words. They see her mouth moving, the strain on her face as her lips open and close. Their car slows down on the long driveway and the driver opens his window.

"Calm down," he says. "We got your call. Just calm down and tell me what happened."

The woman stops suddenly and leans on the hood of the car. "Oh my God," she says, panting, "you wouldn't believe."

The driver starts to get out of the car but ducks back in when the woman looks angrily at him. "Go now," she says. "Don't get out. Go to the house." She points up to the large mansion. "He's up there. Go. He's in the pool." She waves her hands.

"Is anyone else there? Where's Emma Fine?"

"No," the maid pants. "No. He's all alone. I don't know where she is."

The driver says something to his partner. He radioes the station and requests backup. The car moves up the driveway, pulling around a pickup truck, a blue tarp covering the contents in the back, towards the huge house. The police leave the woman standing alone, her arms hanging by her side, her chest rising and falling.

"Nice day," Martin says to Joe as they walk around the pool, looking down into the waters.

The police officers, Frank and Gerry, and the plainclothes

detectives, Martin and Joe, are inspecting the scene at Emma Fine's house.

"It's beach weather," says Martin.

Frank radioes the deputy coroner.

"I think it's supposed to rain tonight."

"Doesn't look like rain."

Martin looks up at the clouds and then looks down at the pool. He can see the clouds reflected in the rippling water. "Poor guy," he says.

Joe says, "It's way too nice out to die."

"The weather has nothing to do with it," Gerry calls over from where he's leaning on the gate around the pool and looking up at the huge house. "Even a tornado wouldn't make it a great day to die."

Frank says, "The coroner is coming. Who else is in the house?"

"Just the maid," Gerry says. "And she's still out on the driveway. I can see her from here. She's sitting down. I think she may be in shock."

"I'll go talk to her," Joe says. "I speak a little Spanish."

"I don't think she's Spanish. She looks Greek."

"How would you know?" Frank asks. "She spoke English to me, that's all that matters. I'm half Italian, but do you think I speak a word of it?"

"Go ask her what happened."

"I can say *cappuccino*. I can say *buon giorno*. I can say *mamma mia*."

Joe walks away from the others. He leaves the side of the pool and closes the gate behind him.

Gerry says, "Shit, we shouldn't have touched the gate. We all touched it when we came in and then Joe just did it again."

Frank says, "I just saw him floating in the pool and I opened the gate quickly and came in. I wasn't thinking."

"It's such a nice day," Martin says. "It's hard to think

when it's such a nice day."

"We should call forensics," Gerry says. "See if there are any prints. Dust."

"It's a suicide."

"How the hell do you know? And, besides, it doesn't matter. Forensics will still want to look at this."

Martin radioes the police department. "Forensics will be here soon," he says. "I bet they'll be here before the coroner. The coroner is just about as slow as an ambulance."

"What is it with ambulances?"

Gerry nods. "My wife's best friend had a heart attack a couple months ago and the ambulance didn't come. Her husband drove her to the hospital. Then, the next day, the ambulance showed up at her house. The next day." He shakes his head.

"What happened?" Frank asks.

"Her husband told them they were too late."

"She died?"

"No, she's okay. She's recovering."

The men stare down at the pool. They are mesmerized by the reflection of the house in the blue liquid. The breeze picks up and ruffles the water.

"You think it was a suicide?" Gerry asks.

"Yeah," Frank says. "Drugs or something. An overdose."

"Why would you say that?"

"Look at the house. It's huge. Anyone with a house this big must be into drugs. Her friends are into drugs. Her friends do a little too many drugs. You've seen it before, Gerry. This happens all the time in Hollywood. People go overboard." He laughs. "Literally." He points to the body. "Splash."

"Cut and dry," Gerry says.

The men look at the pool and then at the mansion before them. The entire back of the house, looking out at the pool, consists of glass windows, three storeys of glass windows. The property around the house is expansive. There are fences and gates and hedges blocking anyone from looking in. The pool is large and deep and clean and blue and surrounded by matching lounge chairs and umbrellas. Nothing is out of place. Everything is well taken care of.

"It could be a hit," Martin says.

"Mafia?" Frank laughs. "A hit?"

"You could say that."

"I'm Italian," Frank says. "There's no way this is a hit. I'd say it has something to do with drugs. Jilted lover. Suicide. You can smell it."

"Emma Fine's house," Gerry says quietly. "I saw her on 'Entertainment Tonight' a couple of months ago. She was interviewed by the pool here. You could see all the windows of the house and the umbrellas and lounge chairs." Gerry itches his neck. He shrugs. "My wife watches the program. If you ask me, it's all pretty stupid, but my wife likes to watch it."

Martin looks around. He is standing in the backyard of Emma Fine's house. Standing by her pool. He looks down at the dead body and then up again. "Do you think we'll get to meet her?" He swivels his head as if he expects to see her standing directly beside him.

"Emma Fine, Jesus Christ." Frank smiles. "Marty's got a hard-on," he says, laughing.

Joe is with Maria Candalas, the maid, out in front of the house. They are standing under a tree in the shade. Maria is nervously shaking her head back and forth. She is a small, thick, older woman with black hair and big brown eyes. Joe notices that her ankles are swollen. Her feet look as if they have been squeezed into shoes that are too small. Joe thinks this may explain the awkward limping as she ran down the driveway. Maria is wearing a black uniform and a white apron. The apron is slightly damp, as if she were just drying her hands on it when she caught sight of the body in the pool. Joe towers over her. He is holding a notepad and a pencil, the nib of which keeps breaking. He is scratching things down in his notepad with the blunt pencil. Maria is talking fast, moving her arms about, waving them in the air. Joe looks towards the cars and wonders if he has another pencil in the glove compartment.

"I came in early to do laundry. Mother of God, there was a lot of laundry. Last night she was throwing things around her room, getting things dirty. Towels from washing her hair. You know. She couldn't decide what to wear to the party. And then I was in the kitchen doing the dishes. Everything dried on. From two nights ago. You'd think she'd at least soak overnight. You'd think she'd listen to me once in a while. I say, 'Soak them, soak them. It makes my work easier,' but she never listens. She just leaves them on the counter. Everything dried on. Like a crust, you know. Like picking at a scab trying to get it off. Look at my hands. You see these hands? Too much soaking in hot water. That's the problem. Look."

Joe notes her Spanish accent in his little book. He doesn't know why he writes it down. He just does.

Her hands go down to her sides. "And then I heard a noise. A loud noise. I jumped."

"What kind of noise?"

"A loud one."

"A bang? A smash? Glass breaking? A gun firing?"

"A noise." Maria looks angry. "Just a noise. I don't know. What do you think I am? You think I'm a big Hollywood writer? You think I can describe a sound like that? You're like my doctor, my God. My doctor, he says to me, 'Tell me where it hurts, Mrs. Candalas,' and I say, 'Here,' and he says, 'And what does it feel like? Like a knife? Like a dull pain? Like a twisting pain?' and I say, 'It hurts here. That's all. It just hurts.' What am I? A book?"

Joe writes "Talks a lot" in his notepad. He chews on the

end of the pencil, waiting for her to say something more. She looks up at him. She squints in the sun.

"And then what happened?"

"I looked out the window."

"Does the window face the pool?"

"All the windows face the pool. Didn't you go back there? Didn't you see the whole house is windows? What are you, an idiot?"

Joe writes, "All the windows face the pool."

"Go on," he says.

"I looked out and saw someone running across the grass."

"You saw someone?" Joe perks up.

"Yes, but not clearly."

"Was it a man or a woman?"

"I couldn't tell."

"Tall? Short?"

"I couldn't see."

"Black? White? Asian?"

"I couldn't see."

"You couldn't see?"

"The person was so far away and running. I couldn't see. I have eye problems." Maria points to her eyes and Joe bends a bit to look at them. Large, brown, the pupils are jet black and large. "I have no vision. I can't see."

"What?" Joe straightens.

"I'm partially blind, I think. Just a little bit. I'm waiting to see someone. To see an eye doctor. Ms. Fine wants me to wear glasses but I think I'm blind. I think it has nothing to do with glasses. I think that the sun is making me blind. It's a curse." She raises her hand, fist closed tightly, at the sun.

"What about the running person?" Joe asks. "Did you notice anything else?"

"I only looked for a minute. I thought it was one of the pool cleaners. I thought for a minute that it could have been a dog."

"A dog?"

"Sometimes dogs get on the property and the pool cleaners chase them off. Sometimes they squeeze through the hedge."

Joe sighs. "And Ms. Fine?"

Maria looks around. "Ms. Fine? Where?"

"The owner of the house. Where is she?"

"She doesn't have any dogs," Maria says.

"Yes, but where is she?"

"She's gone out for the day, I guess. I don't know where she is. There was no note. She doesn't tell us."

"When did she go out? Who is 'us'?"

"The pool cleaners," Maria says. "Who else do you think? Oh, and there's the driver. He lives above the garage." She points. "And the house cleaners come on Thursdays. What day is it?"

Joe scratches his head. "Where is the driver then?"

"I don't know," Maria says. "What do you think I do here? Keep track of everyone coming and going? I have things to do. I run around cleaning up after everyone, keeping things in order, cooking meals, doing laundry and dishes. I have no time to check up on everyone's whereabouts. My feet are so swollen I can't move half the time. I'm the maid for the house. Not a babysitter."

Joe and Maria look at each other.

"About the body in the pool," Joe says.

"I thought it was a towel."

"A towel?"

"Yes, sometimes there are towels floating in the pool. Sometimes after big parties the whole pool is filled with different coloured towels. You should see it. What a mess. And I say, 'You know it'll plug up the filters, Ms. Fine,' but she just laughs. She laughs because she has money and one broken pool filter doesn't bother her at all."

"So what did you do after you heard the noise and saw the person running?"

"I think I thought it was a dog," Maria says.

"With a pool cleaner chasing it?"

Maria looks confused. "No, just a dog. There was only one thing running across the grass. What are you talking about?"

"Let's start again," Joe says. "Let's start from the beginning. You were in the kitchen and you heard a noise. You looked out the window."

"I might have looked out the window before I heard the noise."

"Why would you look out the window if it wasn't for the noise startling you?"

"The noise didn't startle me. I always look out the windows. The whole house is windows. I told you that already. You can't help but look out the windows. Sometimes a bird hits the window and falls down stunned. The dogs come to eat the birds, I think, or to carry them away. That's what the dogs are doing there."

"I didn't think dogs ate birds," Joe says, more to himself than to Maria.

"I don't know," Maria says. "Dogs are a mystery to me. My husband's family has a dog and he's always sleeping with his feet in the air. You should see it. Back to the floor, feet stretched high in the air."

"So you looked out the window, with or without the noise."

"Yes."

"And you saw something running across the grass. Where did that thing go?"

"What thing?"

"The thing you saw running?"

"Oh, the person."

"You said it might have been a dog."

"A dog couldn't kill a man, could it? Don't be silly." Maria laughs. "What do they teach you in police school?"

Joe rubs his temples with his hands. The pencil scratches

on his face and leaves a mark. "Where did the person go?"

"Into the bushes."

"Is there a way out through the bushes?"

"There must be," Maria says. "The dogs get in."

Joe nods. He writes all this down.

"And then what did you do?"

"I dried my hands on my apron," Maria says. "I couldn't find a clean dishtowel."

"Is that when you noticed the body in the pool?"

"Not for a while. I mostly dried my hands and looked out the window towards the bushes where the person disappeared. I was a little nervous because I couldn't see well and because I was all alone."

Joe nods. "But you said you didn't know if anyone else was home. How did you know you were alone?"

"What are you saying?" Maria asks. "I said Ms. Fine was out. She didn't come down for breakfast and she wasn't in her bedroom, the pool cleaners weren't there yet, the house cleaners come on Thursday, and today isn't Thursday, is it? And the driver was out too."

"But you said —"

"I think he was out. I didn't see him for breakfast. He always eats breakfast at the same time. Come to think of it" — Maria puts her hand up to her mouth — "I think he has a girlfriend. I think he stays there overnight. But I don't live here. I don't know what happens when I'm not around."

"Go on," Joe says.

"Well, then I turned towards the pool because I caught something out of the corner of my eye. I thought it was a towel in the pool. But I told you that."

"Were the pool cleaners scheduled for today?"

"They come every day," Maria says. "They'll come this afternoon, I think."

Joe writes this down. His pencil breaks again. He fishes around in his pockets looking for another pencil. A car pulls up in the driveway. Maria and Joe turn and look at it.

"She likes a clean pool," Maria says as she looks at the car. "She likes a very clean pool. There's no crime in cleanliness."

"Is that the driver?" Joe asks, pointing to the car in the driveway.

"No. Dan drives Ms. Fine's convertible when he goes off on his own. She lets him."

"Dan," Joe says. "Does he have a last name?"

Maria shrugs. "Plubbs? Pluggs? I can never hear him correctly. I think my hearing is going too. Probably the weather. The sun. The wind. Everything hurts my eyes and ears. The doctor says nothing is wrong but you can't trust that man. He's too young. Just a boy, really."

A man gets out of the car and moves closer to Joe and Maria. "Forensics," he says. He waves his badge in the air.

"It's about time you got here. The body's out back," Joe says. "In the pool."

The man shuffles around the side of the house as if he is wearing slippers. His feet rarely leave the ground. He opens the gate carefully with latex-gloved fingers and he closes the gate behind him. He joins the other men by the side of the pool.

In front of the house Maria says, "So then I saw the towel in the pool and I went out to look more closely at it."

"Yes? How long after hearing the noise was that?"

"About an hour. Maybe more."

"You waited that long to check the situation out?"

"I didn't know it was a situation. I had laundry to do. Dishes to wash. I won't tell you how to do your job, so don't you tell me how to do mine."

Joe looks up at the sky.

"And it wasn't a towel." Maria pauses. "But you know that."

"So what did you do?"

"I called the police."

"You didn't touch the body?"

"Should I have touched the body?"

"No, it's just — didn't you want to know if the person was still alive?"

"He wasn't alive."

"How did you know?"

"I could tell."

"What if he were drunk?"

"Ted Weaver never drank."

"Ted Weaver?"

"The man in the pool."

"So you know the man in the pool?"

"I knew him," Maria says. "He's dead now." She crosses herself and looks up to the sky.

"Who was he?"

"A friend of Ms. Fine's." Maria stresses the word "friend." She rolls it off her tongue.

"A good friend?"

"Yes, you could say that. You should ask her, though, sometimes she hated him."

Joe looks at Maria. She stares back icily.

"And this Ted Weaver? He never drank?" Joe finds this hard to believe. He's a man who likes his beer after work, his Scotch and soda on the weekends or before bed.

"Never."

"What if he just fell into the pool?"

"What if? Maybe he did. He was dead. He is dead. Can't you see that for yourself?"

"But why didn't you try to pull him out?"

Maria sighs. "I've watched enough TV," she says. "I know that you shouldn't touch any evidence."

"Evidence? You think this was foul play?"

"What do you think? A running person, a noise, a dead man in a pool. It was foul play. Besides," she adds quietly, "when you saw him you didn't try to pull him out of the pool, did you? You left him there."

Joe has to admit that it all sounds suspicious. However, he's been at too many places where rich people take too many drugs and fall into pools or off balconies or drown in bathtubs. Where they are depressed because of their riches or because of their fame, something Joe can't even fathom, and they do themselves in. Just because Ted Weaver didn't drink it doesn't mean he didn't do drugs. It doesn't mean he wasn't sad about something. He's seen all of this before. Still, the fact that someone was running off through the bushes, that tells him something.

"You said you were alone in the house, didn't you?"

"Mr. Weaver had left."

"So he was there with you? Before he died?"

"Yes, he was with me," Maria answers, "until he was dead in the pool."

"I thought —"

"What did you think? That it was someone I didn't know in the pool? If it was someone I didn't know, would I be so upset?"

"Where was Mr. Weaver going? What kind of a mood was he in? Was he with Ms. Fine?"

"No, I told you. Ms. Fine must have gone out early. I didn't even hear her leave."

"Do you think she stayed out all night? Where was she last night?"

"At some party. A cast closing party. Mr. Weaver stayed here, I think. He said he was going to stay here. She wouldn't have stayed out all night if he was here."

"And Mr. Weaver? What was he doing in the morning?"

"He was eating breakfast when I came in. Messing up more dishes. He used every pot in the house to make oatmeal. Every pot that wasn't already dirty from before. He was making oatmeal with brown sugar and maple syrup. He said they were going camping. Up to the hills. His truck was all packed and he said he was picking her up at the studio."

"So you knew she was at the studio?"

"I didn't know anything. I just did the laundry and listened."

"And then he left?"

"And then he left."

"And then what?"

"And then I heard the noise."

Joe sighs. "Did he say anything to you before he left?"

Maria thinks. "He told me to have a nice weekend. He was excited about going camping." She sniffs a bit and rubs at her eyes. "Oh, he's dead now. I didn't like him much but he didn't need to die."

"He was happy, then?" Joe says. He writes everything in his notepad but he can barely read the writing because the pencil is completely broken. Chicken scratches dent his page.

"Wouldn't you be? It's such a fine day. A nice day to go camping."

Joe excuses himself from Maria.

"Don't go anywhere. You'll have to answer more questions later," he says.

Maria nods.

Joe walks back to the pool.

Maria stands in the driveway with her arms crossed in front of her chest. She looks up at the sun, her eyes open wide. Then she closes her eyes and watches the sunspots dance behind her lids.

Chapter Three

Bruce is walking with his head down, his hands moving in his shorts pockets, his shirt pockets, searching for his sunglasses, walking down the street to Business World, trying to remember which direction to turn, trying to imagine what it would be like to be someone else, when he glances up for an instant, looks across the street into the glare of sunshine, and suddenly sees her. And even though the sun is blinding, he is sure it is her.

Emma Fine.

"Jesus," Bruce breathes out. He stops fumbling around and stands completely still. Slowly he begins to notice the street signs, the neighbourhood around him, the recent developments, stores, and restaurants. It's like he walked into a new world. Bruce thinks he should have checked out this side of Pasadena years ago.

Emma Fine. She's aged considerably in ten years but Bruce is absolutely certain that it is her. He catches the tilt of her head, the fullness of her lips, the swollen breasts, the way she carries herself. All echoes of the past.

Life throws curveballs at you sometimes, Bruce thinks. One minute you're dragging your feet down the street, blinded by the sun, feeling lost and hopeless and pissed upon, feeling that life is unfair, but preparing yourself because you're going to get fired from your job, and the next moment you see her standing in a store doorway, your big scoop, dressed all in black, one hand on her hip, the other hand clutching a shopping bag. You see her bend just a little to shut the door handle because she's so damn tall and you decide quickly to follow her as she disappears down the street.

Bruce picks up his pace, racing to get nearer to her as she turns corner after corner after corner. Suddenly it seems as if all of Pasadena is one big corner. Bruce is out of breath. He can't get his bearings straight. His heart is beating wildly. He wonders if she always walks this fast or if he is just out of shape and then he thinks that he really should check into his health club membership and see if it has expired. He has to start working out again, taking care of himself.

How old is she now? Bruce thinks that she was somewhere in her late thirties when everything happened. The newspapers called it a scandal. Now that was something. At the peak of her career and the cops find a dead man in her pool. Then the disappearances and the DA taking Emma Fine to court and losing because of faulty evidence and weak witnesses. If only he'd been a reporter back then.

Emma Fine's mansion. Bruce was one of the realtors who went through with the rest of the riff-raff when it was on the market. Everybody pretending to be someone else so they could get a peek at how she lived before she fell out of grace. Emma Fine. At the top of her career she disappeared. She lost everything. Bruce remembers the windows covering the back of the house, the huge pool, empty of water, police tape strewn on the fence surrounding it, the star's bedroom, cleared of furniture, of any evidence of a crime. Bruce wanted to live like her. He wanted to have what she had before she lost everything. He thinks that may have been when he decided to change his career. That might have been just around the time he applied for journalism school at the college. Just after Shelley took off. Three years of night school and, blammo, he was a bona fide journalist.

Whoopee.

Ten years ago. Bruce remembers her story broke when he was slowly realizing that something was happening between

Shelley and Michael, their affair still just lingering outside his vision. His kids were so small and fragile then. And then Shelley left him and Emma Fine disappeared. Bruce roamed through Emma Fine's mansion, sock-footed on the plush, white carpet, imagining what her movie-star life must have been like, wanting to do something else with his life. He remembers reading the newspaper each morning, checking to see if the police had found her yet. At first she disappeared for a couple of days and then resurfaced to an army of flash-bulbs and investigators. A dead body in her pool. A married lover. And then, after firing her staff and staying hidden within the house, after the absurdly quick trial, she disappeared again for good.

Bruce remembers that the wife of the murdered man was involved somehow but she was never found. And there was something about the chauffeur but Bruce can't remember exactly what it was. The maid created a stir on the stand, if he recalls correctly, but Bruce doesn't know what she said.

He's digging in his brain for the answers. Movie-star sighting, he thinks mechanically.

Story.

Emma Fine is in her late forties now. He watches her body move up the street from him and he thinks that, despite aging, she has held up very well. But then he thinks that forty-something isn't really old any more. It's quite young, actually.

Bruce jogs some more to catch up. It's like following a horse. Her legs are so long. She hasn't noticed him yet. He's so out of shape he's surprised she can't hear him panting.

Her teeth. He remembers her wonderful teeth. She had a toothy grin and he wonders if she still has it. He remembers her body then, the large breasts, the slender waist, and flat belly. You see one movie with her in it and you'll never forget her body, Bruce thinks. There was something so different about her body, it was unreal. No one had bodies like that then. Now they are everywhere. Plastic surgery. Adding on, taking off. Shelley's body was warm, real, lying beside him in bed, often turned from him that summer she started to see Michael, who was down in Pasadena researching unidentified bones someone found in the valley.

It was Bruce's fault she met Michael. He was searching for a place to rent and they hit it off immediately. Michael came over for dinner almost every night and Bruce would drink with him, beers and then Scotches, and watch the kids run through the sprinkler. Shelley would drift in and out of the kitchen like a ghost. She began to move farther and farther away from Bruce in bed. She distanced herself from him, from the kids, from life in general. And Michael stopped coming around as often, caught up in work, he said, too busy, he said, old bones to be discovered, dusted off, cared for.

It was easy to see why she fell in love with him. A big man. A quiet man. A man with old bones on his mind.

It was the end of that summer, when Shelley was packing their bags into Michael's car and Bruce was hiding behind the shutters in the townhouse they had just purchased — unshaven, hungover, angry at himself for yelling at Shelley in front of the kids the night before, hiding there watching his family leave him — it was that day that he heard on the radio Emma Fine had cancelled the contract on her latest movie. Bruce remembers she paid the advance back to the studio and just disappeared. No one knew where she went. The police looked for her. What friends and colleagues she had left looked for her. Turned out she was financially bankrupt and her West Hollywood home went into receivership. It was sold to a computer tycoon. Bruce read the papers every day searching for her face, for a glimpse of her exquisite body. He searched for her in print but she never turned up and was soon forgotten, another casualty of Hollywood. But Bruce never forgot her. Not for years. For a time she was as important to him as Shelley. He spent countless days reading the paper and watching her movies, searching, drinking, as if her tragedy contained all his sadness. Because her tragedy *did* contain his sadness. In one fell swoop, both his life and Emma Fine's life collapsed.

Now he is following her down the block, his head aching from the sun in his eyes. And he is sure it is her. It has to be her. But what is she doing here in Pasadena? Shopping for bread and vegetables? Bruce can see carrot tops sticking out of the bag, a loaf of French bread. She is dressed in clothes that are shabby and ill-fitting. Black clothes, all black. Head to toe. Like an Italian widow. But even with these clothes, with the ten years on her face, on her body, Bruce still thinks she looks fantastic. Her bearing is almost majestic as she moves down the street, her head held high. Bruce notices that her shoes don't fit. They are a couple of sizes too big and she shuffles a little to keep them attached to her feet.

Bruce wants to call out. He wants to shout, "Stop, I know you," but he knows he will scare her, she will run. She's been hiding somewhere for ten years. She doesn't want to be caught. Bruce watches. She ducks into a store on the corner, a flower store, and Bruce idles outside, waiting. He lights a cigarette and doesn't take his eyes off the store entrance.

Bruce bounces his leg up and down quickly, nervously, and he thinks, *This is what I've been waiting for.* And the thought makes him suddenly feel sick to his stomach. So plain and direct and easy. Years of waiting for something like this to fall into his lap and then, at the end of his rope, when there doesn't seem to be any more answers, it does. Bruce couldn't have written this better if he were a screenwriter. He will write a story about Emma Fine. No, *the* story about Emma Fine. The knockout story. This will be it, he thinks. His big scoop happens to be exactly what he wanted it to be. With the addition of ten years of mystery.

Bruce throws his cigarette down and thinks of how he will have to do research, look into what really happened. Police reports, eyewitness accounts, trial data, psychiatrist notes — that whole messy summer will have to be dragged through the mud before he can sit down to write about her. He will have to know the story inside and out before he can even interview her. Because, once approached, she might bolt, she might disappear again as quickly as she resurfaced. A tall woman in black clothing appearing out of a store, distancing herself from him as she shuffles down the street.

Bruce will follow her to wherever it is she is staying, and then he will slowly work his way into her life, into talking to her, getting to know her, getting her to trust him. This will take time. Bruce looks at his watch. He hopes she has time. He hopes she isn't just jetting through California on her way back to Paris or Barbados (or even Italy, judging from the widow attire), to wherever it is she lives now, in obscurity.

She comes out of the flower store carrying a sad bouquet of carnations, pink and red and white flowers, and she walks past Bruce, cuts up a side street, and continues on. Bruce stamps on his cigarette, sucks in his stomach, and follows.

Bruce remembers that she played a Mafia wife in one of her early movies. He remembers her standing by the grave of her son, who was shot point-blank by her husband, and he remembers watching her shoulders sag as she dangled the flowers over the black hole in the earth and threw them down. As she stomped off through the wet grass, her hair plastered to her head in the rain, her large breasts heaving as she sobbed (all overacted, but she looked fine), her husband following closely behind, Bruce recalls that the camera panned back to those flowers on the lid of the coffin. And then the camera closed in on the flowers until they were only mists of colour and then darkness. Cut.

Bruce picks up his pace. Sure, it would have been easier, he thinks, to have stayed in the realty business, to have continued to sell houses, to have met a nice woman, settled again, maybe even had more kids. But now it seems that the daily grind of boring reporting has finally added up to something, meant something, made life worthwhile. Here, in front of him, is the story he's been waiting for, working for, ignoring his life for. Here is something that he can hold up to the light and, for once, see a human element behind the glamour. Here is something big.

The last seven years. The big scoop. And now Emma Fine has walked right into his life, carrying flowers and carrots and bread.

She turns into the front lawn of a huge building, all stone and Gothic windows. As Bruce approaches he sees that the building is a church. A Catholic church with side buildings, portables, surrounding it, attached to it. Emma Fine enters through one of these portables with a key, and as she turns back to shut the door, she glances over and sees Bruce standing there looking at her. She shuts the door quickly behind her. Her shadow behind the mottled glass of the door lengthens and then disappears.

Bruce runs his fingers through his hair until it is sticking up oddly on his large head from the sweat of his brow. He tries the door. It is locked. He stands there. Still. Watching. He sits down. He walks the steps up to the front doors of the church but they are also locked. He sits on the steps. He waits. He looks at his watch. And, after a long time staring at the empty door, almost expecting her to come out for an encore, he turns on his heels, shoves his hands in his shorts pockets, and starts the long walk back to his townhouse, squinting in the late afternoon sun. If she has a key, he reasons, she belongs there somehow and he will find her again. But, for now, he has to phone Will before he loses his connection to the magazine that will publish the story of Emma Fine.

Back at his house Bruce sits for a while in the living room, his drapes pulled against the low-angled sunshine. He opens a beer and drinks out of the bottle. He takes a cigar from the box on the coffee table and lights it. He doesn't want to rush things. Bruce wants to savour the moment, he wants to be able to remember this, remember when he had nothing, before he had everything. But after a minute he gets jittery and nervous. He must get moving. What if she disappears again? How could he have just left? Just assumed that he would find her again? He has to face Will and tell him about Trash, about the article that is scheduled to run in tomorrow's edition. Bruce goes into his office and picks up his phone. He leans back in his chair and sips on his beer, his feet up on the desk. He listens to the ringing of the phone through the receiver. Although he's slightly nervous, Bruce also feels proud and cocky and stirred up. He feels mildly lustful. He feels full of himself, as if seeing Emma Fine on the street was something that should have happened to him, that did happen to him, because he's so great and talented and pure. Because he's the best damn entertainment reporter in L.A. This wasn't luck, Bruce tells himself, it was fate. This was supposed to happen. Bruce has been paying his dues and now he is going to collect. He turns to his computer as he waits for the person on the other end of the phone to transfer him and deletes all the interview files he has on Trash. He doesn't need that any more. Who gives a crap about some multi-million-dollar, adolescent pop group, singing their backstreet lyrics, blond hair falling in faces that have never seen a razor. Emma Fine is out there. Ready to be rediscovered. And only Bruce knows where she is.

"Hey, Will," Bruce says into the phone. He sits up straight in his chair.

"Bruce."

"Listen, I've got something to tell you."

"You haven't finished the article yet, have you? You know it was due for publication last week. I've delayed once already."

"Screw the article, I've got something better."

"You know I can't keep you on, Bruce, if you aren't going

to deliver. You know this was the last chance. Get it in today. By five o'clock."

"Listen, Will."

"No more excuses."

"I've got something much more important to tell you."

"I don't want to hear it. I want to see that article on my desk in an hour. Christ, it's already four o'clock. I want it on my desk by five."

"It takes an hour to drive to your office this time of day. Let alone printing it out or —"

"Get moving then. Get going. Or fax it in. E-mail it."

"Will."

"Now. I mean now."

"But …"

"Come in, Bruce. I should see you face to face if I'm going to fire you. I'll see you in an hour."

"But, I …" The phone goes dead in Bruce's hand. He shakes his head. Will's anger has dampened his mood somewhat. Bruce takes a large gulp of his beer and heads into the living room to light another cigar. He puffs on it for a minute and then he walks back to his office and puts it out in the ashtray beside his pen holder.

Taking his keys from the hook beside the door, Bruce leaves the townhouse once more and skips — this time he skips and hops and bounces — down the stairs to his car, parked on the street. If Will won't listen to him on the phone, he reasons, then he'll surely listen to him in person. It's better this way. He can explain everything face to face.

Bruce needs to know what happened that day, in the beginning of the summer, the day they found a dead man in her pool. And where was she? They couldn't find her for several days and when they did find her … well, she was a mess. He remembers that. He can still see the picture of her being led out of that alley and into the bright day, one cop on each side, holding her arms as if she were a common criminal.

The alley. He'll have to go back to the alley and look at it to set up his scene brilliantly.

Bruce starts the engine in his car and listens to it idle for a minute. Then he puts the car in first gear and pulls out onto the street and heads in the direction of downtown L.A., towards his editor's office. He is sure that once Will hears him out he will be congratulated, proudly thumped on the back. Will just has to listen.

Chapter Four

In the backyard of Emma Fine's house the detectives split up from the plainclothes officers. They are all highly suspicious now, knowing this may not be just another suicide, conscious of the fact they have been touching things, worried about destroyed evidence. Martin and Joe head towards the house to see if the driver is inside or perhaps in his apartment above the garage. Gerry and Frank start along the hedges and bushes around the property, looking for a gap or for clues.

The forensics officer is dusting the gate of the pool for fingerprints. He is writing in his notepad. He jots down the details that surround the scene, the position of the body in the pool. He notes what the dead man is wearing, he notes where the sun is in the sky, the placement of a glass of water (he bends at the waist to sniff it) placed on a side table. He takes his camera out of the case he has slung around his neck and he snaps photos of everything he can see.

"Damn," he says when he lifts five sets of prints, all smudged, from the gate. He looks over at the two police officers who are wandering the property. "Fools."

Martin is opening the door that leads into the kitchen from the pool.

He whispers, "I can't believe I'm walking into Emma Fine's house."

"What's with you?" Joe says. "She's just a person."

"She's Emma Fine."

"And she's missing. I called the studio and she never showed up for work today."

They walk into the kitchen, wiping their feet, self-consciously, on the mat by the door. There is a dirty oatmeal pot resting in water in the sink and Joe tests the water with his finger to feel the temperature.

"She was washing dishes," he says. "The water's still warm."

Martin shrugs. He looks out at the pool. He can see the forensic man out by the pool, bending over, looking in. He can see the cops walking along the bushes around the property, bending every so often to pull apart the plants to see if there is a hole in the fence.

"Do you think she'll come home? Do you think he was her boyfriend? I thought she was single."

"The maid says they were *friends*." Joe enunciates the word.

"Friends?" Martin laughs. "You couldn't just be friends with Emma Fine."

"I wouldn't know. I don't watch TV."

"This isn't TV, Joe, this is movies."

"I don't go to the movies." Joe starts walking through the hallway that leads off the kitchen. "Come on."

"You don't go to the movies? How can you live here and work here and not go to the movies?"

"One has nothing to do with the other," Joe says, his voice fading as he gets farther away.

"Sure it does. Movies, West Hollywood, L.A. It all fits." Martin shakes his head and follows Joe. "I can't believe you don't go to the movies. Why did I never know that? We've been working together for two years and I didn't know that."

"I guess it never came up," Joe says. He looks into a guest bedroom, a bathroom, a recreation room. Everything is in its place. Joe stops for a minute in the recreation room and looks at the size of the TV. A door off to the side reads, "Movie Room," and Joe opens it to reveal a small theatre complete with velvet theatre seats, a fairly large screen, and a small popcorn concession stand. "Christ."

"Would you look at that," Martin says. He is standing on the circular staircase leading to the next level. He is pointing at the glass cases lining the walls. Each glass case is home to an award, a statuette or a medal or a plaque. "Would you look at that." He runs his finger along a glass case. "Just look at that."

Joe and Martin continue throughout the house. The master bedroom is the only room that looks lived in. There is a woman's dressing gown lying on the floor, half into the ensuite bathroom. In the bathroom are opened cases of makeup, contents spilling, lining the counters which are stained with brown eyeshadow and red lipstick smears. There is a hairbrush and a basket of hair clips. Martin touches the hairbrush. He touches a long blonde hair that is tangled in the bristles. The huge bed hasn't been made and the sheets are half pulled down and jumbled. A man's watch lies on the bedside table along with a box of Kleenexes, an empty bottle of wine, and one glass.

"I thought he never drank," Joe mumbles. He picks up the glass to sniff it.

"Don't touch that."

Joe quickly puts down the glass. "Where the fuck is my mind today?"

"Maybe it's her glass," Martin says. "I think she drinks. I think she has a bit of a drug problem, actually. I read that somewhere."

Joe nods. This doesn't surprise him. He looks out the window of the bedroom and he sees the deputy coroner and his assistant pull their van into the driveway. The maid is still standing by the tree, her arms still crossed over her chest. She points the way to the pool to the deputy coroner and then she looks up at Joe and waves. Joe waves down. He scratches his head. If she can see him up here, why couldn't she see the person running from the scene of the crime? Behind the van two police cars drive up and the officers get out and pull police tape across the end of the driveway. The tape says, "West Hollywood Sheriff Station — Crime Scene — Do Not Cross" over and over. Black on yellow. Joe can see TV crews, cameras and trucks, already lined up in front of the house. The police officers wave away questions and push back the gradually forming crowd.

"This is getting messy," Joe says.

Martin looks out another window. "Damn. I thought this would be routine. Drowned rich guy. Drugs. Depression. Suicide. Easy."

"Let's keep moving." Joe heads out of the bedroom and down the hall. "We should check out that apartment above the garage."

"Hey," Martin shouts. "Come back. Look what I've found."

Joe hurries back to the room. Martin is holding up a pair of jeans. "Dead man's? They were under the bed. They're slightly damp at the knees."

"Check the pockets."

Martin empties the pockets and two small pictures in plastic fall out. "Hey, look at that — it looks like he's married."

"Married?"

"Here's a photo. Doesn't it look like a wedding photo? City hall, sure, but she's got a bouquet of flowers. And maybe they have a kid. No, this picture is from a while ago. It looks like the same guy here as a boy. Maybe a brother or something with him. Look, they're in a canoe."

"We'll have to notify her quickly, before she sees the news." Joe looks at the back of the photo. Theodore Simon Weaver and Bridget Amelia McGovern. The date. He writes her name down in his notepad.

"I hate doing that. Telling the wife."

Joe nods. He hands the photo back to Martin. "Is there anything on the back of the other photo?"

"No, nothing. Not even a date. It's old though. It's crinkled and yellow."

"Forensics will want to see them," Joe says, as he walks out of the room. "Put them back exactly as you found them."

Martin shuffles the jeans around and shoves them under the bed right beside a woman's pair of black running shoes. He follows Joe out of the room.

The two police officers push through the bushes. They have been walking around and around. They have almost circled the property.

"Nothing," Gerry says. "I can't even see how a dog could get through."

"Over, maybe?"

They look up at the tops of the bushes. "It'd be hard. You'd have to climb up the bush somehow and then propel yourself over. I can't imagine it."

"And fast too. The maid said the person was gone fast."

Gerry shakes his head. "We must be missing something." He looks back at the pool, at the forensics officer standing by the glow of the water talking to the deputy coroner and his assistant. "This here would be a direct path." He lines up the pool with his hand and traces a path to where he is standing. "And the maid could see it all from here." He looks over at the house, at the windows, the kitchen now lit up with the sunshine.

"Feel that breeze," Frank says. "It's gorgeous out. I wanted to take the kids to the beach this afternoon."

"You won't be going to the beach this afternoon."

"Yeah," Frank says.

Gerry continues bending down and peering through the bush. "From the way you're behaving," he says, "you'd think we never have a sunny day here. You'd think we were living in the North Pole or something. Canada maybe. I hear up in Canada they have snow all year around."

Frank says, "It's crisp out. What do you want?"

"Crisp? Shit, Frank." Gerry straightens up.

They begin walking.

"Let's go back to the pool. There's no way out here. The person must have run around a bit and then headed out the front driveway. Or maybe there was no person. Maybe the maid didn't see anyone at all. Joe said she has bad eyes. Can't see a damn thing."

"Let's go back and help them with the body." Gerry looks over towards the pool and sees the deputy coroner trying to fish the body towards him with a large pool net. He is stirring up the water. Gerry and Frank walk together towards the pool. They open the gate around the pool and enter the deck.

The forensics officer stands up after kneeling in front of a lounge chair, looking underneath, and he says, "Can't you guys keep your fingerprints off anything?"

Gerry and Frank stop and look at their hands.

Inside the house Joe and Martin have seen every room. They are standing in the front entranceway.

"I swear she only lives in her bedroom," Joe says. "Nothing else looks lived in."

"I'd do that," Martin says. "If I lived with her, I'd only live in her bedroom."

Joe says, "Keep your mind on the business at hand. Let's check out the driver's apartment."

The two men leave through the front door. The sun is blinding. They walk to the side of the house, to the seven-car garage, and look around for the stairs up to the apartment above.

"Over there," the maid shouts from down on the front grass. She is sitting under a tree, leaning up against it. She shades her eyes with her hands. "To the side." She is watching the reporters behind the front gate fighting with the police officers for any tidbit of information.

"Thanks." Joe waves. Again he wonders how she can see him.

"I have a key if you want one," Maria shouts. "Do you need a key?"

Joe walks to Maria and takes a key from her outstretched hand.

"I don't want you to break any doors," Maria says. "And wipe your feet on the mats provided. The cleaners don't come until Thursday."

"How did you see me up in the window?" Joe asks.

"What?"

"Your eyes." Joe points to Maria's eyes.

"What about my eyes? I see shadows. I see a blurry shadow and what do I think? I think there's a police officer in Ms. Fine's room. I wave. Do you have a problem with that?"

Joe glances down the driveway at the large crowd huddled around the entranceway. "I'm a detective," he says, "not a police officer."

"Well, la-di-da." Maria looks away.

The two police officers at the road are standing guard, their hands crossed over their chests. When he starts to move away from Maria, Joe sees a flurry of activity, cameras positioned, flashes popping. He heads back up to the garage.

Joe says, "It's a fucking circus out there."

Martin follows. They enter Dan's apartment after knocking once. The apartment is very large, spanning the width and depth of the seven-car garage. The furniture is old but still fairly nice. Again, the area does not look lived in. Everything is dusted, everything is organized. Even the bed is made, the shower clean.

"Do you think he lives here?"

"The maid says he might be living with a girlfriend."

"Shouldn't a driver be around at all times? What if Emma Fine needed to go somewhere in the middle of the night?"

"They must have some pre-arranged deal."

Martin looks at the framed photos above the fireplace. Pictures of cars. "This must be him." He points towards a photo of a handsome man dressed in black standing before a Rolls-Royce. "And there she is." He hands a publicity photo of Emma Fine to Joe. "Nice, right? Didn't I tell you she's nice?"

"Yes, nice."

"You've seen her before, haven't you?"

"Yes, sure," Joe says. "I recognize the face. Besides, there are pictures of her all over her house."

"You can't help but recognize her. She's famous." The photo is signed in the corner. Martin holds it up to read the writing: "Dan. Take care of my cars. Love, EF."

"Sweet," Joe says. "Her cars." He roams around the room. He opens a closet door. "Will you look at that?"

Martin puts his head in the closet and whistles slowly. "Holy shit."

Inside the closet there are shelves and on these shelves are pictures of Emma Fine. All framed. There are candles, burnt down, and a pair of woman's dress gloves in a box. There is a tube of lipstick and a woman's angora sweater.

"You think we have our killer? Little jealous maybe. Drowns the lover?"

"Too easy," Joe says. "Or he's just stupid. But we certainly have some sort of psycho here."

Suddenly they hear a commotion outside. Someone shouting. Joe looks out a front window. He sees the two police officers trying to stop someone from coming within the police tape.

"That must be our man," Joe says.

"Who?"

Joe signals back towards the closet.

Martin and Joe head out of the apartment and walk down the large driveway. Maria joins them.

"That's Dan. Back from his girlfriend's house."

Joe nods. He tells the officers to let the man through. Dan walks through, short and angry and muscular.

"What the hell is going on?"

"There's been an incident," Joe says. "Please move away from the media cameras and we'll tell you all about it." He motions Dan up the driveway.

"I had to park down the street," Dan says. "I had to leave the fucking BMW down the street. Do you know how bad that will look? What if something happens to it? I could get fired for leaving it down the street."

Martin signals to a police officer. He takes the keys from Dan. "This officer will get your car for you and bring it into the driveway."

Dan nods. "Be careful with it," he calls to the receding figure of the officer. "The clutch is temperamental." He looks at Maria. "It's not my car," he says.

As the men walk towards the house, Joe leans into Dan and tells him about the body in the pool. Maria excitedly recounts her story of the noise, the dogs, the towel, the body, the police.

"Where's Emma?" Dan asks. "Is she okay? Ted Weaver is dead?"

"No one knows," Martin says. "Do you know where she is?"

Dan shakes his head. "I was at my girlfriend's last night. I drove Emma home from the party and then stayed the night at Cheryl's."

"I told you," Maria says.

"Can we get the name and address of your girlfriend?"

Dan looks confused. "Yeah, sure. Cheryl Calhoun. At the yacht club. Her houseboat is called *Sweet Marie*."

Joe scrapes the name and address into his little notepad.

"What condition was Ms. Fine in when you dropped her off? What time was it?"

Dan pauses. "Around two in the morning, I think. She was pretty wasted, but otherwise okay. She said good night at the door. I didn't watch her go in. I just turned around and left."

"You're a suspect," Maria says. "Can you believe it?"

"That's not true," Joe says. "We just need to check his story. Like we need to check your story."

"My story? It's not a story."

"How did Ted die?" Dan asks.

"We don't know yet," Joe says. "There's no blood so I have to assume it was either an overdose or maybe he was whacked on the head with something blunt."

"Whacked on the head?"

"Maria saw someone running away from the scene."

"It might have been a dog," Maria says.

"I'd like it if you two would go inside and stay away from the windows. We don't want to give the news anything to play up right now. And don't go anywhere else for a while. We will need to question you more thoroughly. There are some things in your apartment we need to talk to you about."

"My apartment? You can't go in there. Did you go in there? Don't you need a search warrant to go in there?"

Joe shrugs. "We were just making sure there weren't any more dead bodies. We needed to make sure you were okay."

Maria says, "I bet Ms. Fine is getting her nails done. I bet she's picking out colours right now." Maria laughs.

"We're calling around. We've got everything covered," Joe says.

"I can't believe you went in my apartment. I should call a lawyer."

"That might be a good idea."

"I need a shower," Dan says.

"I'm sorry," Martin says, "but you'll have to wait for that."

"Why?"

"You'll just have to wait."

"Am I a suspect?"

"It's always the men they suspect," Maria says, more to herself than to the others.

"I didn't do anything."

"We know that," Martin says. "It's just better if you stay in the living room right now until we straighten everything out. There are more police coming soon."

After seeing Maria and Dan into the house, Joe and Martin head back to the pool through the kitchen.

"Where the hell is Emma Fine?" Joe asks as he pauses in the doorway. "I'd like to ask her some questions right about now."

"It could be an open-and-shut case," the deputy coroner tells the two plainclothes officers and the two detectives. "Or it could be more complicated."

"What do you think?"

"I think it'll turn out to be very straightforward."

"Like?"

"Like a drug overdose or a suicide. Something like that."

"That's what we thought."

The men watch the coroner's assistant pull the wet body out of the pool. The assistant is soaked. He is grunting but no one offers to help.

"Can I get a hand over here?"

Martin and Frank move towards the body. They help pull it up onto the deck. They roll the man over and look into his face. His eyes are open, as is his mouth.

"He looks like he's trying to say something."

"Tell us who did this to you," Frank says in a ghostly voice. He laughs.

"If you pressed his stomach right now," the deputy coroner says, "a whole shitload of water would come out. His lungs are full of it."

"How long has he been dead?"

"I'd say at least a couple of hours from the look of him. Rigor is just beginning to set in."

Joe nods his head.

"You've got pencil on your face," Martin tells Joe. He licks his finger and tries to clean Joe's face but Joe pushes his hand away. He rubs his face with his own hands.

"Don't you ever lick me," Joe says. "Don't you ever get your saliva anywhere near me."

Martin laughs. "I was just trying to help."

"There are no noticeable contusions," the deputy coroner says. "But I'll have to examine him more thoroughly. It's hard to tell. He's got too much hair. Guess I'll have to pull back the scalp."

The assistant nods.

"Scalp him," Frank says.

"Full autopsy."

"He looks huge."

"He seems to have been a large man. Tall. Looks like he used lots of weights."

"He'd be hard to overpower, wouldn't he?" Joe says. "I mean, it'd take a large person to knock him over the head and dump him in the pool. The person had to drag him in, I assume?"

"Yes, I'd say so." The deputy coroner stands up, cracking his back. "Or it could have been someone small really surprising the shit out of him. You'd be surprised at how powerful you become when you're panicked. Let's get him out of here."

The deputy coroner and his assistant unfold the stretcher and everyone helps load the dead man onto it. The body bag is zipped up. The outline of the body is visible. Drips of water slide down the stretcher legs to the wheels.

"That Dan guy is pretty big," Martin says to Joe.

Joe nods. "He's short but muscular. Like a pit bull."

"I do think it was an overdose," the deputy coroner says. "That's what it usually is in these cases. Suicide, depression. Ironic, isn't it?" He signals to the house. "But I'll get back to you with the results of the autopsy."

"Yeah, sure," Gerry says. "Thanks."

The four officers watch the deputy coroner wheel the stretcher down the driveway. The forensics officer shuffles along behind them. Down at the end of the driveway there is movement among the media. Frank can see news reporters doing live coverage, he can see satellite vans parked up on the curb, he can see cameras flashing and people scurrying. A helicopter circles the property.

Joe looks up at the house, at the glass windows. He sees Dan and Maria standing on the second floor, looking out at the pool. Maria waves. Dan turns away from the window and disappears. His hair looks wet. "Shit," Joe says. "I think he's had a shower." He motions with his chin up to the second floor but by now Dan is gone and Maria just stands there waving her thick arm in the air and shuffling from swollen foot to swollen foot.

"Why the hell did you leave him alone?" Frank says.

"Shit," Joe says.

"Where are the other cops? We need more cops here."

"Don't blame the cops," Frank says. "You two left him alone."

The coroner's van manoeuvres around the BMW, the forensics officer's car, the truck, the detective's car, and the police cruiser in the driveway and heads out to the street and disappears. Several camera crews follow the ambulance. The helicopter flies above. The forensics officer stands by the BMW, looking in. He borrows the key from the police officer and opens the door. Frank and Gerry and Joe and Martin watch as he pops on latex gloves and begins a thorough investigation of the car. He takes pictures using a Polaroid camera. Then he moves towards the truck and continues searching. A tent, stove, sleeping bags: the forensics officer takes everything out and puts it on the grass. He snaps pictures and works steadily. The media at the end of the driveway love this. There is so much activity down there that

Martin thinks for a minute everyone is dancing.

The sun is getting hotter and higher in the sky. The clouds are billowing and beautiful. The breeze picks up. Frank takes a deep breath, steps over the puddle of water at the side of the pool from where they dragged up the dead man, and starts to walk down towards the driveway.

"Come on," he says. "We've got stuff to do."

"I'm going into the house to talk to the jerk," Joe says, nodding towards the glass windows. "Martin, come with me."

The police officers split up from the detectives to do their work just as more police arrive on the scene. Soon the house, the pool, the gardens, and the driveway are overcrowded and congested. A tow truck arrives to take the truck away to the lab.

"Like maggots on a rotting corpse," Dan says to Maria as they look out the windows around them. "Where is Emma?"

"I don't know where she is," Maria whispers, "but they'd better not mess up the house trying to find her."

Chapter Five

"Emma fine?" Will shouts. "Who cares about Emma Fine? That was ten years ago, Bruce. Where's the article on Trash?"

Bruce sits in a chair in Will's office, across from the large man behind his desk. Will's face is pockmarked, there is sweat on his brow. There is always sweat around Will, under his armpits, running in rivulets down his temple, behind his ears. His hands are wet, his feet sweat and stink.

"Don't you get it?" Bruce says. "She disappeared. Now she's back. No one else knows."

"Trash," Will says, trying to stay calm. He is chewing on the lid of a pen, chewing hard and fast and furious. A reformed-smoker kind of chew. "Our readers care about Trash. You were supposed to deliver the article. You were supposed to make them big."

"But they're shit, they're a drop in the bucket. They'll be gone tomorrow. They don't even write their own lyrics. This, Will, is huge. Don't you understand? This is really, really big. This is Emma Fine."

Will stands up. He shakes his head. Bruce watches tiny droplets of sweat spill around the desk. He can hear the muted conversations, the mumblings, of people in the hallways around the office, the constant blur of white noise. He can smell stale coffee in the machine down the hall, he can smell photocopy ink and the burning stench of printers left on too long. He can smell Will's feet.

Will is walking around his office in his socks. He is ranting. His face is turning red. Bruce isn't paying attention. He is thinking about Emma Fine and wondering when it would be safe to actually approach her, when it would be appropriate. He is thinking about what he will say to her when he first meets her, what would be the right thing to say? He can barely imagine it.

Will is talking about responsibility to the newspaper, about owing the rock group for their interview — "They made a special effort to be here for you" — about owing Will for all the faith he's had in Bruce, for all the times he's covered when Bruce is late. "This is it," Will says. "I can't believe this is finally it."

"Who else are you going to get?" Bruce asks. "Be realistic. You can't fire me. There's no one else in all of L.A. like me."

"That's for sure. Other reporters get their stories in on time."

The men look at each other.

"What if I do the article on Trash really quickly, right now. I'll use your computer." Bruce signals to Will's desk. "You go and get two coffees."

Will nods. "Then?"

"Then we'll talk about Emma Fine. We'll talk about her and you'll let me into the archives, you'll set me up with research and information, photos and stuff."

Will groans. "Fuck Emma Fine."

"In my dreams," Bruce starts.

"I don't want to hear it," Will says. "I don't want to hear about your wet dreams."

Bruce laughs. "Get me a coffee. Two sugars, no cream. I'll be done by the time you get back." Bruce stands up and moves over behind Will's desk. "Where's the on button? Does this thing have an on button?"

Will shakes his head, again scattering moistness, and turns on his computer. He sets Bruce up with a blank word-processing page and then he leaves the room. Shoeless. He shuffles in his socks, his black socks, down the corridor to the coffee room. Bruce can hear him go. Hear his large bulk sway. Hear a few choice words he throws at the people in other offices.

Bruce sits down at the desk and begins to type. He sees Emma Fine in his head (perhaps a big photo of her now, front page, splashed next to a picture of her ten years ago, at her peak), but he writes about the young band from Westwood. He writes about their dimpled cheeks, their pre-Raphaelite curls, their hard bodies — stuff the teenage girls will soak up. He writes about their rhythm and mentions several key lyrics.

Will comes back into the room with two coffees and Bruce doesn't stop typing. He lets the coffee rest on the desk and he doesn't stop typing his article until he is all finished and the coffee is cold. Will leans up against the desk and reads over Bruce's shoulder. It always amazes him that people can concentrate so fully — Will spends so much of his time worrying about his increasing size, his inability to stop sweating, his nerves, his bank account, that he can never concentrate on one thing for more than five minutes.

"I don't know why I'm letting you do this," Will says. "I should be telling you to get lost. I should have fired you. I should have kicked your ass out onto the street." Will stands and looks out the window, looks down at the street below.

"Shhh," Bruce says, still typing.

"It's just that I've always had a soft spot for you," Will sighs. "Can't help myself."

"Quiet."

"It must be your hair."

Bruce groans.

"And this Emma Fine thing does sound all right. It's not a big story, mind you, but it's a page filler, something for the back page, perhaps."

"Shit." Bruce turns away from typing the last line of the

Trash article. "A back page? Filler? Don't you know anything?"

"She's a has-been, Bruce. She's not big news any more. No one cares."

"She will be big news if I break the story. If I tell what really happened. If I show where she has been. Christ. A murder, a disappearance, a court case that was never resolved. What more can you —"

"I thought the case was dropped. Wasn't it dropped? Wasn't the suspect dead or something?"

"See? See — you're an editor for an entertainment newspaper, the biggest in L.A., and you don't even remember what happened. See? This is big stuff. This is bigger than anything you've ever had before. Bigger than that chili dog you probably washed down at lunch."

"All right, calm down. It was a burrito, not a chili dog." Will leans down and begins to read Bruce's article. "Let's see what you've got here." He skims the sections he has already read. "Good. Good. Yes."

Bruce stands up and stretches. He drinks his cold coffee down in three gulps. He rubs his nose with the back of his hand.

"This is not perfect. It's not even great. But it will do. It will please the band, it will please our readers."

"What more can you possibly want? Great literature?"

Will shrugs. "That'd be nice every once in a while. A poetic phrase here and there. A plot."

"Not everything has a plot," Bruce says.

"Not a consistent one, at least."

"Not everything has an easy ending."

The men look at each other.

Will says, "I'll have Sally dig up everything she can find on this Emma Fine by tomorrow at noon. All right? That'll please you?"

"Yes," Bruce says. "That will certainly please me."

Bruce turns to leave the office. At the door he turns back. "My hair? It's my hair that you like? You don't think it's falling out?"

"It could be your ass," Will says, looking out onto the street again, wondering what he's going to buy for a snack before he goes home to his wife's overdone vegetables and mashed potatoes. He thinks he may get a falafel or maybe a pakora. Something exotic, spicy. "Or it could be your chin. I do like a man's chin."

"Shit," Bruce says. "My chin." He rubs his chin as he rides down the elevator, as he enters the parking garage, as he climbs into his car, and as he drives slowly, awkwardly, down the street, stuck in evening traffic.

Part Two

The photo is in full colour. The caption reads: "Emma Fine, dazed and confused, led from alley by police." In the bottom corner of the photo there is the back head of a newspaper reporter, one hand balancing notepad and pen, the other hand raised high, trying to get the star's attention. His hair is yellow and looks like straw, thick and uncombed. He is wearing a jean jacket and the blue is bold and new. Emma Fine is blinking in the sunlight, bright after the dark of the alley, she is stumbling slightly, leaning on the arms of the police, her soft green dress dirty and ripped, stained. She is barefoot. Her hair is held up in a loose bun, strands of it falling into her face, bits sticking up in the air. The police are looking down at the ground, they are holding up the movie star, they are leading her straight towards the photographer, leading her out of the dark. The police look remarkably similar, like twins, their hair the same, their moustaches the same, their body build and height the same. Each one has an arm bent crooked to hold Emma up and they are both glancing humbly at the ground, avoiding looking at the star.

TRANSCRIPT OF FORENSICS OFFICER'S TESTIMONY:

Q. Would you please review your findings, Officer Jessup.

A. May I refer to my notes?

Q. Please do.

A. The Coroner believed that Theodore Simon Weaver had been hit on the head with some type of blunt instrument weighing approximately ten pounds. There was no bleeding but, according to the Coroner, the blow caused some internal hemorrhaging and the victim lost consciousness. He was then dragged towards the edge of the pool and rolled in. He must have drowned immediately, water filling up his lungs and restricting all breathing. The victim had been in the pool for approximately three hours before any of us arrived.

MR. WRIGHT: Objection. Why is he giving testimony we've just heard from the Deputy Coroner?

JUDGE LIONS: Sustained. Can you continue with answers relevant to your line of work, Officer Jessup?

A. Yes, sure. Sorry.

Q. Let's start from the beginning. Who was at the house when you arrived?

A. There were two police officers and two detectives on the scene when I got there. There was the maid, a Mrs. Maria Candalas, out front in the driveway. And the driver had just arrived or arrived shortly after I got there. The Deputy Coroner came with his assistant about that time, I think.

Q. Go on.

A. Mr. Weaver was wearing green work pants, a

white T-shirt and work boots. The fingerprints of the four police officers at the scene, of the maid, and of the victim were all identified on the gate leading into the pool and in several key areas around the dead body -- the ledge of the pool, for example, and the tops of tables surrounding the pool. There were also fingerprints of the owner of the house, Ms. Emma Fine, scattered around the pool area and the scene of the crime. If there were footprints in the short grass leading away from the pool, the police officers' own prints obstructed any identification. There seemed to be no way of escaping through the backyard -- all areas of fence and bush were checked -- and so it is assumed that the perpetrator disappeared down the front driveway.

Q. And the vehicles in the driveway, sir?

A. On close inspection of the car the chauffeur drove up in that morning, I came up with small samples of hair and blood belonging to Ms. Fine. There wasn't any evidence in the victim's truck. The back was full of camping equipment, newly bought. A new pistol was also found in the glove compartment. It was not loaded and no bullets were found. There was a bag of cocaine also in the glove compartment.

Q. What about any evidence in the house?

A. The master bedroom of the house was also closely inspected and was found to contain: seminal stains on the bedsheets belonging to the victim, possibly from the night before; hairs on the pillows of the bed which, upon microscopic examination, were consistent with Ms. Fine's and Mr. Weaver's; two laminated photos in the pockets of the pants belonging to the victim tucked under the bed, and a wineglass with red wine residue beside the bed that contained both a police officer's prints and those of Ms. Fine. There were also many different kinds of drugs in the side table. Amphetamines, steroids, Valium, antidepressants, lysergic acid diethylamide --

Q. Could you describe the photos found in the pocket of the jeans? We've entered them as Exhibit F.

A. One of the photos was of Mr. Weaver and his wife, Ms. McGovern, at their wedding, and there was another of Mr. Weaver as a child with another child. From the likeness between the two, we can suppose the other child is his younger brother. There was really nothing out of the ordinary in the master bedroom. The maid, the only other occupant of the house at the time of death, heard nothing but a "loud noise," which she can't seem to explain. She heard no arguing or screaming. No fighting.

Q. And where was Ms. Fine all this time?

A. I don't know. She wasn't at the house. No one knew where she was.

Q. Did you have any questions after your search of the premises or any questions regarding all the information you had been given?

A. Well, yes, I did have questions.

MR. WRIGHT: Objection.

JUDGE LIONS: Sustained.

Q. But your report noted that you asked for a suspension of the detectives present at the scene of the crime.

MR. WRIGHT: This has nothing to do with --

Q. If Officer Jessup found it necessary to ask for a suspension of the detectives and the police officers at the scene --

MR. WRIGHT: This is not admissible --

Q. Evidence was destroyed. Two of the officers were suspended for two weeks, no pay. The detectives were reprimanded. It was shoddy police work --

MR. WRIGHT: Your Honor, I object to this line of --

JUDGE LIONS: Sustained. Are there any more pertinent questions for Officer Jessup?

The day after Ted Weaver's dead body is found in Emma Fine's pool the headlines on the entertainment pages of the three major newspapers read:

Where Is Missing Suspect?
Foul Play in Pool: Where Did She Go?
Was It an Act of Passion or Revenge?

Chapter Six

"Would you look at that?" A police officer stands before the alley, looking in at two other police officers who are helping Emma Fine up from the ground and beginning to walk her out into the light. "That's definitely Emma Fine."

A news reporter walks up to the officer and stands beside him. He snaps a picture. The officer tells him: "Step back, let the lady have air."

Emma emerges from the alley. There are stains on her clothes and she is limping. The police lead her to the car and one officer gently holds her head down as they help her in to the back seat of the cruiser. They shut the door and Emma Fine looks vacantly out the window at the crowd of reporters and police officers. She tries to smile but her lips are cracked and dry and swollen and the smile comes out lopsided, like a grimace. She has a black eye and a cut running down her cheek.

"Is she hurt?" the news reporter asks the police officers. "Has she been hurt? Is that blood on her dress?"

The officers get into the car and start the engine. They do not answer any questions. They drive slowly away from the alley, away from the crowd of onlookers and cameras which have started flashing again. The one officer left on the scene disperses the crowd as quickly as he can. He tells the news reporters to take it easy on Emma Fine. To let her be.

In the car, one of the police officers says, "Are you seriously hurt?"

"I want to go home," Emma says from the back seat.

"We have to take you to the hospital. The sexual assault unit."

"We'll notify people. You'll have people you know there."

The police settle into their seats, settle into the drive. They are both quiet. One of the officers occasionally looks back at her as she looks blankly out the window.

Emma Fine can't remember anything but what is happening right now, what happened from the moment she stepped out of the dark alley. She looks down at her lap and sees the stains on her dress. She looks at the soles of her feet and sees the dirt caked there, the blisters that have formed. She notices that her toenails and fingernails are chipped and cracked. Emma Fine touches her hair with long fingers and tries to smooth it down on her head.

"I need a shower," she says. Her voice is hoarse.

"Yes," says an officer. "You should get cleaned up. But first we'll have the doctors check you out."

"I'm not hurt."

"You might have been raped," the officer says. "Were you raped?"

"Raped?" Emma touches her stomach. She can't remember. Surely she would remember something like that. "I don't know."

"You don't know?"

"I can't remember anything."

"Nothing?" The officers look at each other. The one who isn't driving looks back at Emma Fine. "You don't remember anything?"

Emma shakes her head. She looks again out the window.

"What about Ted Weaver? Do you know what happened to Ted Weaver? Or Bridget McGovern? What about her?"

"Don't ask her questions now," the driver says. "She's in shock. Wait until we're at the hospital."

"Ted Weaver?" Emma asks. "Bridget? I don't know anyone named Bridget."

The officers shake their heads. At first Emma thought they were twins but now she can tell they aren't even related. One officer has reddish hair under his hat, the other officer is shaved bald. Sitting behind them she can see that their heads are different sizes and that one officer has a double chin, the other a bony chin.

Emma feels like she's waking up from a long sleep. She feels headachy and angry. Still tired. Overtired. She wants to take a shower and have a cup of coffee. She needs an orange juice. She wonders again where they are taking her, and then she instantly remembers things, the images in her mind shooting towards her like a fast-forward video: she remembers the house where she lived as a child, her mother's face. Like an electric shock. Everything is suddenly apparent. "I'm Emma Fine," she whispers.

"Yes," one officer says. "You certainly are."

"I'm a mess," she says. "Shit, I'm a big mess. You can't let anyone see me like this."

"It'll be all right, ma'am. No one will see you."

"Do you remember what happened?"

"What day is it?" Emma says. "What day is today?"

"Thursday," the officer says. "It's Thursday today. You've been missing since —"

"Missing?"

"Since Tuesday morning."

"Tuesday morning? What have I been doing?"

"We're not sure, Ms. Fine," the officer says. "We've been looking all over for you. You went to a cast party and then you just disappeared."

"Ted Weaver," Emma says. "Who is this Ted Weaver?"

"You don't know?"

Emma shrugs. "Should I know that name? I know lots of people."

"He was ..."

"Let's do this all at the hospital," the driver says. "Let's let her rest for a minute."

"You said *was*?" Emma asks. "He *was*?" She feels hollow suddenly, like she's famished. "I'm starving." It's like the wind has been knocked out of her. For a moment she can't breathe.

The officers look at each other. "It'd be best if we didn't say anything else until we get you to the hospital, all right? They have doctors there, psychiatrists and such."

"All right. But I want to go home." Emma sits back and touches her hair again. "Oh my God," she says. "My hair. And my nails. Look at my nails. It looks like I've been climbing up a brick wall with my nails." Emma holds her hands out and the one police officer turns in his seat and looks at her fingers.

The police car pulls into the hospital and the men lead Emma to the sexual assault unit on the fourth floor. She feels like she's under arrest. One officer on each side of her. She looks down at her naked feet. She wonders what will happen next.

Emma is in a private hospital room with a doctor and two nurses. Her agent, Max, and her manager, Doreen, are outside, pacing up and down the halls. The doctor is puttering around, trying not to stare. He is standing by the window, his back to her, as she unbuttons her dress. For her whole life Emma has been surrounded by people who like to watch her undress, or just like to watch her, so she is used to his furtive glances. The doctor turns towards her when she is covered with a gown and he motions for her to lie on the bed. He is stuttering and nervous. He is blushing. He stares at a hole in his shirt-sleeve cuff which seems suddenly to give him great concern.

"What are you looking for?" Emma asks.

The nurses shuffle around the room, straightening things, peeking carefully at this famous woman before them.

"Looking for?" The doctor is still looking at his shirt. He

seems startled that she has spoken.

Emma sweeps her hand over her covered body. "On me."

"You?" The doctor moves towards the bed. "Oh, on you."

"I don't know why I need to be examined. I just want to have a shower."

"Yes," the doctor says. "A shower would be nice." His face darkens to an almost burgundy red and he stammers some directions about what he will be doing. He questions her nervously as he examines her.

The doctor feels Emma's forehead and then checks her glands to see if they are swollen. He looks into her eyes, her ears, her nose, her throat and he makes her say, "Ah." He is on call today and he is amazingly grateful, suddenly, for the technology behind his pager. He can't think of anything he'd much rather be doing. He thinks of the guys at the golf course he just left, playing their small game.

"Ah," says Emma. She finds this whole thing ridiculous. This is her body. She should be allowed to shower whenever she wants.

The doctor takes a small bag from the table and he proceeds to scrape dirt out of her fingernails and place it in the bag. Then he cuts her ragged fingernails and puts them into the bag as well. He is wearing latex gloves. The nurses are wearing latex gloves too.

"A manicure," Emma says. "I didn't know doctor's gave manicures."

"I'm taking samples for the lab," the doctor laughs. "Manicures are extra."

"Do you know anything about the man everyone keeps mentioning?"

"Ted Weaver? Nothing more than what I've read in the papers."

"Who is he?" Emma sits up. "Why was he in my pool?"

Suddenly a nurse comes towards Emma and eases her down to lying again. All Emma wants is a shower.

"I need to take some swabs," the doctor says. He clears his throat.

"Oh, Christ," Emma says. "Down there? I had a pap test only six months ago." She tries to laugh. The nurse beside her laughs awkwardly.

"I have to take samples. I'm sorry."

"I think I should have a lawyer present. Wait a minute. Do you think I should have a lawyer?"

"Did the police tell you to call a lawyer?"

"No."

"Then you should probably call a lawyer." The doctor shrugs helplessly.

The nurse lets Emma go and she stands and holds together her gown. Emma has a private room. She picks up the phone. "I know a good lawyer," she says. "I know a lawyer who can talk circles around anyone."

"Good," the doctor says. "It's best to be safe." Suddenly he notices her outline, the way her breasts and hips and legs are tight against the fabric of the gown. He clears his throat again. He coughs a bit, choking on phlegm. The nurses look at him. He blushes.

Emma calls her lawyer and leaves a message with his receptionist. The woman says she can transfer Emma to another lawyer in the firm but Emma wants only to speak to her lawyer. Emma hangs up.

"I really want a shower," she says.

"You can't do that without being examined first," the doctor says. "I'm sorry, but that would be destroying evidence. We can wait until your lawyer calls."

Emma looks around the room. She feels trapped, caged. "I want to brush my teeth," she says. She is almost crying. The doctor leads her again to the table.

"Just lie down. I'm sure you have nothing to worry about. We can wait."

"I want to go home. I want this over with. I don't want to

wait. Just be quick."

Emma climbs on the bed again and lifts up her gown. She puts her feet in the stirrups. The doctor's hairs in his nose quiver. Emma watches him as he examines her. He takes swabs from her vagina, from her anus. He studies her feet. He presses on her stomach. He is quiet and patient and kind. Emma lets him do this, lets him touch her, because she has done this all her life. All of her life she's had men touching her one way or another and this feels no different. His hands are cold and clammy. The nurses watch intently. Emma thinks that tomorrow there will be descriptions of her naked body in all the local tabloids.

"There are marks on your upper thighs," the doctor says. "Can you tell me how they got there?"

"Marks?"

The doctor studies her thighs. "Some small cuts that look infected. Also some newer scars. Right here. Plastic surgery?"

Emma sits up and bends to look at these marks. "No," she says. "I don't remember getting the cuts and bruises. They aren't sore." She touches her scars. "And I'm a movie star. Of course I've had plastic surgery."

The nurses look at her.

"Everyone has had plastic surgery," Emma says. "Haven't they?"

"There are cuts on your legs as well. As if you had climbed something. Or run through something sharp. A bush, perhaps?"

Emma looks at her legs. "That's going to hurt when I need a wax," she says. "They don't really hurt right now."

"Some of these are infected as well. Wash them carefully, okay? I'll give you some medicine."

"If I'm ever allowed to wash."

"And that?" the doctor clears his throat and reaches up to point at her breasts. "What happened there? Plastic surgery?"

"What?" Emma looks at her breasts. Both breasts are

bruised. "Oh, God. Now that you point this all out I'm feeling sore and achy. I wasn't feeling bad before."

"Did you have them enlarged recently? That could lead to bruising."

"No. A long time ago."

"It could be a sign of rape," the doctor says. "Rapists sometimes get violent with the private parts of their victims."

"There, there," a nurse says.

"You don't remember anything, do you?"

"No," Emma whispers. "Nothing."

The doctor looks at her. Studies her face. Looks into her eyes.

"You'll have to talk to someone. A psychiatrist, maybe. And I have to take some blood. Is that all right? And a saliva sample. Are you doing okay? Do you need a break?"

"Let's get this over with," Emma says. "You've taken everything else from me. Take my blood." She tries to laugh. When she laughs her breasts ache. She touches them. They do feel almost as bad as when she came back from the breast augmentation she had done. And then she suddenly remembers all the plastic surgery, her doctor, the nurses hovering over her, and the change it made to her body. They took her at the clinic and formed her like she was clay. She shakes her head trying to get rid of the image. The pain of recovery was unbearable.

The man takes her blood in small glass vials. "Are you tired?"

"Yes, of course," Emma says. "That's a stupid question."

"I'm sorry, but you look like you might be anemic. Have you given blood lately? You're very pale."

"Not that I know of." The tears are swelling up in her throat.

"You have needle marks on your arm."

"Yeah, well." Emma shrugs the doctor off.

"Drugs?"

Emma says nothing.

"I need to cut a piece of your hair. I also need to run a comb through it."

"Ah, a hairdresser too. What next."

"Just a piece. I'll get it from under there, by your neck. You won't notice it missing."

Emma reaches up to her head. "I guess."

The doctor takes a small pair of scissors out of his pocket and proceeds to cut a sample of Emma's hair. Then he quickly reaches down and cuts a sample of pubic hair. He takes a comb to both head hair and pubic hair. He places all the samples in bags and labels them.

"Hey," Emma says. "You should have warned me you were going to cut down there. You might have stabbed me."

The doctor straightens his back. "I'm sorry."

Emma turns away from him and looks at the nurses. They are plain, mousy-brown hair, nondescript women. Emma sighs.

"We're going to have to take a few pictures."

"Pictures?"

"Just a few close-ups. Your face won't be identifiable. The bruises. The cuts."

Emma lies still. She puts a pillow over her head. The doctor removes the pillow to take a picture of her cheeks. He clears his throat and wipes his forehead with his hand. He is hot, damp. The air conditioning is lovely but the doctor is still sweating. "Thank you for your cooperation. I'm very sorry this has happened to you. I'm sorry you had to go through this."

"You can't publish those, right?" Emma says. "They are confidential."

"Of course."

The nurses help her get dressed. Emma feels scattered and emotional. She wants to cry. She wants to lean back in the shower, curl up on the floor, and sob. "Can I have a shower now? Can I go home?"

"We'll just need you to talk to a psychiatrist for a minute and then you can go home," the doctor says. "I'll give you some antiseptic for those cuts on your legs."

"Christ," Emma grumbles. "I just partied too hard. What is everyone so uptight about?"

Max and Doreen follow Emma around the hospital, talking a mile a minute, touching her black eye, her cut cheek, asking her all kinds of questions. Max says she looks different with her deformities and Doreen hopes to hell she'll recover completely. Emma has a movie to shoot, of course, and there are the public appearances she'll have to make because of the scandal in her pool. The police officers who drove her to the hospital drive her home and Emma is grateful for their quiet company. They help push her through the throngs of journalists waiting in front of the hospital doors, and into their squad car.

Inside her living room Emma Fine walks around touching things as if she's been travelling for a great many years and has finally come home. She feels the absence, the break between knowing these things around her and not knowing anything at all. Absence. That's all she can call it. A chasm in her mind. Something missing.

"I've come back from the dead," she whispers to herself. She catches her maid, Maria, walking into the room. "Maria?" Emma says.

Maria rushes towards Emma and begins to cry. "Where were you? We were so afraid."

"Afraid?"

"He was dead in the pool and you were missing."

"Afraid of what? I'm here. Just slightly dirty."

There is silence in the room. The two police officers who have driven her home are waiting for some of their colleagues to arrive before asking questions.

"Let's let Ms. Fine get settled back in now," one officer says.

"I want to shower. I want to brush my teeth. I didn't want to shower at the hospital. I just wanted to be home."

Maria stands by Emma, holding her hand. Maria looks at Emma's hand. She squints to see it up close. She looks confused suddenly. Emma drops the maid's hand. She turns towards the police officers.

"Could you get me a coffee, Maria? Send it upstairs? And some food. Maybe get these gentlemen something too?"

Maria backs out of the room, wringing her hands on her apron. "I'm so glad you're safe," she calls back. "Everyone was so worried."

Emma shakes her head. She's been gone inexplicably before: the time she went into rehab without telling anyone; the time she visited her childhood home by herself, just to sit on the large front porch and touch the walls she grew up surrounded by; the time she was shooting a film in Germany and she couldn't take all the shit from the director and so she drove out into the country and stayed at that little hotel in the Black Forest, listening all night to the small rivulet of water that made its way down the rocks outside her window. She looks down at her dress.

"Did you find my shoes?" she asks the police officers.

It was true that the other times Emma Fine disappeared she knew where she had gone when she returned. She had returned clean and whole, shoes on. She even gave interviews about her experiences. They were published everywhere. Everyone knew every detail.

"Who is Ted Weaver? Why was he dead in my pool? You have to tell me what is going on."

The police say nothing. A car pulls into the driveway and a detective comes into the house. He is a tall man with stooped shoulders and greying hair. Emma notices the hairs coming out of his nose, out of his ears. What is it with men, she thinks, can't they pluck? She cringes. He confers with the police officers and then kindly asks Emma if he could talk to her.

Emma feels self-conscious suddenly.

"You can clean yourself up first if you'd like."

The thought of the smell of soap on her body makes her feel teary-eyed.

She walks slowly up the stairs and into her bedroom. She closes the door.

The police officers look at each other. "I wouldn't mind watching that," one of them whispers.

The other nods. "Lucky shit, the doctor at the hospital. To be a fly on that wall."

"They get paid well too. What are we doing in this business?"

They laugh. Maria brings the coffee in and then goes back to the kitchen. She's had enough of police officers lately. She'd rather sit alone in the kitchen than try and make conversation with them. She thinks police officers are stupid and boring and mean. She heard them talking on Tuesday about Ms. Fine, talking about how they suspect her of the murder — as if Ms. Fine would be strong enough to kill Mr. Weaver. As if she were that strong. Maria tsks. The house cleaners are working in the hallways and in the recreation room. She can hear the vacuum running. The pool cleaners have been told by the police to stay away from the pool for a little while. Maria looks out at the water and wonders about how dirty it must be. She hopes Ms. Fine will get it drained, get rid of that dead-body water and put clean, sterilized, fresh water back in. She can't bear the thought of Ms. Fine swimming in the same water Mr. Weaver's dead body floated.

"Oh my," Maria says to herself as she bustles around the kitchen cleaning up the coffee things. Something was wrong with Ms. Fine's hands. Something was different.

Upstairs Emma locks the door behind her. Then she undresses and kneels naked on the floor beside her bed. She begins to cry. Her body shakes. She rests her head on her soft bed and sobs.

After a few minutes she gets up and looks out the window of her bedroom. She sees the police tape stretched across her driveway and two officers pacing back and forth. There are media vans lined up down the street. Emma thinks it's odd that she didn't notice all of this when the police officers drove her into her driveway. She was looking out the window. She just wasn't seeing anything. There seem to be more media people arriving now. News of finding Emma Fine has travelled. Emma watches the small crowd gather for a while and then she walks into her bathroom. She turns on the light, the fan, the shower, and then she stands before the full-length mirror and looks at her cut and bruised body. She examines herself. She brushes her teeth, her hair, and then she steps into the shower and sits on the floor. The water streams down upon her, hot water, and she sits there, soaked, letting it run down her face and into her mouth and nose and eyes. She sits there. Quietly. She is trying hard to remember what has happened, to remember everything she can remember. She sits in the shower and lets the water run.

Chapter Seven

Bruce waits by the church at the same time the next day. And, amazingly, Emma Fine comes up the front walk with her funeral flowers and disappears into the church. Bruce walks home. He waits for Will to send him all the information he needs, and when it arrives by courier, boxes of photos and trial transcripts, newspaper clippings, and even the post-mortem report, he sits on his patio overlooking his overgrown garden and he sips on a cold beer from a mug and he reads everything, front to back. Everything. He pores over every word: forensics reports, newspaper articles, magazines, trashy tabloids, police reports, the trial papers, hundreds of photographs.

"How'd you get all this stuff?" Bruce asks Will. He is phoning from his cordless phone and the reception is full of static. A plane passes overhead and the neighbours are hammering something ceaselessly.

"Where are you?"

"On my patio."

"Jesus, I pay you a salary and you sit outside and drink tequila and bask in the sunshine. I'm in a stuffy office. I'm sweating like mad."

"You're always sweating, Will," Bruce says. "And I'm drinking beer, not tequila."

"I got a lot of stuff from our files. We had some reporters working on this ten years ago. I sent Amy Branco down to the courthouse for the trial transcripts. They are public property. And the pictures? Our reporters ten years ago had no problem digging those up."

"What happened? Why did you stop reporting on the case?"

"The story died out, I told you. You can't keep writing about something that is old news, Bruce."

"Who were the reporters? Should I get in touch with them?"

"Some woman who got married and moved to Seattle and a man, Fred Traverse, remember him? Fred died of lung cancer a couple years ago."

"Got her phone number?"

"Yeah, sure," Will says. "But don't hassle her, okay? She's a mom now, she has no time for this. There's a lot of stuff there. Don't go bothering people about an old story."

"It won't be old for long."

"Did you tail her today? Did you see her?"

"She's still going into that church. I think she prays all day or something."

"Atoning for her sins?"

"Right," Bruce says. "That's probably it." He riffles through the papers on his lap. "These stupid people next door have been hammering all day long. I can't hear myself think."

"Poor you," Will says. "You come sit in my office all day and I'll sit out on your patio and drink beer and listen to the bang of hammers."

"No thanks."

"What the hell did you phone for anyway?"

"I don't know," Bruce says. "I think I just wanted to say thank you. This is a lot of stuff. I appreciate it. You've saved me tons of time."

"Well, I'm all choked up," Will says. "I think I feel a tear coming on."

Bruce hangs up the phone, gets another beer, and sits back down on the patio and looks out into his yard. He looks into the neighbours' yards too. The mix of people surrounding him astonishes him. The Italians on one side, in a townhouse like his, with their cemented backyard and grapevines and vegetable garden, their clothes hanging from ropes strung everywhere. Orderly, but at the same time chaotic. The woman behind him with her luxury pool and hot tub, her guest house and guard dog. The couple on the other side of him, in a detached home, Mexican style, clay tiles on the roof, with their landscaped topiary, bushes shaped like dogs and cats and crocodiles. And Bruce in the middle, with weeds climbing the fences and dandelions in the overgrown grass. There is an old barbecue tipped upside down back by his fence and a broken lawn chair that he threw over his patio onto the lawn when he was drunk one evening. The cats from all around shit in Bruce's backyard and he hates cat shit and so he never goes out there to clean anything up, to cut the grass, to pick weeds. Dirt scares Bruce. It always has. Funny that his wife ran away with an archeologist, a man who spends his days wrist-deep in dirt. But soft, dry, clean dirt, not cat-shit dirt. Bruce can understand clean dirt somehow. He can almost understand what his ex-wife can see in a man with clean dirt under his fingernails.

Bruce looks up at the sky, trying to clear his head. He really should get going on this Emma Fine, approach her at least, let her know that he knows who she is. He is afraid she may only be passing through California, she can't possibly live here. Someone would have discovered her years ago.

Bruce wonders if his fear of dirt comes from his fear of death. He thinks he remembers someone saying that to him once but he can't remember who it was. Bruce can't even imagine being buried six feet under dirt, having cats shit on your head, worms crawling around you. He wants to be cremated, and as he looks down at his protruding belly and stares at the beer in his hand, he decides that he has to remember to get this down in a will, make his wishes be known. Before it's all too late. Bruce once told his ex-wife that he wanted to be cremated but she's probably forgotten that by now. And, even if she has remembered, Bruce wonders if, in all likelihood, she'd even come to his funeral. He wonders who would arrange everything. Who would even care? Maybe Will. Will's the closest thing he has to a friend.

This thought strikes him as funny. The profusely sweating fat man who is his boss and editor is his best friend. Bruce has known the man for over six years and he's never met his wife or kids. He's never seen his home or even listened when Will mentions his life outside of the paper.

Of course his ex-wife would come to his funeral, Bruce thinks. She'd have to bring the kids. They can't travel alone, can they? He can't imagine them travelling alone. Although he has seen them as recently as a year ago, he sometimes forgets that they have grown up. Ten years have gone by.

Opening one of the boxes, Bruce begins again to read the evidence set forth at the trial. He skims transcripts and looks at pictures. Bruce can't believe how badly the cops bungled all the evidence. The cops on the scene at the beginning, the detectives, even the forensic guy. And he has no idea why they couldn't get an older doctor, a doctor more used to movie stars, to examine Emma Fine at the hospital, why it had to be a young doctor who was so caught up in her beauty he forgot to label some of the evidence, he forgot to send a bag or two to the lab. His testimony at the trial had less standing in the eyes of the jury because he couldn't stop staring at Emma Fine. Bruce is sure of that. He was star-struck. Jurors are simple people. They would have listened to an aloof doctor, someone who cared more about the patient than the patient's career. But this guy was shaking like a leaf, turning red, stuttering. By all reports he'd been bragging on the golf course that he saw her naked. And all he came up with, considering the evidence he took, was that Emma Fine had had sex twice in the days previous to her appearance. That she had been in some sort of struggle, had two samples of semen in her, and had suffered temporary amnesia. She was loaded with drugs. Full of them. Bruce notes that the doctor didn't even test her blood type or do any DNA testing on the hair samples he took. And the lawyers didn't question this. But then, why would they? This was Emma Fine. She was rich. The dead man was drowned, perhaps even accidentally, not stabbed or shot to death. The doctor merely looked for sperm and for signs of the movie star's presence at the murder (there were none). No blood under her fingernails except her own. There were scratches on her legs as if she had climbed a tree, but no one could prove they came from climbing the hedge around her house.

Bruce feels sorry for Emma Fine. She had it all and then in one swoop everything was taken away from her. She was raped, battered, destroyed.

No evidence, no evidence, no evidence. Nothing conclusive. The semen samples were tested and one came back inconclusive. The other came from Ted Weaver. That's what all the papers said. All the final sentences. Nothing, no proof. The samples were sealed for five years and then, because there was no appeal, destroyed according to Emma's wishes. And Emma Fine couldn't remember what had happened to her. People at the cast party the night before remembered her passed out in the bathroom, remembered her doing lines of coke with the leading man. The leading man got off easy. He said he refused the coke from Emma, he said she was always trying to push it on him, he said she was always trying to break up his good marriage.

Or could she remember? She was, after all, an actor, Bruce thinks. And a damn good one at that. She won all sorts of awards for her acting. Was she playing a part in some scene, perhaps? He's seen her play drunk so convincingly, why couldn't she play drugged? The huge doses of drugs in the blood couldn't be faked, however. He's seen her play a cowering child, an older woman, a hip, young teen. He's seen her die of cancer, chase the bad guy, get punched in the face by a jealous husband. Why couldn't she pretend she was an amnesiac? Is that even possible?

Bruce stands up and stretches. He breathes in deeply. The smog is getting thick in the late afternoon but Bruce has lived here all his life and so he does not even notice it. The only time he notices smog is when he has to clean the windows of his townhouse, when the dirt and grime roll down the walls and stain everything brown. And he hasn't cleaned the windows in years, not since a year or two after Shelley and the kids left, and so the smog doesn't bother him at all.

Bruce has the urge to call Shelley in Canada. Call her up and tell her about Emma Fine. But Shelley was driving across the country the moment Emma Fine's story broke, the moment the details came out, and so she probably didn't even care about it. She had already left him. Bruce wonders if, after leaving your husband and stealing the kids, a person would even bother to watch the news. He wonders if maybe the news becomes second-hand, becomes boring, compared to the excitement of the person's own adulterous, back-stabbing life.

Bruce decides it's time to continue following Emma Fine again, see where she lives, how she conducts her life. She seems to be going to the church in the morning. He wonders what she does for the rest of the day. So he walks to the bathroom, brushes his teeth, and pees with the door open, sitting down, his elbows resting on his naked, hairy knees. He finds he pees slower sitting down, the pressure off his legs, and it gives him a slight rest, a chance to rethink things. He ties on his running shoes at the front door. He makes sure he has his sunglasses and then he locks his townhouse and moves down the front steps to the sidewalk. He feels jaunty and alive. A morning spent researching, a morning spent in blissful busyness. He hasn't felt this way in a long time. It's as if his life finally has purpose. No more teenage rock groups or divorces of the stars to cover, no more Academy Awards, no more dress fabrics and diamonds to price. This time he has an important moment of history grasped in his palm and all he has to do is spread his fingers wide and let it sail. But first he'll hold it tightly, milk it for all it's worth. Maybe later he'll write a book. Bruce has always wanted to write a book.

He thinks: *The Life of Emma Fine*, or, *Woman Gone Missing*. Or maybe something not so obvious.

A book on what happened and what is happening now. Bruce likes this idea. The thought of spending a year or so researching and writing, throwing himself into something tangible, makes him want to whistle. A bestseller. He whistles a tune as he walks down the street.

But for now Bruce will write the article to beat all articles. He'll give Emma Fine back to the world and then he'll take her story and make it bigger than any newspaper, than any tabloid.

Bruce is so caught up in his thoughts that he doesn't know where he is until he turns the corner and comes upon the church. He almost walks into the locked gates out front. Locked. He wonders if there is a law against banning people from religious places. Why would it be locked? It wasn't locked this morning. Bruce rattles the gate. A large, iron one. Black. Ornate. Too high to climb without making a fool of himself.

"Shit," he mumbles. He looks at his watch. Three-thirty. He'll wait half an hour and then, if nothing happens, he'll come back tomorrow. Or maybe he should wait all night. But if he's locked out, then surely Emma Fine is locked out as well. Or locked in. But maybe she has gone already. Bruce sits down on the curb of the sidewalk and he thinks. He'll wait for a little while. Even if she isn't here, surely there are other people, priests and the like, that he can question. Surely they've seen the attractive woman in black bringing flowers and food into the church. And tomorrow he'll come back early and spend the day here watching for her, following her.

Bruce picks up a stick and traces lines in the dust on the side of the road. He watches the ants. The afternoon sun is thick and hot. He wipes at his forehead and chin with a Kleenex he finds in his pocket and the Kleenex rips with the sweat and leaves tiny patches of white on the stubble on his face.

As he waits Bruce thinks about his life and how it is turning out. He is thinking about Shelley and the kids a lot lately, ever since he saw Emma Fine yesterday. They seem to dominate his mind now. He thinks about how one image of the star knocked the past back into his life. It's odd that he almost misses his wife more than his kids. They seem like such foreign objects to him now. Ten years gone, they've grown so much he doesn't know them any more. But he remembers that intense ache in his gut the first year they were gone, the feeling that part of him was ripped away, was physically missing. He remembers longing to touch his little girl's head, to touch Amy's head, her soft, downy hair. Wanting to kiss them both good night and smell their smell, an odour he'll never forget — soap and sweat and dirt and fresh air. Nothing can duplicate that smell. Or the image in his mind of Tyler running haphazardly in a field, stopping to kick a ball. And it's not that he really misses Shelley more, it's just that he can imagine her more fully. He can feel her body and sense her mind. She didn't change that much but the kids did. They have become objects he no longer recognizes. Shelley sent him pictures last Christmas. Tyler with his long hair, a hoop earring in each ear. Amy with her hair pulled back, severe, bright red lipstick, and sad, puppy-dog eyes. Those aren't his kids any more. They are Michael's children now, although he knows they don't call Michael Dad and that pleases Bruce as much as it can.

Maybe after he publishes his book he could fly up to

Canada and surprise them. See them all together and not be angry. They flew down to see him a year ago and all he did was drink and argue with Shelley in her hotel room while the kids swam in the pool and avoided him like the plague. He spent no time enjoying their presence. But next time it will be different. Not only has he thought things through a little, but he will have published something substantial, something he can be proud of. Bruce is tired of not being proud of himself. And his kids will be proud of him. Next time he will bring his swim trunks and join them in the pool.

Cars go past quickly and Bruce breathes in their exhaust.

Suddenly there is a clang and Bruce looks up and sees an older woman coming out from the locked gate of the church. She scurries off down the street, leaving the gate open behind her.

Bruce stands up. He walks onto the grounds around the church, feeling like a criminal. His shoes crunch in the gravel.

"Can I help you?"

Bruce looks up. A nun is standing on the church steps just in front of him, smiling down.

"I thought I'd just look around," Bruce says. "If that's allowed."

"Of course it's allowed." The nun laughs. "We were just closed for cleaning. The pews needed polishing." She turns back on the stairs and disappears into the church.

Bruce moves towards the doors that Emma Fine used yesterday. He puts his hand over his eyes to shade the glare of the sun and he peeks into the mottled, wired glass. He can't see anything. All he sees is darkness. Bruce tries the door but it is locked. He remembers that Emma Fine used a key. Maybe you have to be part of the congregation, one of the faithful, before you get a key. Or maybe she knows someone. Stars always know someone who will get them things, keys, hotel rooms, into the best clubs. And the fact is, Bruce thinks, that even if they don't know someone, everyone knows them. So they get everything they want. Hence the murder. Bruce thinks, first of all, that if Emma Fine had been anyone else, she wouldn't ever have been placed in a situation where her lover was found dead in her pool. She wouldn't even have a pool. Secondly, it's because she was a star that the news paid attention to her. Bruce knows that many people are murdered each week in L.A. and he doesn't give a damn about most of them. No one does.

He walks away from the door and then moves up the steps into the cool, dark church. Churches always impress Bruce. The huge pillars, the stone, the stained glass, the beauty of it all. They knock the socks off Bruce. Churches are one of the rare things Bruce can't imagine being built by people. They seem invincible and stable, as if they were always standing. As if they will always be there. As a kid, Bruce used to love to hear his feet echo on the marble floors of the churches in Europe his parents would drag him through. In fact, the church around him now reminds him of his parents, of his solitary childhood summers following his parents through art galleries and cathedrals and museums. Bruce enjoyed the trips, the airplane rides, the different smells and feels of old cities, but he was always lonely. His mother, a seamstress, brought back fabrics that were new in California. Too new, in fact, to impress her customers who would try on her dresses in the family's bathroom while Bruce, an adolescent, watched TV in the living room. And then they would argue the price down a dollar or two. His father, a factory worker, saved every year for the trip, scrounging every penny, making Bruce wear shoes that didn't fit, cutting his son's hair himself.

Walking through the church now, looking at the holy items around him, Bruce thinks that it was all worth it, even the loneliness. It was all worth travelling to Italy, Greece, Germany, France. Maybe he'll travel again after his book comes out. Maybe if he'd just taken Shelley and the kids more places, they would all still be together. She could have found the exotic within him, not in someone else.

And then he sees her, Emma Fine, standing stiffly by a confessional. She is wearing a handkerchief on her head, dressed all in black again, and her arm is moving back and forth, doing something that Bruce can't quite see. Her back is to him and Bruce hurries up the aisle towards her and reaches her just as she turns, hearing his footsteps, to face him. She stares. Bruce stops. He looks at what is in her hand, he looks at her face, the handkerchief on her head.

"Yes?" she asks. She looks nervous.

"I —" Bruce stands, breathless, before her. "I —"

She glances around the church as if she senses something, and Bruce looks at her lovely teeth, her pale pink lips. He ignores what she is holding and he tries to remember those lips on the chest hairs of Johnny Stallini in the movie *Up in Paradise*. He remembers how she lightly grabbed Johnny's hair with her white teeth and pulled teasingly. She wasn't wearing a handkerchief on her head then.

Bruce turns quickly and walks back down the aisle. His heart is beating madly. He stumbles out the front doors of the church into the blinding sunshine and the heat of the day and he rests his head against a stone pillar until he can pull himself together.

Later, back in his townhouse, a hot dog in the microwave, a cold beer in his hand, Bruce wonders again, for the hundredth time since he saw her only an hour ago, how the great, beautiful, powerful Emma Fine could have sunk so low. Find a dead body in your pool, Bruce thinks, and you might as well give up on everything life has to offer.

Part Three

In the picture Emma is a small baby, perhaps not even one year old, and she is being held up by her father over the stone wall that protects people from falling over the side into the torrents of Niagara Falls. She is being held with one hand clutching her arm, the other hand scooped under her diaper, her fat baby legs waving in the air. Her father is laughing at the camera, but there is an unmistakable glare in his eyes. As if he would toss the baby girl off the Falls in a minute if someone looked at him the wrong way. The baby looks as if she knows already that she shouldn't cry, that she shouldn't let out a sound, not a peep, not a whimper. She looks stoically at the photographer, almost daring herself to care if her small life is ended in a second, in a rush of water and rocks and rapids.

Notes from the Report of Detective Joe MacLean, 22nd Division

Bridget McGovern, twenty-eight, born in New York to a middle-class family. Mother, Susan Runaldo, was a housewife; father, Ryan McGovern, was a schoolteacher. Both died in a car accident when Bridget was twenty-one. Met Ted Weaver while filming a commercial in Ontario, Canada, two years ago. Married him within months. No kids. Moved down to L.A. together. Wanted to be a serious actress. Has been in many commercials. Working her way up. She hasn't been seen or heard from since last week. Neighbours heard some loud noises from the house around the time she may have disappeared but they didn't bother to report them. One neighbour said it sounded like a gunshot, another said like a hammer, another said glass breaking. No evidence. No sign of a fight. No blood or gunpowder residue or glass. Everything in the house, furniture, all clothing, food, etc., is gone. The house is empty. Cleaned out.

Chapter Eight

"Pose for me, darling. Show me your legs."

Emma Fine, just five years old, pushes her little chubby legs out of the slit in her evening dress and smiles at the camera.

"Sell that cereal," the writer hisses. "Little Miss Tart eats Fruit Fruities for breakfast in her evening gown."

"Stop being a jerk," the producer says. "She's doing fine."

"She looks ridiculous. I don't even know what you are trying to say here."

"Fruit Fruities are for the sophisticated kids," the director shouts back at the couple arguing. "They are for the kid who's got taste. Right, honey?"

"Then you shouldn't have put her in a purple taffeta dress. If she had taste, she'd be wearing something a little less prom-like."

"Jean, take a break," the producer growls. "Get off the set for a minute and cool yourself. We're not always going to use what you write."

"The problem, Jake, is that you are using what I wrote. But you've changed it all around."

Emma stands silently on the set. Her little leg pushed out, her hip at an angle. She feels as if she is stuck. Something seems to have locked in her bones. She feels herself on the edge of tears. They are welling up inside of her, and if someone, anyone, were just nice to her for one measly minute, she would sob and cry and pout.

But no one is nice to her and her hip comes unlocked and

she continues to smile for the director. Everything she has learned is in her head: Stand straight, lick your teeth so they shine, don't lick your lips or the lipstick will come off, touch your curls every so often — men think that's cute. Her acting coaches, her agent, all of them are stuck in her mind like a skipping-rope song. Going around and around. Don't trip, Emma thinks. Listen to the beat. Hop. Emma thinks that if she just smiles nicely, if she just gets this one over with, she can go back to her bedroom, with her cat named Joe and her paints and crayons and easel. She can maybe relax.

"Show some more of your thigh, sugar," the director shouts. "I want to see the tip of your panties."

"Jesus Christ," the writer says. "This is a five-year-old you're talking to." She storms off the set.

The producer and director look at Emma. They look at each other. "Come on, now, honey. Show us your panties."

And Emma complies. She'll do anything to see herself on TV.

Emma is smoking a cigarette at the back of the studio with Donny, one of the grips. She is seventeen years old. Donny balls phlegm in his throat and then spits on the ground.

"Bug flew in my mouth," Donny says.

"Yeah?" Emma makes horking noises and then spits out a gob of phlegm, landing it precariously close to Donny's puddle. "Me too. A bug." She laughs.

Donny smiles.

Just fifteen minutes ago Emma smoked what seems like her billionth joint in the back dressing room with a druggie named Francine. She inhaled and exhaled and giggled. She's hungry and has to pee.

And now, suddenly, her mother comes around the back, behind the wooden set structures, and starts shouting and pushing her around. Her mother, out of nowhere, seems to be attacking her and Emma stands still, her cigarette in her hand, a spot of saliva on her chin, and giggles. She can't stop laughing. Donny is grabbing her mother, pulling her away from Emma.

"Hey, stop it."

Emma is standing still and taking the weak blows. She can see them coming at her but she can't feel them.

"You little tramp. You're doing drugs. You're smoking. You tramp."

All she can think, her arms down, the cigarette burning a small hole in her pink miniskirt, is how lucky she is to be in the movies, to be living the Hollywood dream. She thinks about her paycheques and her new car. She thinks about the girls who scream when they see her in the mall. Her mother yells at her and Emma Fine thinks only, Me. Emma Fine. I'm the luckiest person alive.

Emma is working at a nightclub in Los Angeles. She is stripping. This is what all actors do while they make their way to the top, she thinks. This or waitressing, and stripping pays better. Lap dances sometimes make you fifty dollars, if you have a generous client, a drunk client, if you let a hand roam ever so gently up your thigh. And in between sets onstage you walk up and down the club in your G-string and push-up, leaning down and chatting with the men, fetching them drinks for an extra dollar tip.

This is an upscale club. Sometimes a wife or a girlfriend will come but she is usually high and will rarely get a table dance. It's the single men who pay for these, the single men with that look in their eyes, Emma can't decide whether it's anger or pain or fear.

Emma used to work in a different club, where the clients were usually covered in drywall dust or had paint stains on their hands, where they were a loud and laughing bunch. But here, in the Paradise Club, the clientele is quiet, contemplative. The suits fit perfectly.

Emma walks onto the stage wearing next to nothing and slowly gyrates her hips and slips out of her clothes, her legs wrap around the pole, her breasts pushed together with her dead hands. Because all of her is dead to this, to the quiet eyes staring up at her, to the clink of glasses and the heavy beat of the music. The black lights are glistening off her body, making her look airbrushed and perfect, an image the men take home to bed, put to use while their wives underneath them feel suddenly less than beautiful, knowing they can't compete with the image their husband has brought home — it doesn't matter how many damn dinners they cook to perfection, how many shirts they iron, or kids they feed. The mystery is always the girl onstage.

One night Emma danced in front of a drunk woman who cried quietly into her martini. The tears rolled down her face, dripped from her chin into her lap. Her husband held tightly to her hand but didn't see her crying, watched instead as Emma peeled off her black leather bra and panties and faced away from the audience, bending forward, her hands on the wall.

"Never let them see you high," Trish tells Emma the first night. "Never let them catch you off guard."

And so Emma starts with the hard drugs, stuff to take the edge off, stuff that won't make her stumbling drunk.

After hundreds of commercials, many stand-in theatre performances, dance spots, and small bits in low-budget Hollywood movies, after the studio owned her, schooled her, fucked her, and sent her back, Emma is twenty-one years old and stripping in downtown Los Angeles. She strips in the evening and takes classes on technique and movement and performance in the day. She occasionally sleeps with the up-and-coming screenwriters and directors after midnight and she auditions for them at ten in the morning. Emma's mother is working on divorcing her seventh husband and she calls her only daughter twice weekly and demands, no cajoles, no pleads, for Emma to stop stripping and move back home.

"I'll get you an agent," she says. "I'll get you noticed."

Emma's naked breasts hang low before the operations. They swing easily and lightly as she turns around on her high heels on the stage. Her naked stomach and hips are tight and toned and tanned from the California sun. Emma closes her eyes and pretends she is with her lover, last night's catch. She pretends she is standing before him, stroking herself, and he is casting her in the next big movie. She dreams she is living in a mansion in Beverly Hills and her neighbours crowd around her at parties, insisting she come for dinner.

A man in the front row smiles at Emma and puts his finger up, requesting a lap dance. Emma finishes her dance and bends to pick up her clothes and leave the stage. She runs quickly to the dressing room, picks a silver sequined number off her rack, and puts it on.

"I've got a lap dance," Emma says to Trish.

"Use table six. Table seventeen is sticky. Some guy spilt his beer on me."

Emma walks casually back onto the floor and approaches the man who has signalled. He is surrounded by women. Four of them. All beautiful and tall and lean. Models, Emma thinks. Why didn't Emma notice them before?

"Hello," the man says to Emma. He stands and the women stand with him. Emma leads them up the stairs to the back. The women sit around the man in section six. They lean back on the long leather couch. Emma stands in front of them. She looks at the women. They look back.

"The rules say only one customer per dancer," Emma says. "Sorry."

"Don't you worry about the rules," the man says. "We've spoken to your manager." The man takes a wad of money from his pocket and begins to count one-hundred-dollar bills into a pile on his lap. He counts out five bills and then he picks them up and gives them to each of the women and keeps one for himself.

A song comes on and Emma starts to dance. She dances slowly, wonderfully, seductively. She twists and turns, rubs her hands over her body. She tries to ignore the women who are watching her intently. They are expressionless. Suddenly a woman stands and puts a bill in Emma's G-string. Another stands and shoves one in her bra. Another stands and sticks one, folded, in the toe of her high-heel shoe. Then the last woman stands and takes Emma's face in her hands. She pulls it close. She kisses Emma on the lips. A soft, drawn-out kiss, something so fresh and exciting that Emma feels shivers run down her legs. She tastes garlic and wine. Emma doesn't draw back. The woman then places a bill in Emma's open lips and pushes Emma away. She laughs. Emma slowly peels off the money and her clothing. She moves all the money carefully to a corner and she gives her panties to the man and stretches over his sitting body only inches away from his face.

When the song ends the man asks Emma to join him at a table. He hands her his one-hundred-dollar bill and tells her that the manager said she could take the rest of the night off. Emma looks over at Bob who is half hidden behind the DJ window and Bob nods to her, smiles slightly through parted lips, a cigarette dangling from his mouth.

Emma laughs. "This is awkward."

"Come sit with us. Over here. It's dark. No one is up here."

Emma struggles into her G-string and bra, keeping the money in one hand. She is fully aware of the women watching her, the man watching her. She adjusts her outfit and then stands straight and tries to smile.

The man takes Emma's hand and leads her to the couches across the room. The women follow. Emma is clutching her money. The man sits and Emma sits next to him. She crosses her legs and folds her hands across her chest.

"I'm Frank Dillay," the man says. "And you're Emma Fine."

Emma gasps. "Oh my God, Frank Dillay, the producer? I thought I recognized you."

"I've seen you on the stage," he says. "I've seen your commercials. I've been watching you since you were a kid."

"Oh, God," Emma says. "Shit."

"I'd like you to do something for me."

"Yes, yeah, sure. What?" Emma wishes like hell she'd snorted some coke before coming out to lap dance. She feels shaky and pale. She sniffs.

"I'd like you to be in my movie."

Emma drops her arms from her breasts.

"The movie is about a lesbian woman. A stripper. I would like you to play the part. I would like you to be sexually turned on by women. Do you think this is possible?"

Emma swallows. "Yes, of course, I ..."

"I want you for this movie," Dillay says. "By the looks of things, I think you can do it. You don't need an audition. You exude sexuality. I'll send over a contract in the morning."

Emma looks at Dillay. She studies his face. He stands and snaps his fingers. His women stand. Emma closes herself all up again, like a flower, her arms around her chest, her legs quickly cross. She stands before Dillay and thanks him. She won't look at the women.

"I'll see you soon," he says. "You'll want to quit this job. You won't need this kind of trash any more. I'll send over some money tomorrow to keep you going until shooting starts. Do you have an agent?"

Emma nods.

"I expect you to start taking care of yourself. No drugs, no alcohol. Do you hear me?"

Emma nods again.

"You're a star now, Emma Fine. Start acting like one." Dillay leaves the club with his entourage of women. A few of the men watching the dancing below follow his movements but most of the men can't take their eyes off the stage.

Emma hurries down the stairs and into the change room. She collapses into the couch and begins to cry. She is humiliated and proud and angry and happy.

And for six months she quits drugs, she quits drinking, buys fancy clothes, and gets her nails done and facials and her hair dyed and her eyelashes tinted and some plastic surgery. She works out every day and moves into a nice, new apartment overlooking the ocean. The movie is a hit. Emma Fine wins an award. She moves up in Los Angeles. She buys a house. Stars in another movie. She hires Maria and has the maid tell her mother she's too busy to come to the phone.

Chapter Nine

She is standing at a party surrounded by beautiful, famous men and women, wonderful food, and plenty of alcohol. She is bored. She swallowed a pep pill in the bathroom but she still doesn't feel peppy or happy or excited. She feels tired and hungry. Her stomach growls.

"And then the guy shot out the lights and everyone screamed," a man tells her. She isn't paying attention to what he is saying. "He asked her if she believed in God and she said yes and so he shot her."

"I've heard that one before," Emma says. "Didn't that happen last year too?" She yawns.

People are talking around her, about her, to her, but she is not listening. She doesn't give a damn. She looks down at her dress to make sure her nipples aren't sticking out of the low cleavage and then she shakes her head a bit to loosen her hair from the tightness of the clip holding it up. Her lipstick feels like it's fading.

Emma Fine excuses herself from the conversation and walks towards the bathroom carrying her drink. On the way into the bathroom she sees a man leaning up against a hallway mirror. He catches her eye because he is dressed in faded, ripped jeans and a black T-shirt with a yellow happy face on it. She stops and looks at him. She notes that he is handsome. She notes the wedding ring on his finger. His attire places him outside of the group of overdressed men and women. She stares.

"Hi," he says.

"Hi." Emma goes into the bathroom. She fixes her lipstick. She swallows her drink quickly and waits for the buzz. She takes another pep pill and she thinks of asking around for blow to stem her hunger. Emma wouldn't be at this party if it wasn't for her director leading the cast out of shooting and forcing them to make an appearance, plug the movie, make the whisper of it carry through West Hollywood. And he wanted his star, Emma Fine, to look her best. Sent wardrobe out to buy her this dress, chose the right heels which are digging into her naked feet. Emma turns in front of the mirror. She does look fantastic. The dress is skin coloured and so clingy that she looks as if she's naked. A naked blonde wearing bright red lipstick and high-heel shoes. Emma smoothes some cold cream on her hands, her arms, her neck. She sprays on perfume that is on the counter and she walks back out into the hallway. She can feel the pep pill working. When she looks again at the man leaning against the mirror she almost feels good. He looks good. That's all that matters, she tells herself.

"Hi again," he says.

"Underdressed for this shindig, aren't you?" Emma asks as she walks past him. "Or are you parking cars?"

"You're a bit underdressed too," he says. He stares at her flesh-coloured dress. "And I'm a guest, not a valet."

She laughs. "I guess you're right there." She tries hard not to look down at her breasts. They are covered, aren't they? She is sure they are covered.

"Emma Fine," she says, holding out her hand.

"I know."

"Of course you do." Emma smiles. She wants another drink. She wants to cozy up to this beautiful man and get another drink in her body. "Would you get me another drink? I don't feel like going back in there. I feel like I'm drowning in those crowds."

"The bar's a long way away," the man says. "What if you

aren't here when I get back?"

"Then you'll have to drink it yourself."

"I don't drink."

"I'm sorry for you," Emma says. "I'll have a glass of white wine." She holds out her empty glass. "On second thought, make that gin instead. With tonic."

The man disappears around the corner, into the swell of people. Emma is soon surrounded by well-wishers and her eyes and mind are buzzing and tight. She can't stand for a minute in the hallway without people coming over. She feels excited, sexually stimulated, sick of the people around her. She feels on edge. She wants her drink. She wants the man in the jeans to come back. This afternoon Emma filmed a scene where she had to run from a crazy man who wanted to rape her. As she ran her clothes kept ripping on bushes or from his grabbing hands, and although her character got away, Emma felt as if she had been raped. Her breasts naked to the camera, to the thirty or so people filming the shot. There was something wrong with how titillating the whole scene was. Emma can't shake the feeling out of her mind. She wanted something terrifying and the director went for smut.

Typical.

When she was about five, that was her favourite word: *typical.*

The man comes back with her drink and places it in her hand. He holds her hand for a brief second and she suddenly wants to be with him. But then she realizes that he is doing this because she is shaking. He is holding her hand still. She pulls away.

"Thanks." She drinks quickly.

"You should be more careful of what you put into that," the man says.

"Into what?"

"Your body."

"Aren't you going to say my beautiful, sexy body that you'd

just love to sleep with?"

"No." The man looks away. "But I could say that if you'd like me to."

Emma feels sad all of a sudden. "Sorry," she says. "It's just that that's what everyone always says."

"Everyone?"

"Everyone. Male or female." Emma turns up the charm again. Smiles. Sips her drink.

"Well," the man says, "I guess I'm not everyone."

Emma stares at him. "You're not, are you. Who are you then?"

"I'm Ted Weaver." He holds out his hand.

"Ted Weaver. Would I have heard of you?" She takes his hand for the second time.

"Maybe," Ted says. "If you know anything at all about condominiums."

"You own condos?"

"No, I build them."

"Ah, a construction tycoon."

"No," Ted says. He looks away from Emma when he talks. He never looks into her eyes. "I'm a construction worker. I get up at five in the morning and I put on my hard hat and steel-toed boots and I build condominiums."

"Oh," Emma says. "That's nice. That sounds interesting."

"You're full of shit," Ted says.

"Pardon me?"

"I'm not rich and famous."

"So what? I am. And what does that get me but anything I want?"

Ted looks at Emma's face. Emma laughs.

"I'm married," he says.

"Oh." Emma fakes shock. "And I was going to take you home and introduce you to my gay friends."

Ted Weaver smiles and Emma's heart stops. Just for a minute. His smile is open, wide, trusting, honest. He has beautiful teeth and Emma looks at the dimples that break around his lips. There is something about him, some pull, something about the way he makes her feel like the only one in the room. But she turns from him and starts to walk away. "Thanks for the drink." No more married men. No more confusion.

"No problem," Ted says. "As long as I didn't have to drink it myself."

"I respect you for that," Emma says.

"I respect you for drinking," Ted laughs.

Emma joins the cast of her movie at the bar. Her heart is beating rapidly from the pep pills and the alcohol, from Ted Weaver. She feels sweaty but when she touches her face she feels only warm, dry skin.

"Emma," the director says, his arms wrapped around her. "Where have you been? Randy here wants to meet you." The director pushes Emma towards a tall, sleek man, a man dressed in black. He extends his hand and Emma grabs it, almost falling from her high heels.

"Do you have anything?" Emma whispers to the man. "Any blow? A joint?" Marijuana would calm her down, would make her see things more clearly. Would take her mind off him, Ted Weaver, as she watches him walk across the room. His back is strong. He is a big man. Muscular. Emma would like him to hold her. She would like to feel his arms around her, she would like to wrap her arms around his back and hold on tight. She shakes her head. She doesn't know why the hell she'd be fantasizing about a man in ripped jeans.

Her director and the man back away from her slightly. The director shrugs. "She's tired, I think. We've been shooting all day."

"I'm not tired," Emma says.

The man dressed in black disappears into the crowd.

Ted Weaver walks up to a woman with red hair. A tall woman. A woman who looks strikingly familiar. Emma can't place her. Emma's eyes feel thick, as if she's looking through the bottom of a bottle. Ted puts his arm around the woman and whispers in her ear. The woman turns and looks straight at Emma.

"Christ, Emma, he was going to give us money for the movie. He's not a drug dealer," the director says.

"He looked like a drug dealer. All that black. Besides, what did you want me to do? Sleep with him?"

For just an instant the director's face gives him away.

"Oh, shit, Mark, you wanted me to sleep with him. I'm an actor, not a prostitute."

"Keep your voice down. Of course I don't want you to sleep with him."

"I'm leaving this party. I'm leaving." Emma walks away from her director and the rest of the cast. She can feel the red-haired woman's eyes on her, following her every step. Emma moves slowly, feeling as if she's swimming. One foot in front of the other. She's had many more drugs in one evening than she's had tonight but she feels strange and overwhelmed and scared. She wonders if Ted Weaver put something in her drink. The thought strikes her suddenly and she can't shake it from her head. That's it — he drugged her.

"Shit," Emma says. She collapses in a chair by the front door. Then she sees Ted with the woman again, closer now, his arm still draped around her. There is something so perfectly well known about this woman, as if Emma is looking at her own face in a mirror. Ted says something to the woman. They are alone across the room. Emma watches as the woman pulls away from him, as she shakes her head, no. Ted looks angry and grabs at her arm. He turns and notices Emma watching him and he lets go of the woman and looks straight at her. He smiles. The woman flicks her hair over her shoulder and looks away. Then she looks straight at Emma. She says something to Ted.

Emma gets up from the chair and walks to the door. She picks up her wrap at the coat check and she stumbles out into the evening and waits for the valet to bring her car. She told

Dan to stay at home tonight, that she wanted to drive by herself, feel the wind in her hair, but now she feels like shit and wishes she had her driver here to take her home.

She fumbles with the door, asks the valet to take down her roof.

"You shouldn't drive," he says, but he presses the right buttons anyway and accepts her gracious tip.

"What do you know about anything?" Emma says as she climbs into the car. "You're too young to know anything. You're fifteen."

"Eighteen," the carhop says. "And I know a lot about drinking and driving."

"I'm not drunk." She slams her door. "I'm high."

And then Ted Weaver is there, and he helps her from the driver's side and carefully leads her over to the passenger side. He takes her keys and gets behind the wheel. He starts the engine.

"I'll get you home safe," Ted says. "But you'll have to tell me where we are going. I don't know where you live."

Emma looks over at Ted and sees, behind him, in the window at the party, the woman with red hair. She is looking out at them. The woman has no expression on her face. It's as if she is wearing a mask. Emma can't place her. She looks like someone Emma once knew.

"Your wife?"

Ted looks at the window.

The woman with red hair turns away and disappears back into the crowd.

Ted pulls quickly out of the driveway. "Where are we going?"

"Did you drug me?" For some reason she isn't scared. She doesn't want to call out or get him out of her car.

"What?"

"Did you put something in my drink?"

"No," Ted says. "Why would I do that?"

"I just feel so weird."

"I'll take you home. Don't worry. You're safe with me."

Emma reaches up and pulls the clip out of her hair which falls free over her shoulders and blows in the wind surrounding the car. Ted drives carefully and wonderfully. Emma feels comfortable with him there. He reminds her of one of her mother's many husbands, she supposes. One of the nice ones. All men remind her of them. Each in their own way. A parade of men through the house when she was a child, some of them predatory and possessive, some sweet and kind, others horribly abusive.

Emma takes him back to her house. "You're not a stalker, are you?" She giggles, leaning on the front door.

"Not that I know of."

"There's been a lot of stalkings lately. Brian Silvardo had a woman sitting on his bed when he came home from a shoot one day. She was just sitting there."

"Why is that a stalking? That's more of a break-in."

"She was naked. Did I forget to say she was naked?"

Ted laughs and helps Emma with her key in the front door. Emma walks in first and immediately takes off her shoes.

"Christ, these hurt."

Ted stands at the door. He holds out Emma's car keys and her house keys. He leans towards her and kisses her on the cheek.

"Bye."

"Aren't you coming in?"

"No," Ted says. "I don't think so."

Emma looks at his face. She notices a small mole at the far right side of his cheek. She wants to kiss that mole.

"Why don't you just come in for a coffee?" Emma wonders if she sounds like she is begging.

"If I do," Ted says, "will you respect me in the morning?"

Emma laughs and walks away from the open front door

and towards the kitchen. "Come on. I think I know how to make coffee. If I could just see straight."

She turns on the kitchen lights and the outside pool lights and she looks out the glass windows at the blue glow. She feels an intake of breath beside her.

"Nice," Ted says quietly. He puts his hand on her shoulder. "I love pools."

"Want to go for a swim?"

"Now?"

"I have suits. I have men's suits."

"Of course you do. You have everything."

"Go ahead," Emma says. "Over there. I'll bring out coffee."

"Maybe a Coke instead," Ted says as he opens the patio door and walks outside into the warm night air. "It's too warm for coffee. And make yourself a drink. Your hands are shaking."

"Shit," Emma says to herself. But she pours herself a drink and a Coke for Ted Weaver and she walks outside and stands by the pool and watches his muscles, his large chest, his long legs, as he swims in her pool. She places the drinks beside the pool and goes to the changing room in the cabana and puts on her bathing suit. She wipes some of her makeup off.

Ted doesn't even look at her as she climbs into the pool. He doesn't look at her body. He stares only at her face and he laughs like a boy and he talks about how great the water feels, how if you stay down far enough the mosquitoes aren't bad, how he grew up in Ontario, Canada, and how his parents had a small cottage on a lake just outside of a huge city. He says they spent every summer up there, his father working in the city, coming up on weekends, his mother the housewife, dutiful and patient and kind. And then his face becomes unreadable and he swims away from Emma, towards the other side of the pool. He is quiet.

Emma watches him and she sips on her drink. She kicks

her legs in the water, leaning on the edge of the pool. She feels the shakes slowly leaving her hands and she feels warm and clear. Her lips are thick and numb. She wants so badly to kiss this man. It's been a while since she's made love to anyone, ever since she broke up with Nick Smythe, the tabloids going wild with the story. And he never made her feel desperate like the man before her is making her feel. She thinks it must be the pep pills and she makes a mental note to check the label on them in the morning.

"I had a boat," Ted Weaver is saying, "and my brother and I would drift out into the lake late at night when our parents were sleeping. We would lie in the boat and just look at the stars and drift."

"Sounds wonderful."

"The mosquitoes and blackflies were bad," Ted says, "and you had to make sure no other passing boats hit you in the dark. They couldn't see you. We were just two little heads on the top of the water." Ted floats on his back and Emma watches the swim shorts he is wearing puff up with air. "And then my brother died and I would lie out there alone wishing the boats would hit me."

Emma stares at him.

"But I was young," Ted says. "I was young and angry."

"And then you met that redhead and fell in love." Emma doesn't press the death of his brother. She doesn't want to go there because she can feel the sadness in his voice. She doesn't want to become sad right now. There might be time for that later.

"Something like that."

Emma thinks about how different her childhood was. She never lay flat in a boat by herself on a lake late at night. She was always surrounded by talent scouts, agents, her overbearing mother, her many stepfathers and infrequent stepsiblings, directors, other actors. She was schooled in the studio rooms with other child stars. She never had a moment alone. But this man has nothing now, Emma reasons, and look at all she has. Emma looks up at her house, lit up behind her. She looks deep into her pool. She looks at the drink before her.

"I need another drink."

He has a marriage, but obviously that's not working.

"Would you like me to make you one?"

He has his freedom. The freedom to come and go without being watched.

Emma smiles. "That would be wonderful."

He has a nice smile and wonderful teeth and a glow surrounding his body that Emma writes off as the alcohol she's had but still thinks that it is magical and special and telling her something.

"This time I won't drug it," Ted says, as he splashes playfully past her and climbs out of the pool.

Ted walks into the house with wet feet and a dripping bathing suit. He doesn't dry himself on the towels Emma provided. Emma floats on her back and looks up at the dark sky. She has no idea of the time, or of how much she's had to drink, or what the next step in this evening will be. She floats peacefully, her long hair strung out behind her.

Emma wakes early the next morning, her hair still damp and smelling of chlorine, the covers tangled around her naked legs, her naked body. She wakes alone in her big bed with a horrible hangover, with a pounding in her head. Her mouth is dry, like sandpaper, it hurts to swallow. There is no sign of Ted Weaver, of his presence, and Emma wonders if, after all, he was really there last night. And she wonders what happened after the swim in the pool. She feels her body all over, between her legs, looking for a sign. Did she sleep with him? She can't tell. Her bathing suit is hanging from the open bathroom window latch, drying in the morning sun. She walks around her room, looking for clues — perhaps a condom in the wastepaper basket? Would a man who drugs and rapes you use a condom? Signs of his body in her bed, hairs, stains on the sheets? Nothing. She can't find anything.

"Oh, God," Emma groans, holding her head in her hands. She enters the bathroom and swallows aspirin with water, something she knows will make her vomit, but she wants to vomit, get all the alcohol out of her body.

Maria is in the kitchen making coffee.

"Good morning, Ms. Fine."

"Is it?" Emma whispers.

"Is it what?"

"A good morning?"

"Oh, yes," Maria says. "Look out the windows. The sun is shining. It's glorious. Not too hot, not too cool. Just right."

"Humph." Emma sits at the table, her bathrobe slightly open at the neck, and she picks at the grapefruit Maria places in front of her.

"Are you shooting today?"

"Shooting?"

"The film?"

"Oh. I don't know. Am I shooting?" Emma gets up and gathers her papers and datebook from the kitchen desk. She riffles through them. "Yes, I'm shooting today at three."

"Three? What does that mean?"

"Three o'clock." Emma sits again in front of her grapefruit. She wishes Maria had a better grasp of English. That or she didn't talk so much, ask so many questions.

Maria whistles while she serves the coffee. "Do you want toast? Cereal? What do you want?"

"Just grapefruit and coffee. That's it. Like every other morning."

"You're so skinny. You have to eat more. You're going to waste away." Maria throws her arms up. "Every morning I tell you to eat breakfast, I tell you to eat healthy, and you never do."

"Grapefruit is healthy. I tell you that every morning."

Maria grunts. She pats her rounded belly. "Look at me. I'm the picture of health. If I wasn't too old to have a baby, I'd look just like a woman who can have a baby. You look like a stick figure. You look like those drawings my son used to bring home from school when he was little. The sticky-looking Mama, the sticky-looking Papa." Maria sighs loudly.

"Maria," Emma says, putting her head in her hands again. "Let's do this tomorrow. I'm not in the mood today."

"Suit yourself," Maria says. She bustles out of the kitchen, tsking as she passes Emma.

"Oh, Maria?"

"Yes?" Maria stops and looks back.

"Did you see anyone leave here this morning when you came in?"

"As in a man?"

"Yes," Emma says.

"No, I saw nothing. I saw no one. My eyesight is bad. You know that. You know I can't see anything."

Emma stares at Maria. Maria leaves the room.

"She's insane," Emma says to herself as she picks at her grapefruit.

At the shooting, in the afternoon, he is there, standing by the entrance to the set, watching Emma in character slap her ex-husband across the face and accuse him of stealing her child. Emma sees him standing there, leaning up against the wall, wearing the same ripped jeans and black-and-yellow T-shirt from the night before. She doesn't know how he got on-set but she can't stop the shooting and go and ask him. She feels uncomfortable. She feels naked even though this is the one scene where she is dressed the most. Emma doesn't know what is worse: sleeping with a man and not enjoying it or sleeping with a man and not remembering it.

By the coffee cart he comes up to her and kisses her on the cheek.

"Hello."

Emma stands back, sipping her coffee, she looks up into his face. "Hi."

"That was good," Ted says, indicating her scene.

"It was shit. I'm hungover."

"Couldn't tell."

"I'm an actor," Emma says. "I can act like I'm not hungover." She laughs.

"I had fun last night," Ted says. "I just wanted to tell you that. It was nice talking to you."

"Did your wife have fun last night?"

Ted looks away.

"How did you get in here?" Emma asks.

"I know people," Ted says. "I know lots of people."

The director calls for the cast.

"Well, here I go again."

"Can I see you again? Can we do something?"

Emma stops walking away from Ted. "When did you leave last night?" she asks in a whisper.

Ted smiles. "Just after we swam in the pool. I left you by the front door. You were wet still."

"And dressed?"

"Yes, and dressed." Ted laughs. "You insult me," he says. "You don't remember all we talked about? Your family, my family? You don't remember the small kiss on the lips by your front door? You think I took advantage of you?"

Emma looks confused.

"Cast call," the director shouts.

"Can I come over sometime?" Ted says. "If you'd like. We could be sober together."

Emma pauses. "I would like that. That would be nice." For some strange reason she believes everything he says. She wants to say, "What about your wife," but she can't get those four words out of her dry mouth. She doesn't want to ruin this. Something is happening. She can feel it. She likes this man, and the mention of his wife, the thought that he is married, makes her shudder. Emma has been involved with married men before, more than once, she has watched her mother move from married man to married man, and so she knows the consequences of her actions, she knows what she's getting into.

She swallows her coffee, puts it down just off the set, and waits for the call to slap her ex-husband. When the call comes she raises her hand and slaps hard. Very hard. Harder than she's ever hit him before.

"Perfect," the director shouts. "That's a wrap."

"Shit," the actor says, rubbing his face. "That hurt."

Chapter Ten

Bridget Mcgovern throws the vase at Ted's head. She misses. The vase crashes down near him, but doesn't break. It is a heavy, leaded vase, too heavy to shatter on the soft carpet.

"Where the fuck have you been?"

"Calm down." Ted looks at the vase.

"Where have you been? Where did you go with her last night?" Bridget is wearing a nightshirt and her legs are long and shapely. Her red hair is wild and unruly. "It's been two months, Ted. You're out every night with her. You stay over. You're never with me any more."

"You know what I'm doing. I told you what I'm doing, Bridget."

"I've been filming commercials. You don't even know that. You know nothing about my life any more. All I do is film stupid commercials."

"They bring in money. We need money right now."

"But they're stupid. I hate them. They don't have anything to do with acting. They aren't acting."

Bridget sags down on the couch. Her whole body folds into the pillows. Her shoulders are shaking. Ted realizes that she is crying.

"Christ," he mumbles. "Don't cry. Please. I've got to take a shower. I've got to get to work. Everything is fine. Just think of the future. Remember what I told you. We've got so much to look forward to. The way I planned everything. Everything will be fine. I'm doing this for you. For us."

"I want to act," Bridget says. "Some serious acting. I

want to be someone."

"You are someone."

"You know what I mean. And I want you home. I can't take this. I picture you with her at night when I'm alone. I can't deal with it."

Ted suddenly turns on her, throws a punch at the wall, almost breaks his hand. Then he turns to her quietly and says, "You can't have everything. You weren't satisfied with our life. You wanted money."

"I didn't want this."

Ted leaves the room.

Bridget stays on the couch. She stops crying just as quickly as she started. She wipes her eyes with the backs of her hands and blows her nose on a Kleenex. She can hear the shower start up. Bridget walks over to the vase and picks it up off the floor. She studies it. Not a single crack. She places it carefully back on the shelf beside the other vases she bought herself for wedding presents a couple of years ago. There was no one else to buy her anything. A ceremony at city hall. Relatives all dead. Ted paid a man on the street to be the witness. But she wore white, a long gown. She wore her hair up, a small white veil covered the red strands. She walks to the bathroom and opens the door.

"How long do you think it will take?" she asks Ted through the steam.

"What?"

"How long will you be sleeping with her?"

Ted is quiet. The water hisses around him.

"Tell me, damn it."

"I don't know. Just relax. You've got the surgery. It'll be a while."

"I can't relax, Ted."

"Well, what can I do? The whole thing is in motion. It's started. Your surgery will take time. Recovery could take months. I can't stop it now. I'm not stopping now."

Bridget walks over to the toilet. She looks into the empty bowl. She flushes. The water pressure drops suddenly and Ted shouts and jumps around in the shower. She can see the shape of his body behind the shower curtain.

Bridget leaves the bathroom and goes into the bedroom. She lights a joint. She stands in front of the mirror and looks at herself. Bridget knows she'll have to quit smoking cigarettes. She'll have to gain a bit of weight, some more muscle. The surgery will be painful and long. Bridget hates Ted right now. She hates him so badly she wants to kill him. She touches herself, between her legs, and imagines Ted entering Emma Fine.

"Fuck," she screams.

Ted comes in from the shower, a towel around his waist. He stands behind her and looks at himself over her shoulder in the mirror. Bridget moves over and lies on the bed and Ted lies beside her. He tries to take the joint from her mouth but she inhales deeply and then holds it away from him. Ted opens her nightshirt and starts to kiss her tight stomach, her small breasts. Bridget stares at the ceiling and smokes. She tries to ignore his movements.

"I can't stand it any more," she whispers. "I miss you."

"Hmmm ..." Ted says. "I love you. You know I love you."

"I want you back."

Ted kisses Bridget's belly button, he runs his hands up her thighs, stroking softly. "I'm not stopping this, baby," Ted says. "I'm in the middle right now. I want what she has."

"We could, you know. We could stop." Bridget rolls over towards him and opens his towel. His back is still wet from the shower. She pushes him down on his back and then straddles him, her joint dangling close to his chest.

"Careful with that."

Bridget holds the joint close, almost burning some of his hairs.

"Shit." Ted reaches up and grabs hold of her wrist. He twists it. She cries out.

"I can't sleep at night," Bridget whispers, rubbing her wrist. "I stare at the ceiling all night and I can't breathe. I feel like someone is sucking my breath out of me. I feel like someone is sitting on me. I don't think it's worth it. Nothing is worth this."

"Do you know what she has? Have you seen where she lives, what she owns?" Ted takes the joint out of Bridget's hand and puts it out in the ashtray beside the bed. He grabs her hips with his large hands, adjusts her, forcefully enters her. "We only live once."

Bridget groans.

Ted pulls at her hair, pulls her head back until all he can see is her neck. "She has so many clothes, baby. Shoes and makeup and jewellery and furs. A goddamn fur coat. You want a fur coat?"

Ted puts his clothes on in the bedroom. He is tired, overworked. His construction boots are slipped on at the front door. He gets in his truck and drives off. More overtime. Bridget watches from the front window. She lights up another joint and picks at her fingernails. She bites the inside of her cheek until it bleeds and the smoke from the pot makes the cut sting. After some time she takes a shower and gets dressed.

Bridget can't get by the security gate at the bottom of the driveway. The electronic voice says that "entry is not permitted." She makes up a name but the voice still won't let her by. She says she is a manicurist, a makeup artist, a masseuse, an old friend, a good friend of Emma Fine. The gate stays locked.

"Fuck," Bridget says. She kicks the gate with her open-toed high-heel sandals. She stubs her toe. "Ouch, fuck." Bridget hobbles around the front of the gate, clutching at her toe, almost falling over. She sits in the driveway in her miniskirt and tank top, her long legs forward. She leans back on her hands and looks up at the sky. Her car is parked just down the street. She looks at it. "Piece of shit," she says. Bridget sits forward and lights a cigarette. Her red hair looks orange in the bright sun. There is no way she can quit smoking, Bridget thinks. Maybe Ted could get Emma to start smoking.

A car horn honks. Bridget stands up, shading her eyes. She looks at the car, pulled half into the driveway. A man gets out of the car and walks over towards her.

"Can I help you with anything?" the man says.

"I want to talk to Emma Fine," Bridget says, putting her cigarette out on the driveway.

"Does she expect you?"

"Who are you?"

"I'm her driver. Who are you?"

"Well, driver, she doesn't expect me. If she expected me, that stupid security gate would have let me in."

"If she doesn't expect you, then you can't go in."

"Listen ..."

"Dan."

"Listen, Dan, I've come a long way to get here, to talk to her. It's important."

"A long way?"

Bridget signals down the side of the mountain, towards the valley.

"Oh, a long, long way." Dan laughs. He looks at the woman's clothes, her heels, her cigarette-stained fingers, and red hair. "From the valley." He thinks this woman looks vaguely familiar. He's seen her somewhere. Matter of fact, she looks a bit like Emma Fine. Smaller breasts, red hair, but the same wide eyes and full lips. Approximately the same height and weight.

"Can you get me in?" Bridget turns coy. She sidles up to Dan. "Advice?"

"Yes?"

"Don't be so obvious," Dan says. He steps away from Bridget. "Don't sell yourself short." He gets back in the car. "You'll have to move," he says. "I'm going in."

"I'll follow the car," Bridget says.

"No you won't." Dan presses a button in the car and security gates slowly open. He drives the car in. Bridget stands there, in the driveway, not sure of what she should do. She looks at the car, at the gate, at her feet in such high heels, at the sky. She thinks everything seems so impossible sometimes. She's angry. She's tired. She hasn't slept in weeks. The gate starts to close. She watches Dan drive the car up the long driveway towards the garages at the top.

"What the hell," Bridget says. She slips through the closing gate and walks up the driveway, swinging her purse. Dan comes out of the garage and walks down towards her.

"This is called trespassing, you know. That's what it's legally called."

"Is that what you'll charge me with?"

"Not me," Dan says. "Emma Fine."

"I'm not a threat. I just want to talk."

"About what?"

"About my husband," Bridget says. "About Ted Weaver."

Dan nods. "Ah, good old Ted. So you aren't a stalker? A crazed fan? Just a woman whose husband is sleeping with a movie star."

Bridget laughs. "I've never even seen any of her movies," she lies. "I don't even know what this woman looks like. All I know is that she's sleeping with my husband and I want to get a look at her. Maybe have a nice, friendly chat." Bridget rifles through her purse for another cigarette and then she lights it. "I'm not carrying a weapon, I don't intend to fight or anything. I just want to make myself heard. I'm sick of staying home while they fuck."

Dan smiles. "You should go out more," he says. "It's not healthy to stay at home and sulk."

Bridget says. "Maybe I'll just sleep with someone myself. Maybe I'll just start having affairs." She throws her half-smoked cigarette down on the ground.

"With who?" Dan asks. He straightens up.

"Anyone will do," Bridget smiles. "Even you."

"I don't even know your name, Mrs. Weaver."

"Screw that. I'm Bridget McGovern. I'm not a Mrs. to anyone." She pushes one hip forward and balances carefully on her heels, looking as if she's going to fall.

"I don't think you want to see Emma Fine," Dan says, sighing. He takes Bridget's arm and begins to lead her down the driveway.

"Hey."

"You're just angry now. Talk to your husband. He's the one you should talk to."

"It takes two people," Bridget says. "Two people to fuck."

"Come on, let's go."

Bridget pulls her arm away. "You know where we met?"

"Here, in the driveway."

"No, me and Ted."

"Where?"

"In Canada."

"I think I know where that is." Dan laughs. He's enjoying this afternoon. He always enjoys it when life throws him something new. Dan doesn't like stability, routine.

"In Ontario."

"I thought you said Canada."

"Ontario is a place in Canada."

"Oh."

"I was up there shooting a commercial."

"Ah, another actor. Why is everyone you meet in this city an actor?" He thinks that he must have seen her in commercials. That's why she looks so familiar.

"And he was hanging around the set doing construction, fixing things up. It was a commercial for shampoo but they had this huge set because they wanted to make the shampoo a natural-looking product and so they wanted the set in the middle of the woods. It was great. A big cottage front that looked out on a lake. Ted lived on the lake in the summers with his family. He got summer jobs doing construction. When his family died he bought a little hut up there. This was a couple of years ago. We were young."

"Very," Dan says, continuing to lead Bridget down the driveway. "Everyone was young once."

"Anyway," Bridget pops some gum into her mouth. She offers a piece to Dan, who refuses. "We hit it off. Right away. It was like magic, you know. Obsessive. We couldn't bear to be apart from each other. He followed me down here to L.A. He started his own construction business. And he was doing fine. Doing okay."

"Was?"

"The construction business is up and down," she says. "But we're fine, really. We're okay."

"Just that he's sleeping with one of the world's most beautiful actresses."

"Don't get me madder," Bridget says. "You wouldn't like me when I'm mad."

"I think I'd like you mad or happy."

Bridget stops walking and looks at Dan. "You're something," she says. "You're pretty cute." She smiles, the sun lights up her face. "Really something."

"Shucks," Dan says. "Why don't you come up and see me sometime?"

"I think I will do that. I think I'll come up to the gate and say that I'm here to see Dan. Then the gate will open and I'll come in and find you. Do you live here?"

Dan points to the apartments over the garage. "I'm just up those stairs. Just knock on the door, Bridget McGovern."

"I'll do that sometime. I think that would be fun."

"Fun?"

"Nice." She laughs. She pops her gum. "Like an ice cream cone on a hot day."

"Leave Emma and your husband alone," Dan says. "Concentrate on us." He laughs.

"Hell," Bridget says as Dan pushes her out the gate. "What have we got?"

"Nothing yet."

Bridget watches Dan walk up the driveway. She studies his build, his tight ass. He's muscular. That's useful. She admires Emma's huge house and thinks that someday, if everything works out, this could be hers.

Bridget strolls off down the street to her car, swinging her purse behind her. She wants to be home before Ted gets home. She wants to make him a nice late dinner, maybe run a bath so they can soak together like they used to. He promised her that he would come straight to her tonight. He promised her that he would come right home after his overtime shift. Ted's working weekends and evenings, working early in the morning. When he isn't working he's with Emma. Bridget thinks that he is trying, it isn't all about sleeping with Emma Fine. He wants everything for Bridget too. They are in this together. But tonight he promised he would bring her something — blow, a joint — something special. She stops at her car, and using the side mirror, she runs her fingers over her eyebrows to smooth them down. Bending down, she applies some red lipstick before getting in and driving home.

Chapter Eleven

"She's a maid?"

"She works for the priest. She cleans his office, his house, and helps out cleaning the church sometimes."

"Holy shit," Will says.

"I told you this will make a big story." Bruce stares out the window at his neighbour who is suntanning in the front yard. She is lying on a reclining lawn chair and has covered herself in suntan lotion. She is holding a reflective shield under her chin. Her skin looks leathery and loose. Bruce wonders who she thinks she is. He wonders why she doesn't tan in the backyard, in privacy. Is she trying to achieve something, brown skin, or trying to tempt the neighbourhood?

"Well, write it up."

"I can't just write it up." Bruce feels strange talking about Emma Fine. He feels as if he's betrayed a sacred trust. He feels cowardly and shamed.

"What do you mean? Write it up." Will has left his shoes on today, and as he reclines back in his chair at the office, phone cradled under his chin, he can smell an unpleasant odour emanating from below. His feet are sweating. Will thinks he should move somewhere cold, the North Pole, the Arctic, somewhere where he won't always be sweating. But his wife won't move. His wife won't leave her tennis club, her health club, her spa, her daily juice stands, her monthly colonic. Let alone leave the shopping. Will sweats just thinking of his wife and the amount of money she spends every day, money that he makes working at this shit job, spending his day forcing writers to meet deadlines, coercing the production department to just hold space.

"I have to do more research, I have to get to know her, interview her. Come on, Will. All I've done is run away from her at a church and then get some information from a passing nun. I haven't even spoken to her yet."

"Get going on this," Will says, "before someone else figures it out."

"You're the one who didn't want me to do this anyway," Bruce says, watching the leather-tanning woman turn over. "You're the one who discouraged it."

"Look, asshole. Just do your work."

"Fine."

"Fine."

"By the way," Will says, "Trash loved your article. Their agent called to thank me."

"Yeah?"

"Yeah."

"Did you tell him it was all bullshit?"

Will laughs.

Bruce hangs up the phone and stands up.

"Hey," Bruce says to himself, to the woman tanning on the lawn, "get a life."

Half an hour later, Bruce is writing up questions to ask Emma Fine and the phone rings. It's Shelley calling from Canada. She wants to know if their son, Tyler, can come down and visit, stay a week or two.

"It's a bad time," Bruce says.

"It's a bad time? You haven't seen him in over a year."

"The day you left me was a bad time."

"Let's not get into that right now. Let's deal with Tyler, not with us."

"Why does he want to come right now?"

"He needs to get away for a while. He's having a hard time."

"What kind of hard time?"

"Just stuff, Bruce. A lot of stuff is going on."

"That's right," Bruce says. "A lot of stuff is going on in my life right now too." He hears Shelley sigh. "I'm really busy right now. I'd love to see him. In a month? Would a month from now be okay?"

"Busy with what?"

"Even three weeks. I can do three weeks. If you'd only phoned me a few days ago."

"Now, Bruce. School starts in a month. He wants to come now. What are you busy with?"

"It's not important."

Shelley pauses. Bruce can hear the weighty silence, the heavy thoughts moving from Canada down to California. "What's the weather like there?"

"Sunny," Bruce says. "It's always sunny here. A nice cool breeze."

"It's humid here," Shelley says.

Bruce laughs. "Serves you right."

"Thanks."

Silence.

"Look," Shelley says. Her voice is tight. "Are you seeing someone right now? Is that the problem? Is that why you don't want him to come? Because that's okay, Bruce. I mean, Christ, I remarried. You can see people. It's been ten years, for God's sake."

Bruce watches the neighbour pick up her magazine, her folding chair, her reflective shield, and her suntan lotion and walk back into her house. He watches the jiggle in her thighs, the roll of fat around her hips, the cellulite appear with every step she takes. He starts to think that maybe his body isn't all that bad, that there are worse bodies out there.

"Is that what it is?" Shelley again.

"No, not really. No. I'm not seeing anyone. Not really."

"Yes or no, Bruce. It's a simple question."

"But it's not your business."

Shelley hums under her breath, something she does when she's angry.

"Look," Bruce says. "How's Amy? How's Michael?"

"Fine. Thanks for asking."

"Is Amy still in gymnastics?"

"No, Bruce. That was years ago."

"Oh."

"Look. What's wrong is this — Tyler thinks he might be … he thinks he's … well —"

"Well what? What is he? Gay?" Bruce barks out a laugh.

"Yes," Shelley says. "I knew you'd understand. He thinks he's gay."

Bruce releases a huge puff of air. "Gay? I was just guessing, just making fun of …"

Silence.

"He's too young to know," Bruce says. "He's too young."

"Seems it's not an age thing," Shelley says. "Anyway, Michael doesn't really feel equipped to talk to Tyler about it."

Bruce says. "Did Michael make my son gay?"

"Bruce."

"How the fuck did this happen? Michael isn't equipped to talk about it, but I am? What the hell does that mean?"

"It's part of life, Bruce. It's the way he feels. It's who he is. I thought you'd be more understanding. You're his father."

"You sprung it on me, Shelley. You knocked me on the head with it."

"Yes, I suppose I did. Can he come down? Can he come visit?"

"Yeah, sure." Bruce runs his fingers through his hair. "Yeah, that's fine. Just tell me when to pick him up."

"Thanks, Bruce."

Even though it's August, Bruce imagines Shelley up there in the snow. Bruce doesn't think he's ever seen her in a heavy winter coat.

"What kind of coat do you have?"

"What?"

"Winter coat."

"Down-filled, I think, I don't know."

"What colour?"

"Blue."

"Light blue? Dark blue?"

"Powder blue, I guess. Why?"

"Just wondering."

"Listen," Shelley says. "Be kind to him, okay? This might just be a phase. It might be nothing. It might just have something to do with being sixteen."

"Something to do with living in Canada, perhaps."

"It might be nothing."

"Or it could be the rest of his life," Bruce says.

"Yes, I suppose so. I suppose this could just be the beginning."

Part Four

There is a polaroid photo stashed in a box of Emma's belongings. A picture of Emma's mother and Fred Randolph, her third husband, on their wedding day. It is not a posed picture. It was taken by a friend who was their witness. Emma's mother's dress is long and white and clingy. Her hair is up on her head and she is wearing flowers in it and carrying white lilies. She is turning away from the camera, away from Fred, her hand reaching out to touch him, yet falling off his broad shoulder as she looks at the person behind her. Fred is wearing a dark suit and looking directly at the camera. He is smiling wonderfully. A huge, open smile. In the bottom corner of the photo is a child. It is Emma. She is ten years old. Her mouth is wide open. She is looking straight at the camera and sticking out her tongue. Her eyes are angry and cold.

Notes from Psychiatric Assessment of Emma Fine

Subject appears agitated. Biting lower lip. Sitting with arms crossed, legs crossed. Typical defensive pattern. I mention memory loss directly after body was found in pool. Subject says drinking and narcotics are to blame. Subject says that someone may have spiked her drinks at the party and the mix of alcohol and drugs resulted in memory loss. Subject says she has no memory of deceased or of incident that led to death. No physical evidence of blood injury trauma to the head. No behavioural oddities that would indicate any trauma to the brain. Subject egocentric. Checks lipstick twice, smoothes skirt on legs, full, open, rehearsed smiles. More interested in fact that I've seen her in movies than she is about dead lover in pool. First session ends without any breakthroughs.

Sergeant Erin Flight's Report on the Disappearance of Bridget Amelia McGovern

After orders were given by Detective Joe MacLean at the residence of Emma Fine, Sergeant Bob Bradley and myself visited 1274 Beachwood Drive at 6:42 p.m. to inform the female party about the death of her husband. There was no sign of the female party. The house was closed up. No sign of forced entry. When the neighbours (a Mrs. Butterfield at 1276 Beachwood Drive and a Mr. Random at 1272 Beachwood Drive) were questioned, they told the police that the female party was last seen two nights prior, leaving in her car in the direction of the local shopping district (Trillium Avenue). She put a large shopping bag and a black purse into her car and was wearing blue shorts and an orange sweatshirt. Black running shoes. She was never seen returning. Neighbours said that all was usually quiet at the Weaver-McGovern residence except for the odd domestic squabble where the female party sometimes threw items of furniture or glass vases at the retreating male party. The neighbours also commented on the fact that the male party was rarely home, often not coming home for days. They seemed to be in trouble financially. According to the neighbours, the male party was once seen stealing a newspaper off the steps of the lady across the street. Mrs. Butterfield told Sergeant Bradley that the female party recently had some severe cosmetic surgery and looked quite different from the wedding picture we showed her found in the male party's pocket. Sergeant Bradley filed a missing person's report. After we contacted the landlord and after a brief wait for him to arrive, he let us into the house. We found that all of the furniture, everything, was missing. Nothing had been left behind. We put out an APB on Bridget Amelia McGovern and had Mrs. Butterfield come into the office to give a description to a sketch artist. We got a search warrant and dusted the house for fingerprints and had a forensics officer in searching for evidence. Nothing out of the ordinary was found. It should also be noted that no one else in the neighbourhood really noticed the McGovern-Weaver couple as they had only been living there a year and were rarely home, and when trying to interview friends, relatives, or employees of the couple, we were unsuccessful in finding anyone who had any recent contact. Dan Pluggs, Emma Fine's driver, will testify that he had a brief affair with the female party seven months prior to the murder but that "she didn't say much" during their affair, which ended hastily and angrily. He claims that she knew about her husband's affair with Emma Fine, and although upset at first, she became increasingly satisfied with not doing anything about it. He will tell you that the female party was actually happy that her husband was out all the time as it gave her time to meet with Dan Pluggs. The driver claims he had no further contact with the female party after their affair ended. He said she was always asking for money for drugs and complaining about her acting career going nowhere. All others interviewed said that Weaver-McGovern were an attractive couple. Mr. Weaver's employer said he was hardworking and quiet but was often quick to anger. Ms. McGovern's employees for the commercials she made said that she stopped coming to work for them about six months before her disappearance and that she was usually high on drugs. They said she couldn't really act but that she looked good so they used her for commercials. She told a fellow actor that she was saving up for cosmetic surgery.

Chapter Twelve

Emma Fine's third stepfather, Fred, an executive at a record company, is sitting on the front porch holding a small wooden box in his lap. Emma is sitting beside him. She is ten years old and has been in three movies and over twenty commercials.

"What's in the box?"

Fred looks at Emma, at her blonde hair in pigtails, her full lips.

"Your mother's toes," he says. "I cut them off."

Emma laughs.

"I'm not kidding."

"Show me," Emma says. "There aren't any toes in there. I saw Mom walking around this morning."

"I cut them off while you were at the studio school."

Emma pauses. She thinks. "That's not funny."

"I didn't mean it to be funny. I wanted to teach her a lesson. Now I'm feeling bad about it. So much pain."

Emma squirms. She moves away from Fred. Fred lights a joint. He inhales deeply.

"Don't move away. Come sit close to me."

"You're not funny, Fred. Stop telling lies." Emma stands up. "Mom?" she calls out into the house. "Mom? Where's Mom?"

"Bleeding, I assume." Fred smiles. Smoke pours out of his nose.

"Mom?" Emma runs into the house. Her mother is in the kitchen preparing cocktails. "Mom." Emma runs over to her mother and hugs her. She looks down at her mother's feet inside suede sandals. She looks at her mother's toenails all painted fire-engine red.

"Emma, let go. I'm getting cocktails. Let go of me." Emma's mother pushes her off and moves out onto the front porch with a pitcher of tonic and a bottle of gin. Emma can hear Fred talking and then her mother's high-pitched laugh. They have been married six months. Emma hates Fred.

Emma goes out to the front porch. Fred is sitting on the porch swing with her mother. He is still holding the box. Emma's mother is touching Fred's hair, his ear, his neck, running her long nails softly down his chest. She takes the joint from his fingers and inhales.

"That wasn't funny," Emma says.

"Oh, honey," Emma's mother says, blowing smoke in her daughter's direction. "You've got absolutely no sense of humour. Lighten up."

Emma is five years old and Travis is taking her to dance lessons. He is her mother's second husband. He is a talent scout. He wants Emma to call him Daddy. She won't. She refuses.

"Just once, honey pie. Just call me Daddy for the girls at class. I just want to hear it once."

"No." Emma won't hold his hand to cross the street. She won't touch him. But he touches her. Travis runs his hands over her hair all the time, pets her like a bunny. He likes to kiss her cheeks and the top of her head. Emma doesn't know why she hates him. He buys her nice presents: soft teddy bears and chewy candy and pink ice cream cones. She wants her real daddy back, she wants her mommy to tuck her into bed at night instead of Travis.

At the dance class the teacher says to Travis, "It's so nice of you to get her into her leotard and tights. Most fathers don't know the first thing about putting on tights."

*

Emma doesn't remember when she was a one-year-old and her real daddy punched her mother in the stomach, the eye, the nose, the teeth. She doesn't remember when he threatened her mother with a knife, a gun, a power saw, a screwdriver. Emma doesn't recall when he hit in the wall, the window, the kitchen cupboard, the TV set. And Emma certainly doesn't remember the day he rolled her crib out into the hallway and tried to push it down the stairs.

"Good thing," her mother always said, "good thing the crib was too wide."

"Good thing," Emma always said, "good thing the stairs were so narrow."

Emma is lying next to Ted Weaver in bed. They are both naked. They are both looking up at the ceiling at the mirror that can be hidden behind a retractable panel. They are looking at each other and at themselves.

"Those are shit stories," Ted says. "You had a bad life."

"*Had* is the operative word," Emma says. "It's over now. My mom died five years ago, my stepfathers are all poor and remarried."

"What did your mother die of?"

Emma sits up, her large breasts attract Ted's eyes. He can't help but reach out and touch them. Emma reaches for her glass of wine beside the bed and she sips it.

"She died of breast cancer. Kind of funny, isn't it?" Emma cups a breast in one hand and looks down at it. "She had both of them removed but it still got her."

"I'm sorry." Ted leans up on his elbow and kisses Emma's cupped breast. "I wouldn't want you to lose these."

"They aren't real anyway," Emma says. "Oh, God, I can't believe I said that." She puts her glass down and flops the pillow over her head. Her words are muffled. "Don't tell anyone that. I didn't say that."

"Emma," Ted laughs. He pulls the pillow off her head and

he kisses her neck, her breasts, her lips, her cheeks. "Everyone knows they aren't real. Don't you read the tabloids?"

Emma laughs. "You make me feel like a million bucks," she says. "You make me feel like a movie star."

Ted continues to kiss her. He kneels on the bed and disappears under the covers. In the mirror above her, Emma watches his bulk move slowly under the sheets. She watches her expression as he finds the right spot and she watches her eyes as she reaches orgasm. She is amazed at the fact that she is in her room, watching herself and also on some other plain, floating high. Her eyes seem cold to her, but her lips are flushed hot and swollen.

"I have to go home tonight," Ted says when he comes up from the covers, when he's holding her in his arms, when she's lying her head on his chest.

"Why?"

"Bridget is getting suspicious."

Emma laughs. "Suspicious? She must be smart. You've only been out every night since we met and you've stayed over half those nights. What could she be thinking?"

"Actually," Ted says, his voice getting angry, "I think she's seeing someone too."

"Oh?" Emma sits up. She touches Ted's face. "That would be wonderful. It would make everything easy."

Ted's eyes change. Emma sees a flicker of dark. He moves out of the warm covers and begins to put on his clothes. "That's not acceptable," he says.

"What?"

"She has no right."

"No right? You're with me. I thought you said your marriage wasn't working. And it's not, Ted. It's obvious it's not working, isn't it?"

Ted continues to get dressed.

"Come on," Emma says. "Come back to bed. Let her spend the night with her lover."

Ted turns to Emma. His face is stiff and enraged. His hands are clenched tight. Emma moves back a bit on the bed. She is suddenly afraid. She has never seen him angry.

"I'm going home tonight," Ted says. He can barely control his rage. Images of his father, his mother, his dead brother, and what they did to him, what they did to each other, what they did to the world he was living in. Every time Ted gets angry he sees nothing else. All thoughts centre on these three people and his mind is a blur of red pain.

Emma follows him out into the hallway and down the stairs. She has wrapped a sheet around her body.

"If you go," she says, "don't ever come back."

"Fine," Ted shouts. "That's fine with me."

"Don't go." Emma begins to cry. "I thought you said I was more important to you. I thought you didn't love her any more."

Ted walks out the front door. Emma follows him to the driveway. A car pulls up into the garage. Dan gets out.

"Evening," he says.

Emma is crying. "He's leaving," she shouts at Dan. "Stop him."

Dan stands there eyeing Ted. Ted eyes Dan. Then Ted walks down the driveway, out towards his truck. He climbs in, starts the engine, and drives off down the hill.

"He left," Emma cries. "And you didn't do anything. Why didn't you do anything?"

Dan walks over to Emma. He takes her in his arms and hugs her, comforts her. He touches her hair, her naked back. He wraps her tight in her sheet and he leads her up the stairs and back into her bed. He gives her a sleeping pill which she washes down with wine. "What," Emma says, "does he see in his wife when he's got me?"

"Nothing," Dan says. "Just history."

Dan tucks Emma between the covers and turns out the light.

Ted doesn't visit Emma for over three weeks after their fight and Emma works on her movie, drinks too much, takes too many drugs, lies in her large bed with the retractable panel over her mirror drawn back, and stares at her face, at her eyes, at her lips. This is just the first fight, Emma thinks, and she wishes so badly that Ted didn't have a wife to go home to. Emma is all alone. She should get married so that, in times like this, she'd have someone to be with. Emma stares at herself for hours on end and no matter how much she stares she can't see what she wants to see. It doesn't matter how she moves her face, what angle she tilts her chin, whatever it is she is looking for just isn't there. It's not in the shine of her eyes or in her parted lips. It's not in the curve of her nose or the highlights in her hair. There is nothing hovering around her, no aura, no sense of herself. And Emma wonders, for an instant, if Ted took that thing she is looking for away from her, or if he put it there within her. Maybe, she thinks, maybe she never had it before.

Chapter Thirteen

It is early in the morning. A beautiful spring day. Crisp. The birds are rustling, singing, chirping in the bushes surrounding Emma Fine's property.

A hooded figure crouches in a small hollowed-out area in the bushes and watches through the wall of glass as the maid bustles around the kitchen. She leaves. The figure then watches the sun brighten the day and then follows the movements of the man as he comes into the kitchen and makes his breakfast. Oatmeal. He is having oatmeal with syrup, a cup of black coffee, and orange juice. He makes a mess of dishes and when the maid re-enters she throws up her arms in dismay. The man smiles and laughs. The figure in the bush smiles slightly, lips closed. The maid begins the dishes, running hot water into the sink, squirting in soap. The figure in the bush itches a thigh, flexes a muscle to keep from falling asleep. The figure yawns and then worries about the movement made, the startling of the birds above, worries about white teeth gleaming through the green bush, worries about a sneeze coming on. A bird calls out. The man glances out the window at the pool, at the garden beyond. He talks to the maid. He gets up from the table and stretches. The maid raises her hand in a gesture of departure and then leaves the kitchen carrying a laundry basket, throwing some comment over her shoulder.

Ted Weaver walks out onto the deck of the pool, patting his full stomach. He is wearing green work pants and a white T-shirt. He stretches and smiles. He takes a deep breath of fresh morning air. He bends to put on the construction boots he is carrying, a last-minute check on his condominiums before the camping trip. And as he bends, the hooded figure rushes out from the bushes, races across the lawn in a crouched position, quickly, athletically, without any awkwardness, and hops the fence to the deck of the pool. Ted Weaver doesn't see what is coming. The figure takes a heavy metal pipe from the pocket of the hooded sweatshirt and raises it above the crouched man's head. Once, twice, three times, down on his head. The first blow startling, the pained expression in Ted Weaver's eyes, the flash of recognition, the thoughts colliding; the second blow knocking unconscious, his body slumps over his boots, straightens out on the ground; the third blow for good measure, to make sure Ted Weaver does not get up.

Don't get up.

The hooded figure puts the pipe back into the pocket, drags the heavy body to the edge of the pool, and stumbling and weaving — the body is so heavy — rolls him in. A small splash, some water comes up over the side of the deck, washes over the figure's black running shoes. The body floats, bubbles come out of the mouth and nose.

The figure jumps the fence again, slips a bit as the black glove catches on the fence, stops to pull off the piece of leather that ripped, places the leather in the pocket with the pipe, and then runs, crouched, back across the lawn towards the bushes. Light footsteps on a shorn-close lawn. The lawn bounces back, springs back. No prints. Disappears.

Maria enters the kitchen, complaining loudly about the dishes, sees something moving on the grass, doesn't notice the body in the pool. She sticks her hands in soapy, warm water and says, "Dogs."

This all happens in the time span of three minutes. Three knocks on the head. Three minutes. Ted Weaver is dead. One hooded figure gone. A car starts down the street. The maid does the dishes.

The wet footprints on the deck dry up quickly in the morning sun.

"There was a dead body in your pool, Ms. Fine. How could you not know how it got there? Surely in the last ten years you've figured it out."

"I told you to leave me alone. I don't want to talk to you. Just leave me alone." Emma rushes away from Bruce and out the front doors of the church. Her thick-soled shoes make no sound on the tiled floor. Outside, in the bright sunshine, Emma stands still and wills her eyes to adjust to the light. Bruce is directly behind her. His hands are shaking as he tries to write down observations in his notepad:

— Sunny, bright, hot. Four p.m.
— Black clothes — hair in a bun.
— No makeup — lines on her face are visible — she's aged incredibly in ten years. Still attractive, though.
— Looks slightly different. Face shifted?
— "Leave me alone."

"I said to leave me alone. Who do you think you are coming into this place, this sacred place, and confronting me like this. Who are you?"

— Her voice is deep, gruff.

"Bruce Dermott," he says. "Reporter. *Entertainment Magazine*."

"I thought so," Emma says. She looks up at the church. "How did you find me?"

"Luck, I guess," Bruce says. "I followed you here one day. I saw you buying flowers."

"Buying flowers? How did you recognize me? What do you want?"

"I want to ask you questions. Write a story about you. What you are doing now, how you fell from stardom, that kind of thing. How you ended up in a place like this."

Emma turns from Bruce. She begins to walk towards the mottled glass doors beside the church. "I will ask you once again," she whispers, "to leave me alone. Don't you think" — she pauses and turns to him — "don't you think that I'm here for a reason, that maybe I don't want to be a star any more."

"I don't want to make you a star, I just want to give the readers some answers."

"I don't want to give answers. I did that in a court of law. Leave me alone."

"But you didn't." Bruce walks again towards her. He calls to her as she opens the door, "You didn't give answers. You raised more questions. That was it."

"Look," Emma says. "I'm innocent. I didn't do anything but make movies. I didn't do anything but take too many drugs and I lost everything because of it. Now go away." She shuts the door behind her and Bruce watches her mottled shadow disappear behind the glass.

Bruce sits on the steps of the church and transcribes their conversation. He sits there in the hot sun, wiping the sweat off his face with a cotton handkerchief he finds in his pants pocket. He looks out into the courtyard for shade but there is nothing but brown, dry grass and a circular pebbled-over driveway. Some small trees and bushes in the corner but they aren't producing shade. The large iron gates leading into the church grounds shed patterned shade upon the pebbles. Bruce moves over to stand beside them. He waits. Surely Emma Fine will soon have to go home. Bruce looks at his watch. It is five-thirty. The sun is still brutally hot and the air is still. He can't believe no one else has noticed her in ten years. It seems unreal.

Bruce has to pick Tyler up at the airport in three hours. His gay son. He wonders what the water is like up in Canada, what it does to straight kids. Bruce always thought Canadian water was purer. But maybe there is some kind of hormone, some chemical, steroid, something, pumped into it. Bruce would like to imagine that. Bruce wishes he could even imagine Canada, he wishes he could see the blue coat Shelley is wearing as she drives her car. What kind of car? His parents took him to Europe every summer. Never Canada. When she lived in L.A., Shelley had a thin, blue sweater she would put on in the evenings. A windbreaker on top of that. It was blue too, come to think of it. Bruce guesses that she knows what looks best with her eyes, that even though her hair is dyed red now, blue will still highlight her eyes. And she drove a Volkswagen. Back when he was in real estate and she worked at the bank. When they had some money. A blue Volkswagen.

There is nothing wrong with gay people, Bruce thinks, as long as it's not his son. For some reason his son's supposed gayness makes him feel like a failure, makes him feel as if he is also gay and doesn't know it — where else would Tyler get this from? Is it hereditary? Has Bruce been deluding himself all these years? He thinks of the last time he met a woman he wanted to sleep with. When was that? Last week. Last week at the interview with Barbara Stanley. The producer's assistant. She was beautiful, funny, nice. But is a once-a-week attraction enough? Bruce once read somewhere that men, on average, have some kind of subconscious sex thought two hundred times a day. That's a lot. Two hundred times a day.

Does he? Bruce shakes his head. He doesn't think so. But because it's a subconscious thought, maybe he does.

Or maybe he only has a sex thought once a week.

Bruce sighs.

Or maybe Michael is gay. Wouldn't that serve Shelley right. A gay second husband. She would leave Michael and come running back to Bruce and Bruce would turn her away, toss her out the door.

Or would he?

Michael was feminine. In some ways. Sure he was large and big and muscular. But he was also sensitive. Shelley said he was sensitive. She said he listened to her when she talked. Well, Bruce thinks, that must be a sign. Bruce doesn't know a single man who listens when a woman talks. "Really listens," as Shelley had said. What's there to listen to? Shelley also said that Michael remembers holidays and birthdays and anniversaries, that he always buys her something to celebrate the occasion. Bruce grunts. Real men don't have the time to remember those kinds of things — there's the car to service, the garbage to take out, the golf game next Sunday, the lawn to mow.

Bruce looks at his watch. He'll have to leave for the airport soon. The sun is beginning to cool down, beginning to get ready to set. Where is Emma Fine? Surely she has to go home sometime. Bruce thinks it would just be his luck to have scared her off. Maybe she'll go into hiding again. Disappear.

"Excuse me?" Bruce stops a nun who is leaving the church. "Could you tell me where that door leads to?" It has just occurred to Bruce that there might be an alternate exit. How could he be so stupid? He stands.

The nun smiles. "That's the residence," she says.

"The residence?"

"Where we live. Our home."

Bruce stands still. He doesn't move a finger or toe or arm. His nose itches but he doesn't wiggle it or scratch. If he moves, all of this will be a dream. The perfect, ground-breaking Hollywood story. The title screams at him: "Missing Hollywood Star Is Live-in Maid at a Catholic Church in Pasadena."

"Can I help you with anything?" the nun asks.

"Who lives there?"

"I don't think that's any of your concern," the nun says, looking around. "Are you looking for someone?"

"The nuns? Do the nuns just live there or can anyone live there?" It would make sense, Bruce thinks. She's always here.

"Run along," the nun says. "I'm coming out to close the gate." The nun ushers Bruce off the property. He moves slowly. She pushes him slightly. "Come on now. Don't take all evening. I have things to do."

Bruce stands outside the closed gate and looks in. The residence. Emma Fine lives there. Jesus Christ, what a story. Ex-stripper, drug addict, Hollywood star, Oscar winner, lives in a church.

At least, Bruce thinks as he rushes home to get his car, to drive to the airport, to pick up his son, at least she lives there for now. At least for the next couple of hours, before she packs her bags and disappears for good. Again.

"Damn," Bruce says as he jogs heavily and awkwardly back to his townhouse. Panting, wheezing, puffing. He hopes he hasn't scared her off.

His fridge is a mess of milk, avocado, eggplant, raw steak, hamburger meat, raspberry syrup, cheese slices, pickles, and onions. He's got carrots and tartar sauce and ketchup and cream sodas. His cupboards are full of pretzels and unsalted crackers and white bread and peanuts. There are four mouldy sweet potatoes under the kitchen sink. They are wet and smell like raw fish. In the pantry Bruce has three cases of beer and over seventy bottles of wine. He has two bottles of Scotch, one bottle of gin, and one bottle of vodka.

"Don't you have any cereal?" Tyler asks.

"Cereal?"

"Cheerios? Cap'n Crunch? Even oatmeal or granola?"

"Cereal," Bruce says. "I don't usually eat breakfast."

"You don't eat breakfast? That's the most important meal of the day."

"So I've been told," Bruce says. He is standing by his fax machine, looking at what has just come through. A photocopied newspaper clipping from three years ago. Will is sending it from the office. It's a story about the disappearance of Emma Fine, about a reporter who claimed to have seen her in Italy, about the high lifestyle she was living there, throwing money away at the casinos, spending spring in Tuscany. There are no pictures to accompany the article and it was published in the *West Hollywood Blaster*, a small, local paper, so Bruce doubts the accuracy, although Italy might explain Emma's black-widow attire.

"I'm going to need more food if I'm going to stay here," Tyler says. "I'm going to need the things I'm used to. My stomach can't digest this shit."

"Don't say that word."

"Digest."

"Very funny."

Last night Tyler didn't say very much. He climbed into his father's car, clutching a small suitcase on his lap. He looked scared, as if he thought Bruce would lay into him, scream at him. Bruce was shocked at his appearance. Tyler looks like a girl. Shoulder-length, ratty hair, earrings — too many to count — and thin. Tyler is thin. No muscles on the boy. He wears rings and necklaces and baggy jeans and tight T-shirts. He was carrying a sweatshirt under his arm as he walked into the airport. He has affected a slight lisp. Bruce drove the boy to his townhouse and carried his bag to the guest room where he would be staying. Tyler took a shower and went straight to bed.

Now it is morning.

And Bruce hasn't yelled at him, hasn't even mentioned his homosexuality. Tyler is loosening up, feeling more comfortable.

"I've got work to do today," Bruce says. "Are you going to be okay?"

"Can I come with you? Are you interviewing a rock band?"

"No, sorry, this is touchy business. I'm scoping someone out."

"Oh." Tyler looks into the fridge again and then shuts the door and sighs. "Guess I'll just sit around here all day."

"I'll be back in the afternoon. We'll do something then. Go to the beach, maybe."

"I don't want to go to the beach."

Bruce looks at his son. What kind of boy wouldn't want to go to the beach in California? What kind of a boy?

"What do you want to do?"

Tyler shrugs. He shuffles over to the TV and turns it on.

"Disneyland?"

"Disneyland? Jesus, Dad."

"Tyler, stop swearing."

"Mom doesn't care if I swear. Neither does Michael."

"Well, that's them. I'm me."

"Obviously."

Tyler slumps into the couch. He holds a cushion in front of him, hugs it really. And Bruce suddenly remembers when Tyler was small and how he would sit on the couch, his legs curled up beneath him, his thumb in his mouth, his other hand playing with his belly button. His son liked to touch warm things, soft things: his mother's back, the inside of her shirt, behind her neck, his father's hand, or under the cuff of his pants. Tyler would crawl over and stick his hand up there to keep warm and feel safe. And when no one was around, Tyler would reach under his own shirt and finger his belly button until it was red and raw.

"I don't know," Tyler says. "I thought we'd just be together. Talk and stuff." He is staring at the TV, not daring to look at his father.

Last night Bruce noticed bruises on the boy's arms. He noticed a scar on his neck that he'd never seen before.

"Is Michael pushing you around?" Bruce blurts out suddenly.

Tyler looks at his father. "What are you talking about?"

"The bruises. I noticed some bruises on your arms last night."

"That's just from some kids at school."

"Oh." Bruce looks out the window at the woman next door who has set up her tanning scenario again and is lathering on the oils. He wishes he lived next door to a real looker, someone who would make him think sexual thoughts two hundred times a day, someone who would confirm his virility. His gay son is being bashed around at school. Emma Fine has probably moved away from the church and his chances of a breakout story are gone.

"I have to go. I have to go to work."

"Yeah, whatever." Tyler turns the volume up on the TV and settles back into the couch.

"See you this afternoon?"

"Buy some muesli," Tyler says. "Buy something for me to eat for breakfast."

Bruce gives Tyler an extra key to the house, gives him some money, and leaves, locking the door behind him.

"Muesli? What the hell is that," he says to himself on the way down the steps. He can hear his phone ringing, he can hear Tyler pick it up, Tyler saying, "Hi, Mom," and Bruce continues down the front walk where he stops to politely say hello to the tanning woman as she turns onto her stomach and loosens the top to her bikini. He begins the short walk to the church. The tanning woman's face isn't all that bad, Bruce thinks. He is armed with a file folder full of clippings, a file folder stacked with evidence against the elusive and angelic Emma Fine. And the tanning woman's breasts were alluring as she rolled over. Large and round and soft. Reminds him of the beanbag chair Amy had when she was little.

He should start counting. That was the first sexual thought of the day.

Bridget is lying on Dan's bed, looking up at his ceiling fan. She is fully dressed.

"You've got too many pictures of her," Bridget says. "What are you? A pervert? You obsessed with her? Holy shit, your closet freaks me out. Like a goddamn temple or shrine or something. It's like those murder movies you see on TV."

Dan is standing by the window, looking out on the freshly trimmed lawn. It is noon.

"You want to go out for lunch?"

"Out for lunch? You've finally got me in this place, on your bed too, and you want to go out again?"

"You're asking too many questions. How can I get comfortable with you if you're asking too many questions. And I'm collecting her stuff so that, in the future, if she fires me and I need money, I can sell it. See those gloves? They'd be worth a couple hundred at least." Dan scratches at his head. "And those murderers have the stuff out where they can see it, right? My stuff's all in my closet. It's in no particular order. I don't even really know what I have."

"Come here," Bridget says. She pats the bed. "I'll forgive you for being in love with her. Everyone's in love with her. I don't mind that. My husband's in love with her. Come lie down beside me and watch the ceiling fan spin. It gives you a rush."

"I watch it every night. I'm not in love with her. I'm hungry for lunch."

Bridget leaps up. "I can make you lunch," she says. "I can make a mean tuna fish sandwich. You got tuna fish?"

"Yeah, I got tuna fish. I got bagels too."

"You just stay there, Danny boy," Bridget says, "and I'll make you the meanest tuna fish sandwich you've ever seen."

"There's never been a tuna fish sandwich I haven't liked,"

Dan says. He sits down in the chair by the window and remains looking out.

"What are you looking for?"

"What do you mean?"

"You're staring at the window like you're looking for something." Bridget bangs around in the kitchen.

"It's a nice day. Can't I look out if it's a nice day."

"Danny boy —"

"Stop calling me that."

"You're going to have to win me over if you want to see me naked, you know. If you want me to climb all over you, you're going to have to be a much nicer person."

"It's not about that," Dan says.

"What's it about then?"

"I'm just hungry. I'm just looking out the window and I'm hungry. Let's eat our mean sandwiches and then let's get back on the bed and look at the fan. Okay? Is that okay with you?"

"That's okay with me." Bridget is wearing a halter top, short jean shorts, and black running shoes. When she bends to find the tuna in the cupboard Dan can see the shorts ride up the crack in her ass. He crosses his black running shoes before him and looks out the window. He thinks about how everyone these days has black running shoes. Used to be every pair was white. Now all you see is black. Then Dan sits up slightly when he sees Emma leave the house with that new man, Bridget's husband. They are walking hand in hand towards the convertible. Ted is wearing those damn sunglasses, dark glasses, he wears when he's trying to be cool. He gets in the driver's side and Emma climbs in shotgun. Dan watches as Ted reaches towards Emma and kisses her lips. He pulls her body close to his. He fondles her knee which is exposed from a slit in her flowing dress. Dan suddenly senses something in his own apartment and he looks over at Bridget who is now leaning into the other window, looking out at her husband and Emma Fine. She has stopped breathing. She is holding the can of tuna fish in her hand so tightly that her knuckles are white.

"Come here already," Dan says. He stands up from his chair, kicks off his running shoes, and walks over to stand behind Bridget. He reaches up and takes her red hair in his hands and tugs gently, pulls her towards him. He kisses her neck. She is much taller than he is and he has to pull her down slightly to do this. She starts to breathe again when his hand unzips her shorts and reaches into them and his fingers push forcefully up inside of her.

"God," she whispers. "I thought you were hungry."

"I am," Dan says. "Come here." He takes the can of tuna out of her hand and leads her towards his bed. He closes his eyes and pretends that she is Emma Fine. It isn't very hard.

Outside the car engine starts and Emma and Ted drive down the circular driveway and out through the large front gates of her estate. They drive down the mountain, towards the yacht club, and Emma Fine keeps her hand at all times on Ted's inner thigh, on his shorts. She strokes the hairs on his legs and she lets her hair fly in the warm wind surrounding the convertible.

Chapter Fourteen

Ted is back in Emma Fine's bed. They fight every month or so and then Ted comes back with an apology, some flowers, wine or Scotch or champagne. He comes back with uppers, small bags of cocaine, pep pills, and valium. Emma gives him money. She takes him back into her bed, drinks the alcohol, sniffs the coke, pops the pills, and all is fine with the world.

"Enter the world of better living," Ted says as he comes back into her home. "Open the doors and take in the shine."

He is up in her bedroom, under the covers, the air conditioning cranked high. Emma is shivering beside him. Ted is sure that Bridget is seeing someone, he is sure of it. He's screamed at her but she won't tell him anything. He can see it in her eyes, he can feel it in the way she makes love to him. And there is nothing he can do. He has too much on his plate, he's too far into the grand scheme of things. Bridget's plastic surgery will start soon, in a month, and then she won't have the willpower, let alone the physical strength, to carry on with some asshole. She needs to be carved away upon, moulded, made into something she is not. She can't do that with some jerk hanging off of her. The old Bridget will be dead after the surgery anyway. They can start anew as a couple. With his arm draped around Emma, Ted thinks of the doctors he has lined up for Bridget, the best money can buy. He'll take care of her, he thinks, make all the loans from his managers, all the overtime and extra work, everything else, worthwhile. He's so damn tired from all of this.

He just wants to sleep.

Emma is drowsy from alcohol. She reaches to the side table to find her amphetamines. She pops one and lies back and waits for the effect.

"Why the hell do you take those?" Ted says. "You're fucking your body up."

"My body looks great," Emma says. "If I didn't take these, the alcohol would go straight to my hips and I would want to eat and eat and eat. This way I can be happy and diet all at the same time." Emma laughs.

Ted pulls her to him. "I just don't think you should always be high," he says. "It's not a good way to be."

"You'd rather I be down all the time. I think I can manage that." Emma points to the other side table where she has her downers.

Ted sighs. He wipes the hair off Emma's face.

There is the sound of a car in the garage revving up and then the motor of the garage door opening. Ted lets go of Emma and gets out of bed to look out the window.

"Where's he going with the car?"

Emma shrugs.

"What's he do for you anyway?" Ted asks. "He never drives you anywhere."

"He drives me to work so I can read my lines in the car. When I'm in bed with you, he drives over to see his girlfriend."

Ted nods. "You ever slept with him?"

Emma laughs. "Dan? No, I don't think so." She laughs again.

"You don't think so?" Ted climbs back into bed with Emma. He pulls the covers over their naked bodies, up over their heads. "It's like a tent under here," he says. "You ever been camping?"

Emma giggles. "With bugs and stuff? Sleeping on the ground? No hair dryer or makeup? Think about it."

Ted kisses Emma on the lips. He stares into her eyes. The

car below brakes at the gate, waits for it to open, and then drives off in the direction of the valley.

"How come you never slept with your driver? Don't all actresses sleep with the people who work for them? Paid sex?"

Emma's eyes are closing. She is so sleepy. She wonders if she took the wrong pill, maybe she took a valium, not an upper. Lately, she's noticed her pills are getting mixed up. Ted's been giving her new pills and she's finding the uppers in the downer bottle, the amphetamines mixed in haphazardly. "I don't know," Emma says. "There have been a couple of times he's put me into bed when I'm drunk, but I don't think anything happened. He's a pretty trustworthy person. I've had him around for years. I like him." She smiles to herself and then whispers. "I'd sleep with him if he asked me. He's pretty darn cute."

Ted laughs. "He's short. Short and mean and angry. Like a pot-bellied pig."

"Go to sleep now. I have to be murdered in the morning. I've got three scenes to shoot."

"I'm going."

"Going? Where?"

"To sleep." Ted takes the covers off their heads and then wraps Emma up in his strong arms. "You really have to go camping sometime," he says. "You'd love it."

"Can we turn the air conditioning down?" Emma mumbles. "I'm freezing to death."

"I was going to say that," Ted says. "I was going to say that you'd love camping to death." He looks at his reflection in the mirror above. He sees Emma's body, the outline of it under the covers, and he wonders what Bridget will look like in the long run, after the surgery. Her hips already jut out like this, round to perfect long legs and dainty feet. But he wonders if her breasts will mound under covers like Emma's do, look perky and real and fake all at once. Ted sighs.

"Camping," he whispers, "is the best way to go. It's better than any goddamn hotel suite, better than a champagne-filled bathtub, better than the biggest bank account in the world."

"I'm just cold," Emma murmurs. "I'm freezing."

"I'll hold you tight," Ted says. "I'll wrap my arms around you and hold you tight. Pretend you're in Canada. Pretend this is winter and we're going to make snow angels and go cross-country skiing."

Emma says, "Just open the windows and turn off the air conditioning. I'm no good at skiing."

Ted twists out of Emma's arms and pads naked down the hall to the air-conditioning controls. He adjusts the temperature and then walks back to the bedroom.

"Hello," he says to Maria who is standing silently on the landing watching him. "You startled me. What are you doing here?"

"I was coming up to turn the air conditioning off before I go home," Maria says. "Too many dishes to wash tonight. I stayed late. And there you are, buck naked. You look like a pink monkey."

"Thanks." Ted doesn't cover himself. He stands before her and stares her down. He doesn't like this woman. She is always hovering in the shadows, always somewhere spying on him and Emma. He would fire her if he had the authority. He's told Emma that many times but she just laughs at him, tells him it would be like firing her own mother if her mother were still alive. Maria's been with Emma from the beginning and she runs her house like a ship.

"Do you need anything else before I go home for the night?"

"No, thanks."

"I'll be here bright and early in the morning."

"I'm sure you will," Ted says.

Maria walks downstairs, shaking her head back and forth.

Mr. Weaver's penis is as small as she expected. Her black running shoes make no sound on the thick carpeting.

Maria Candalas is in room 712 in the west wing of the Pine Vista Home for the Blind on Pine Vista Road leading up from the beach. Bruce tells Tyler to wait on the beach, grab an ice cream cone, and check out the surf. But Tyler follows his father into the home and stubbornly insists on being present for the interview.

"I'll be your cover," Tyler says. "They'll let you in if you have a kid. If you say she's my long-lost aunt or something."

"A friend of your grandmother's, maybe. She's a little too old to be your aunt." Bruce itches his scalp. "That may work. But I want you to be quiet once we're in there. I don't want you to say anything. Understand?"

Tyler nods. "I don't see any pine trees," he says to the nurse as she checks the registry for Maria Candalas's room. "Shouldn't there be pine trees if it's called Pine Vista Road?"

The nurse looks up at him from over her desk. She holds her head up with her hands, resting her elbows on her desk, as if her head will fall off. "Does Sunset Boulevard always have sunsets?" she says wearily. Her head is too heavy. "Room 712, take the second set of elevators."

Yesterday Bruce waited again for Emma Fine outside of the church residence. When he saw her she scurried away. He questioned a nun or two, he spoke to the priest. He discovered that she has been working for the priest for over seven years. She has been a model citizen, a clean woman, a hard worker. The priest didn't realize she was a movie star. He said that she came to them with nothing, only a small suitcase and several hundred dollars in cash which she immediately donated to the church. The priest said she is quiet, a loner. She has no friends outside of the church, no relatives to call or visit. Bruce cancels out the Italian luxury theory from that trashy newspaper.

"It's as if she is repenting for her sins," the priest sighed. "As if something is eating her up from the inside."

Bruce wrote that quote down and went home to take Tyler out for a drive. His son, like a puppy following him everywhere, not willing to stay in the car or even run into the store while Bruce stays in the car, just wanting to be there, lingering, hovering around his father. He's afraid, Bruce thinks, of what he looks like to others, of what he has become. Bruce tries to convince Tyler to get his hair cut so that he won't be so obvious.

"I like my hair long."

"I don't like the beach."

"All my friends wear earrings."

"I hate shopping."

Was Bruce that difficult as a child? His parents lugging him from museum to museum to art gallery to historic monument. Did he hang back and sulk and whine? He does remember complaining when his mother's clients traipsed through the house wearing the new designs she had made. They were noisy and interrupted all thought and conversation, blowing hot air and cool wind through each room. Bruce's homework suffered, his television watching suffered, his phone calls suffered. He remembers once complaining about the Louvre, waiting outside instead, in the Paris summer, waiting for his mother and father to go through, hoping to meet a beautiful French woman to take to a café, preferring the sunshine and smells of the foreign air to the stuffiness of fine art inside.

"How many times can you see the same old art?" he said.

Late last night, after Tyler had gone to bed, reading through the files on Emma Fine, Bruce came across something small and hidden, something full of meaning suddenly, something substantial and overlooked and exciting.

First, a transcript from the trial of a Mrs. Maria Candalas, Emma Fine's maid and cook, stating that the Emma Fine who came back to the house after her disappearance was not, in fact, the real Emma Fine. An intriguing notion which was quickly dispelled when the court then cross-examined Mrs. Candalas only to discover that, like Ted Weaver, she had been stealing from Emma Fine for years. It also came to light that Mrs. Candalas had failing eyesight and a history of psychiatric problems including compulsive-lying disorders and severe bouts of anger and depression.

He also discovered police testimony linking Bridget's disappearance to a bag of bloodied clothing found in a car belonging to Bridget McGovern behind the Pasadena Mall just after Emma Fine returns home. The DNA from the clothing matched Bridget McGovern's DNA and she was thus considered murdered and missing as opposed to just missing.

From all the evidence Bruce has collected, it seems that Ms. McGovern's body stayed missing and is still missing.

Bruce thinks it must be awfully hard to hide a body in Los Angeles.

Unless you have God on your side.

Or a hell of a lot of money.

Bruce started this job thinking that he'd write about Emma Fine's life for the past ten years, but he's realizing that he has to understand those fateful days surrounding the murder in her pool before he can even move forward.

Tyler rushes up ahead of Bruce, slides into the elevator, and holds the door open with his foot.

"Come on, you're slow."

"I'm not slow," Bruce says. "I'm just old."

And Tyler looks suddenly concerned. "You're not that old," he says, looking down at his feet.

In Maria Candalas's room there is a four-poster bed, an antique dresser, and a gilded mirror. There are fresh flowers on the dresser and photos of Emma Fine in silver frames. There are also photos of Maria's family: her son, a retired truck driver living in Detroit, her late husband, her brothers and sisters from their home in Mexico. Maria is sitting in a rocking chair by the window, looking at a large picture book. She is a strong-looking, little, grey-haired woman wearing thick glasses. There is a white cane leaning up against the wall.

"I like pictures of hot-air balloons," she says to Bruce and Tyler when they knock on her open door.

"I thought she was blind," Tyler says.

"She's partially blind," Bruce whispers. "She can see shapes, I think."

"I like the colours of hot-air balloons. Have you ever been in a hot-air balloon?"

"No," Bruce says.

"Yeah," Tyler says. "Once over Calgary during the stampede. My mom paid for me and my sister to go up. We just went up and down. There was nothing special about it."

Bruce looks at his son. "I'm Bruce Dermott," he says. "This is my son, Tyler."

"Hot-air balloons are perfect," Maria says. "Even if you just go up and down."

"That's a book about monkeys," Tyler says, standing close. "There aren't any hot-air balloons in there."

"Is that so?" Maria says. "Who said I was looking at a book about hot-air balloons?"

"You did. You said you liked pictures of hot-air balloons, you said —"

"Mrs. Candalas," Bruce starts. "I wonder if you might answer some questions regarding Emma Fine."

"I like monkeys just as well as hot-air balloons, young man. So don't tell me that I don't."

"I didn't say —"

"Tyler." Bruce signals to the boy to be quiet. He points to a chair by the door. "Sit."

"Emma Fine, you say?" Maria squints up at Bruce. Her eyes are milky and out of focus behind the thick glass.

"My lovely Ms. Fine."

"Yes," Bruce says, pulling a chair up to the old woman. "It seems that you claimed that the woman who returned to the house after the murder in the pool was not Emma Fine."

"She wasn't murdered in the pool if that's what you're saying. Who did you say you are?"

"I'm a reporter," Bruce says.

"A reporter?" Maria pushes her glasses back on her face and pats down her hair. "Do I look good enough for a picture? I might need some lipstick, but I can't see well enough to put it on."

"I'm not taking your picture."

Maria looks confused.

"I've come across Ms. Fine. She's working at a church, cleaning —"

"She's not alive," Maria says. "She's dead. She's been dead for ten years."

Bruce looks at Tyler who is sitting quietly on the chair, twirling his long hair around his fingers. The boy is sitting like a girl, his legs crossed gingerly, his elbow on his knee, leaning forward. What happened to good old-fashioned spread legs? What happened to scratching your balls now and then?

"Do you ever think," Maria starts, "that hot-air balloons could go too high. What would happen if they went too high?"

"The passengers would die," Tyler says. "The passengers would die from lack of oxygen. They would freeze. Then the balloon would eventually come back down to earth."

"Oh," Maria says. "Aren't you a smart boy."

"That's not why we're here," Bruce says. "I want to talk to you about Ms. Fine. I want to talk to you about why you think she is dead."

"I know she is dead," Maria says. "I know it. It's a fact. Like I'm blind. Like your young Jimmy here telling me that hot-air balloons freeze and kill people. He knows that. It's a fact."

"Tyler," Tyler says, "not Jimmy."

"Whatever," Maria says. "Does it really matter?"

"The point is —" Bruce begins.

"The point is that someone pretending to be Ms. Fine came back after she had disappeared. She came waltzing straight into the house and she conned everyone, even the police and lawyers, but she didn't con me. She conned everyone because there was such panic, because no one thought to question the changes in her appearance, her behaviour. And then she fired everyone: her agent, her manager, me, the driver. She hid in that house like a criminal until the trial. She never came out. I know what I saw. I know it. That wasn't Ms. Fine. That was someone else. Ms. Fine is missing. Dead. She's gone." Maria points towards the pictures she has of the actress. She crosses herself. "The sun got my eyes and then my dear husband died and my son put me here. I used to have powerful eyesight when I was young as Jimmy here —"

"Tyler."

"Shhh," Bruce says to his son.

"And then the sun sucked my eyesight away. Burned it up. Like those fires that make the hot-air balloons rise."

"I wear sunglasses," Tyler says. "That couldn't happen to me."

"Don't be sure."

"Just a minute here," Bruce says. He glares at his son. Tyler looks away. "If it wasn't Ms. Fine, who was it that came back after her disappearance?"

Maria looks at Bruce. Straight at him. He can see that her eyes are unfocused, he can see the milky sheen covering her pupils, the huge eyeballs magnified in thick glass. She points again at her dresser, at the pictures of Emma Fine. "What are you, a lawyer? I've answered all this before. I answered so much at one time that they put me in jail for several months for stealing, they made me go to a psychiatrist for two years. What are you going to do? Are you going to lock me in this room? I'm already locked inside this hell." She moves her hands around in the air, causing the book to fall from her lap. "They won't even let me take a walk without a nurse any more. Just because I can't see doesn't mean I'm not a person."

"I'm sorry," Bruce says. "But I'm just a reporter. I can't — I wouldn't do anything to hurt you. How did you know it wasn't Emma Fine?"

Maria looks down at her hands. "Her hands," Maria says quietly. "She used to have a freckle on her left hand, her middle finger, right at the joint. It wasn't there any more. Her fingers were a tiny bit shorter too. Emma Fine had long fingers. I know. I took care of her for years. Before she was even that famous."

Bruce thinks. "What did the court say about that?"

"They wouldn't listen to me."

"Surely they had proof, hundreds of films, surely her hand was in one of those films and they could have compared it?"

Maria shrugs. "Would you believe" — she starts to laugh, her glasses falling down on her nose. Tyler sits up — "that there aren't any clear shots of her hands? I watched over and over. My husband watched every film she made, every interview, every photograph taken. Nothing is clear enough to see the freckle. Everything is airbrushed, touched up."

"Wow," Tyler says.

"But surely people can get freckles removed —"

"During a drug overdose? During a spell of amnesia?"

"But —"

"But nothing. And, Mr. Reporter, the awful lawyers, the police, her adoring public, everyone — no one wanted to see what was right in front of them. No one wanted to see what was staring them in the face." Maria looks out the window. "So they didn't look. They didn't look at all and they blamed the maid because she had bad eyesight and a need for money. I wasn't the only one who stole from her, you know. Everyone did. Her accountants, Mr. Weaver, her agents."

Bruce stares at Maria.

Tyler stares at Maria.

"I needed money," she says. "I wanted to put my son through school. I wanted him to go somewhere with his life. But then he became a truck driver in Detroit and he locks me up here. He never comes to visit."

Bruce and Tyler are in the elevator.

"That's not possible," Tyler says. "She can't be someone else. That only happens in the movies. She's ranting."

"I suppose you're right," Bruce says. "It's just the story of a blind, thieving woman. An angry woman. It makes no sense, really. Who would she be if she weren't Emma Fine?"

"It sounds like something from one of those trashy tabloids you see in the checkout line at the grocery store. Aliens invade Elvis's body, that kind of thing."

Bruce smiles. It's a beautiful day when they step outside of the home for the blind and Bruce walks, his arm around his son, to the ice cream truck and buys each of them a cone. Tyler looks a bit embarrassed to be eating ice cream with his dad, to have a large arm swung around his thin shoulders, but he puts up with it silently.

"You know," Bruce says, "like Mrs. Candalas and her son, when you were a little baby I would have done anything to ensure that you had the best life. I did. As a matter of fact, I worked in real estate. What a shitty job."

"Yeah," Tyler says. "Hey, you swore."

"But I mean I would have stolen for you. I would have jumped in front of a train for you."

Tyler nods as if he knows exactly what his father is remembering: the ache of fatherhood, the horrible feelings of guilt and inadequacy, how you can never do enough for your kids.

"And now," Bruce says, licking his cone, sitting high up on the picnic bench, watching the waves break on the sand, "I'd still do anything for you."

Tyler laughs. "You could get back together with Mom."

Bruce pauses. He looks at his son. "Is that what this is about?"

"What?"

"Your gayness — is it about me and your mom? Are you playing with us?"

"I don't know what you're talking about," Tyler says. "What are you talking about?"

"Because if you're playing with us, if this is some joke, it isn't very funny."

"It's not a joke, Dad," Tyler says, his head hanging. "I've just admitted it to myself. I've just figured it out. At the end of school the counsellor said that it would be best if I told you. He said that keeping it hidden would wreck me, give me ulcers and shit."

"Don't swear. What counsellor?"

"The school counsellor. Now I'm just getting beaten up. All my friends are beating me up. Word got around."

Bruce looks at his son, at his cone dripping on the pavement, at the earrings glistening in the sunshine.

"I don't know what to say," Bruce says. "I don't know how to help."

Tyler shrugs.

"What can I do?"

Tyler stands and walks to the garbage can and puts his half-eaten cone in. He wipes his sticky hands on his jeans and he walks back to his father at the picnic bench.

"I can't really get them to stop beating you up," Bruce says. "I can't make that any better." Bruce is amazed at how serious this boy has become, at how mature he is suddenly. Bruce's chest suddenly hurts. Kids beating on his boy. He aches all over thinking this.

"I know."

"I can say I understand, I guess. Is that what you want me to say? You want me to understand you? Because I don't, really. I can't understand how you can know right now. I mean," Bruce pauses, "you've never even had sex with a girl, have you? How do you know you won't like it? How do you know?" And then Bruce looks at his son and sees the last year written clearly all over the boy's face. "Oh, hell," he says. "You have. You've been with someone. Christ. A boy. Who was it?"

"I just know, Dad. I just know."

"Who was it? What other kid in high school knows they're gay? What other kid is ready to admit that?"

Tyler crosses his hands if front of him and avoids looking at his father.

"It wasn't a kid, was it? It was a man."

Tyler looks at Bruce. "How do you know that?"

"I'm an investigative reporter," Bruce says sadly, "I can read faces. I know."

"It's my school counsellor," Tyler says. "But don't get mad or anything. He's a nice guy. He's really nice."

"Jesus Christ." Bruce throws up his arms. He stands up from the picnic bench and walks over to the garbage can. His ice cream cone has melted right down his arms and there is a pool of white cream dripping off his elbow. He wipes himself with a napkin and heads back to the picnic table. "How old is the guy? Is it even legal? Did he make you do anything? What the hell is going on in Canada? God. Does your mother know? What about Michael? Has Michael ever touched you? I bet that asshole is gay."

"Dad, stop."

"We should sue him." Bruce is shouting now. People on the beach are looking up at the boy and the man. The boy looks horrified, anguished. The man is so mad his face is red. "Sue the goddamn school. The school counsellor? He made you do it, didn't he?"

"No, Dad. It wasn't like that."

"Get in the car. We're going home to call your mother."

"It wasn't like that at all. I love him."

"Get in the car." Bruce walks over to the car and slams his fist on the roof. "Get in the car now."

"Hey, buddy, take it easy," says a man walking his dog past Bruce.

"Take it easy? You want me to take it easy?"

Tyler runs over to the car and struggles with the door. He climbs in. "Dad, let's go. Just go."

Bruce sizes up the man with the dog and then gets in his car. He starts the engine. He is angry but not angry enough to get the shit kicked out of him. "I can't believe this, I can't believe this."

"I knew you'd be angry," Tyler says. "I knew you needed someone to blame."

Bruce drives out onto the road, swerving dangerously into traffic. Horns honk. "There is someone to blame. Some old pervert who seduced my son."

"I made it up, Dad. I'm lying."

"What?" Bruce swerves off the side of the road and stops the car on the shoulder. "What?" He is screaming. He can't help himself. Cars beep as they pass.

"It wasn't the school counsellor."

"Who then? Who was it? What are you doing, Tyler?"

"It's just this guy I met at the hockey rink. I play hockey a lot. It's just this guy. He's my age."

Bruce sits and looks at the steering wheel. He regains his breathing. He regains his composure. He can feel his heart steadying. "Why would you tell me it was your school counsellor?"

Tyler shrugs.

"You can't do that, going around telling people, blaming other people. You can't do that."

"I just thought you'd understand better."

"What the hell are you talking about?" Bruce slams his fist

into the steering wheel. Tyler cowers in his seat. "I'd understand you were screwing an older man? What are you talking about? You can never let people believe that kind of thing. Lots of people could get hurt from rumours like that."

"If you thought it was someone smart, someone older, more mature, I thought you might think that it was okay. I thought you'd think it wasn't just some kids fooling around. Besides, you suggested an older man. You're the one who said it. Because this is the way I am, Dad. This is it. I'm not some kid any more. I'm not —"

"You lie to me, accuse your school counsellor, and you say you're not a kid? Christ, you make no sense, Tyler. You make no sense at all." And then it occurs to Bruce that Tyler is just like his mother. She never made sense and always came to confess things in a roundabout way. Telling Bruce she was leaving him because she didn't love him any more. That wasn't the case. She left him, Bruce is sure of it, she left him because Michael convinced her to go, because she was just tired, needed a change of pace, needed something new in her life before she got too old to have anything start again. Bruce has always known that Shelley still loves him.

"I just want you to take me seriously. Mom doesn't take me seriously. Mom says I need help. She says I need to see someone, a psychiatrist or something."

"Is that what your mom says?"

Tyler nods.

Bruce drives again, out into traffic. He is sweating and wants to have a cool wind blow on his face. He doesn't need this right now. He needs to find out more about Emma Fine. He needs to write his article and get on with his life. He needs to have Shelley and Amy and Tyler back again, to have them with him, safe, in his townhouse. To take care of them and help them and listen, he needs to begin to listen, to really listen. Oh, God, he wants so much to bring them all home to him and cover them over with his arms, protect them, help them, save them, put them on the right path, place them tenderly in his heart again. Bruce clears his throat. "We'll just go home now," he says quietly. "We'll go home and talk this all out."

Tyler opens his window and reaches to buckle up his seatbelt. He looks at his father's strong chin, his father's sad face. After some time in traffic, rushing forward and stopping again, waiting for green lights, for the lines to move, Tyler says, "Do you think that old lady could be right? Do you think people are not always what they seem?"

Bruce shrugs. "I don't know," he says. "I don't know anything any more."

Bridget is getting plastic surgery. She goes to one doctor to have collagen injections in her lips. Then, after several weeks of recovery, she goes to another doctor to have her breasts substantially enlarged. She waits again and then goes to another doctor to have her face reshaped, to age herself just slightly.

"Why would you want to age yourself?" the third doctor asked her. "Most women want to make themselves look younger."

"I just want to look mature," Bridget said through swollen lips. "I just want to look like someone who has done something."

Bridget lies on the couch in pain. The Tylenol doesn't seem to help. The stitches itch, her chest aches, she feels nauseous from the anesthetic, her face stings, she can't drink or eat without a straw. When she took the bandages off her face today, she recoiled in horror. It looked as if she had been beaten, her face black and blue, her skin raw and burned from the peel, her lips swollen and angry looking.

Ted is home taking care of her. He brings her the ice bags, he brings her water and milkshakes in large glasses with straws. He brings her the Tylenol and sleeping pills. He brings her cocaine and marijuana and other drugs too numerous to mention. He sits by the couch with his hand on her leg and he flicks the channels on the TV converter and talks to her about what they are watching, about what they are doing, about why she is in pain. And he controls his temper during this. He keeps it at a minimum.

Ted talks to Bridget about Canada, about the loons on the lake, the frogs chirping at night. He tells her again and again about his brother, Ed, and how he died too young, and he mentions his dogs and how every single one of them also died too young. Ted tells her over and over about his mother and father. He remembers how their worlds fell apart after the death of his brother. How it was when his father took the hunting rifle and plastered his brains all over the cottage, shot himself straight through the nose, how his mother knelt by her husband's body and screamed until her voice disappeared, and then, years later, how she wasted away and eventually became too sick to care any more and she, too, died slowly and painfully. Guilt carried her away. It was her fault his brother died. Her fault his father died. He tells Bridget about how alone he was. How he never wants to be alone again.

And Bridget tells Ted again about her middle-class upbringing, the dance lessons, voice lessons, acting lessons. She tells him again about the agents who sucked her family dry. She tells him how much she wants to be famous, to be rich, how she's so fucking tired of doing commercials and going nowhere with her life. She tells him again about shoplifting as a kid. How she ripped the electronic tags off the clothes and sewed up the holes later. Stuffed them into her purse so that every day in high school she would have something new to wear. She couldn't stand to be a middle-class kid. She wanted wealth.

They rework their histories, simplify them, complicate them. They share everything and still nothing. Creating a pattern that makes sense to them, that excuses their present behaviour. Because, as Bridget says, they aren't really bad people. They're just people who never got a break, people for whom life refused to be easy.

There must be an explanation, Ted reasons, because the plan came so easily. Hatched that night at the party, Ted saying, "You look just like her, like Emma Fine," and Bridget opening herself up, standing tall, Ted standing beside her, thinking things through. "You look like Emma Fine." A simple sentence. Jolting through Bridget like an electric current.

There must be an explanation, Ted reasons, because he didn't realize what he was capable of until that night at the party. Because he never thought beyond the ideal of working damn hard to get what he wanted, because he wasn't a criminal, *isn't* a criminal. Because Ted climbed so easily into Emma's car and drove her home so quickly that Bridget didn't have time to rethink everything, didn't have time to beg him to stop.

"What about Emma?" Bridget asks. "She didn't have it easy."

"She has it easy now," Ted says. "Don't forget that."

When Ted is at work Bridget spends her days reading everything she can about Emma Fine's life, every little article, every biography ever written. She studies pictures in back copies of magazines. She goes to the local coffee shop and learns to research on the Internet. She wants to know what she's up against.

Bridget dreams of money. She dreams of big bags of money falling down from the sky, scattering around her. She dreams of being naked in all that money and making love to the money and eating the money, rubbing it into her body, letting it soak in as if it is cold cream. But mostly she dreams about people watching her, smiling at her, people all around her, admiring her. She wakes from these dreams so overpowered by them that she can hardly move, hardly breathe. The painkillers are addictive, Ted's drugs are addictive, and

Bridget takes more than they can afford. Bridget sometimes, in the dead of the night, fast asleep, waves her hand in the air. She lies on her back in bed, Ted asleep beside her, and she waves her hand as if she were the Queen of England waving to her royal subjects. A slight tilt of the wrist. Her hand straight and steady.

Bridget doesn't dream of Ted making love to Emma, of Ted kissing her, touching her, entering her. She doesn't dream of the two of them, her husband, another woman, the two of them fast asleep together in that big mansion in West Hollywood.

"When I first met you," Emma shouts over the traffic noise to Ted as they are driving in the convertible through the green hills down to the yellow beach, "I thought you looked dangerous, out of place, severe."

Ted laughs. "I thought you looked naked," he shouts back. "And I liked that."

"When I first met you," Bridget whispers to Ted as they are lying side by side in bed, the lights off, each one turned away from the other, "I thought you looked so innocent and pure and perfect. Paddling up to the film set in your canoe, that stupid dog — what was his name? — jumping out too soon and landing in water and then shaking all over me. And you laughing, the sun everywhere around you, you glowed. Like a fucking light bulb."

"Lucky," Ted says. "The dog's name was Lucky. He got hit by a car and lay dying in the road until another car came by and finished him off."

"That's not lucky," Bridget says, rolling towards Ted, draping her long arm over his chest, snuggling down into his shoulder. "That's plain sad."

"Depends on how you look at it, I guess."

"I want to know," Bruce says to Emma as she polishes the

ornate wooden altar with oil, "why you would just disappear?"

"I told you yesterday. I don't know. What would you have done?" Emma whispers. "What would you have done in my situation?"

"Not this." Bruce signals around the inside of the church. "I wouldn't have run away to a church. I may have run away, but I would have taken all my money with me."

"What money?"

"What do you mean?"

Emma sits down on the first pew and looks up at the figure of Christ on the cross. Bruce remembers one of her movies when she played a murdering prostitute and she sat for a moment in a church similar to this one and she looked up at the cross before her and she cried. That was a trashy movie. No good. But Emma Fine was amazing as the prostitute. Bruce remembers watching her move in those low-cut dresses and thigh-high boots and thinking that he wished Shelley looked like that. And now he's with Emma Fine in real life and he wishes Shelley were here beside him. Tyler is at his townhouse watching TV, probably looking at gay sex on the Internet, and Bruce is standing before his dream woman and wishing for his old life back. Give me a second chance, he thinks.

Yesterday evening, after the beach incident with Tyler, Bruce came back to the church and saw Emma Fine sitting on the front steps, fanning her face with a song sheet. He approached her slowly, his hand out, like he would a skittish dog, and Emma Fine turned towards him. Instead of running, she let him sit beside her. She said she had forgotten the feeling of being hunted. She said she had forgotten the feeling of having someone to talk to, someone who knows what she went through.

Now Bruce stands beside her as she sits in the church pew.

"The trial," Emma says. "I lost most of my money defending myself. Plus, the movie studio sued me for screwing up their filming schedule and then dumping the picture. Then the studio sued my estate for backing out of the picture I was supposed to do later that year. And then," she smiles slightly, her lips chapped and dry, "and then there were the habits."

"Drugs."

"Yes," Emma says. "Drugs. Lots of them."

"What about your house? Wasn't that worth something?"

"It was worth enough to pay some of the lawyers fees, the yacht was enough to pay the other lawyers. Then there were the sleazy accountants who stole from me. And Ted and Maria, of course, but that was peanuts compared to the accountants. You must have read about them in the paper."

"Surely there was something left."

"Nothing. I didn't realize how in the hole I was. I wish I had known. I wish I had been sober enough to know. It was only a matter of time. The lawyers, the case, the studios, the dead body in my pool, all of that just sped up the process."

Bruce sits down next to Emma. She shakes herself out of her reverie. "I've got work to do," she says. "I shouldn't be talking to you. I don't really want to be talking to you. It's just nice to be known again. Does that make sense? For so many years I've been hiding and then you come walking down that aisle and I feel like everything just happened. I don't know what to do."

"We could do this together," Bruce says. "We could work on the article together and you could gain your credibility back. You could make a comeback. Maybe there's a chance —"

"Play an aging movie star in my own made-for-TV movie? A movie about my life?" Emma laughs.

"You didn't run last night. You didn't leave the church and move on when I found you. You want to be caught." Emma looks nervous. Bruce continues. "You want me to expose how you've been living. This is all part of the game, isn't it?"

"The game? You think this is a game?" Emma stands up.

"You think that seven years here is fun? And run? Where would I have run, Mr. Dermott? I'm doing this because there was nothing else. There was nothing else that would make everything better. Too many people were hurt because of me."

"Did you kill Ted Weaver?" Bruce asks. His voice echoes around the still, empty church. He didn't mean to speak so loudly.

"Please," Emma says. She is crying. "I asked you to leave me alone. Why can't you leave me alone?"

"I'm sorry, I ..."

"Isn't it possible that Ted could have been murdered by someone who was going to break into my house? Isn't it possible that maybe Ted and I had an argument, something we did often, and I took too many drugs and disappeared for a couple of days, that maybe I just wandered the streets, got lost, slept in alleyways? And Ted, coming out of the house after eating breakfast, maybe Ted had a debt to pay in the construction business, maybe he gambled, maybe he had enemies. And one of those enemies, or maybe someone he didn't know, someone after me, a stalker, there were many stalkers that year, maybe that person came upon Ted by the pool, surprised both of them, and hit Ted and drowned Ted. Killed Ted. Because it was a surprise, because it wasn't supposed to happen. Right? It wasn't supposed to happen." Emma takes a deep breath. "Isn't it possible that all of that could have happened at the same time and that, because of the shock of the situation, because I lost someone I loved, I lost my memory of Ted Weaver temporarily? Isn't that possible?"

Bruce looks at the cherry-red glass in the windows of the church. Lit up and glowing, it casts an eerie shine on the pews. "That sounds like the trial — and you got raped — what about Bridget's blood in her car? How do you explain that? What about the fact that Bridget is still missing?"

"The trial? Why do you think it sounds like the trial? Because I was there, because I was telling the truth." Emma wipes her nose with her hand. Bruce hands her a Kleenex that he digs out of his pocket but she refuses to take it from him. "I remember him, you know. I remember laughing with him, loving him, making love to him. I remembered him shortly after everything was over." Emma is sobbing. "And now I can't stop remembering. I can't forget him. And you, you with your questions, with your accusations, you are worse than the person who murdered Ted. You are like all the other vultures at the trial, you are desperate to pick apart my being, pick apart who I am, whatever sense of self I have. You want to break me until you have nothing but a body left, something you can just fuck. Fucking rapist. Like the producers, like the directors. Like whoever it was who raped me. Can't you leave me alone?"

"I guess that means you don't want to work together on a book?"

Emma rushes out of the church.

As Bruce walks home in the twilight, the evening sounds of cars rushing away from work, the exhaust hanging heavily in the air, he thinks about what Emma said. About how she remembers Ted now, and how she can't forget. He thinks about how there are times at night when he is lying alone in his bed, and for an instant there is a warm body lying beside him. Those times when he turns slightly towards the window and can see Shelley, her hip mounded beside him, her back moving slightly, inhaling and exhaling, and he swears that his world is again at peace, that he has someone. That's what hurts the most, Bruce thinks as he opens the door to his townhouse and sees Tyler asleep in front of the TV. All that he shared, that he wanted to keep close, is now, perhaps, discussed at dinner parties, told to Michael in bed as they lie together after sex, laughed about with friends in coffee shops in Canada. All of his life, trusted to Shelley, shared with Shelley, left with her. Bruce feels empty and alone. And scared.

"Hey, Dad," Tyler says, wiping the sleep from his eyes. "I made dinner."

Bruce walks into the kitchen and sees a pot of macaroni and cheese on the stove. It is cold and has congealed. The table is set: two bowls, two spoons, two glasses of juice, and a bottle of ketchup.

"I didn't know if you liked yours with hot dogs," Tyler says. "I like to eat mine with hot dogs."

"Yeah," Bruce says, ruffling his son's hair. "Hot dogs would be great."

Tyler pulls a plate of cut-up, rubbery hot dogs out of the microwave. He dumps them into the macaroni and cheese and stirs. "Did you get anything on her?" he asks.

"Nothing," Bruce says.

"Do you think she did it?"

Bruce shrugs. "Whatever she did, she's feeling pretty lousy about it. Ten years later and she's feeling like it just happened." Bruce sits down and his son serves him a bowl of cold macaroni and cheese. "Thanks. It's nice to have a meal cooked for me."

Tyler laughs. "I thought for sure you wouldn't eat it. I thought that maybe you'd look at this and take me out for dinner."

"Tomorrow night," Bruce says, "we'll hit that great Mexican restaurant your mom and I used to take you and Amy to. Remember? They gave us salad in those tortilla bowls that you could eat? And the drinks were served in fishbowls with two-foot straws?"

But Tyler has his mouth full and just smiles at his father and so Bruce isn't sure whether Tyler remembers anything substantial, anything meaningful, or if Bruce himself is the only one who has collected the past and stored it for comfort.

Part Five

There is a photograph of Emma Fine at her fourth birthday party. She is standing up against a mirror, her back resting on the cool glass, a plastic cup of purple juice in her hand. Her mouth is open, a stained wide smile, teeth gleaming white against purple. She is wearing a pretty white blouse under a blue tunic, the collar of the dress scalloped and embroidered with flowers, black-eyed Susans and daisies. Emma's mother is in the background, reflected in the mirror. She has her hands crossed before her breasts and she looks tired and frustrated. Her hair, caught up in a ponytail, is fly-away in a halo around her head. Springy curls let loose, falling free. And, although Emma's mouth is open for joy, her eyes, looking directly at her mother, seem concerned, seem much older than the eyes of a girl celebrating her fourth birthday.

> LOS ANGELES – Noted plastic surgeon Nathaniel Trapser was discovered drowned in his Hollyroad Manor pool late yesterday evening. Dr. Trapser was the surgeon for the stars, having performed all types of plastic surgery on the likes of Michael Jonson, Brad Fillmore, Susie Spantz, and Emma Fine. Foul play has been discounted as Dr. Trapser had a history of severe depression, matched with insomnia, and had recently told a patient that he felt suicidal. He is survived by his third wife, *Playboy* centrefold, Estelle Trapser, and his six children from previous marriages, Tommy, Jack, Bill, Cindy, Susan, and Trevor. Funeral services will be held at the Chapel Hill Resting Home in Beverly Hills at three p.m. on Thursday.

Photo of Emma Fine on the front page of a tabloid newspaper. She has been photographed walking towards her house. Ted Weaver is close behind. Emma is wearing a flowered miniskirt and a backless halter top. Ted has his hand on her naked spine. She looks back towards the front gate and the corner of her breast is visible. The image is grainy and unfocused. The headline reads, "Hollywood Starlet Caught Once Again in Tangled Web of Adultery!" and the caption below the picture reads, "Emma Fine escorts her new love, construction worker, Theodore Weaver, into her five-million-dollar mansion. Does his wife know what he's doing here? He's certainly not installing toilets."

Chapter Fifteen

Ted is standing in an unfinished living room trying not to listen to the woman before him as she yells about the mess his workers have made in her bathroom, the mess they have made tracking dirt in and out of the condo. It seems one of the workers even looked around the entire apartment, which would have gone undetected had he taken his boots off. Ted is exhausted. He's been working overtime for months, sleeping with Emma Fine, rushing back to take care of Bridget, and still he has no money. Every cent he makes goes towards drugs and plastic surgery. He is thinking of Bridget and wondering how the most recent surgery is going. He is wondering what her face will look like, if the doctor can perform the miracle he said he would. He is thinking about how much he hates doing this, standing here taking shit from people. He is thinking that he'd like to reach out and punch this woman, smack her right on the nose. But he needs the money.

"Common sense," the woman says, her voice shrill, "just plain common sense and a little bit of courtesy. That's all I ask for. Couldn't you tell them to take their boots off. Or move the pictures from the walls. The dust is everywhere." The woman throws her hands up, indicating the dust as it filters through the bright sunshine coming in from the patio doors. "And handprints on the walls. What were they thinking? To get my floors done I now have to paint the walls? I didn't ask for this. I didn't pay for this."

Ted thinks of Emma and then he quickly shuts his mind

to thoughts of the movie star and thinks again about Bridget. The guilt creeps up every so often but, like swallowing a pill, he struggles only slightly to get it down. He has this way of switching his memories to his parents' cottage on Lake Simcoe. He can go there in his mind, go there before his brother died, and remember how at night in the summer the loons would call so noisily that he'd have a hard time sleeping. He remembers his canoe and the soft splash of the paddle in the water around the pond, the frogs leaping off water lilies and diving into the black bottom.

His workers were stupid. They should have taken their boots off before parading around the entire apartment. And Ted hopes no one stole anything. He hopes they weren't casing the place, looking for the easiest entry into the apartment. Ted doesn't need any more hassles in his life. The plastic surgery bills are coming out of his ears. Emma's money only goes so far. There's only so much he can steal when she's drugged, only so many things he can get her to buy for him, only so many overtime hours in a day. He nods his head to the woman's high-pitched voice. She is trying to whisper but is so upset the sound is coming out of her throat as a whistle. The workers bustle around Ted and the woman. Like schoolchildren, they make faces behind her back.

When Ted started working in this business he liked the warmth and burning smell of the wood as it passed through a saw, he liked the feel of unfinished houses. He knows construction is a dirty business, but the freshness, the cleanliness of exposed joists and beams, of drywall leaning up against a porch, used to make him happy. He was playing boy again, putting things together. Lego. Fitting the pieces into some sort of logical pattern. Something solid and useful. But now he wants out. He wants to lie on the beach on the weekends instead of touring construction sites. He wants to do something with his mind, exercise the brains that he knows he has, stop the pain in his muscles at the end of a day. And,

God, he wants money. Bridget wants to act but she also wants money. There is that incessant snarl close in his ears: "Money, money, money." He sees Emma with her money, loosely giving it out, not thinking about where the next dollar will fall. So much money. And Bridget can't act. There is no way he will let her act. When they finish what they started they will go away, move to Europe or Canada or somewhere, cash it all in. One day on-set and Bridget would be discovered. She's a shitty actor.

"I'm talking to you. You're not listening."

"I'm listening," Ted says.

"You men are all the same," the woman shouts. "You respect no one. You don't give a damn about anyone but yourself."

Recently divorced, Ted thinks.

"I'm not paying you the final bill until you clean up this mess. I'm not paying you a penny more."

"You know," Ted says quietly, "it's not good to threaten the workers. They could walk out."

"They won't walk out. They want their money. They have to finish the job."

"They could very easily walk out. Disappear. Just leave."

"No, they won't. They won't walk out. Don't you see? There is so much that needs doing. They won't leave my place like this." The woman looks frightened.

"Look," Ted says. "Your apartment is under construction. It's bound to be messy. There's sawdust and stuff. It's a messy business."

"But my walls —"

"Your walls will wash clean. Just a little soap, some water."

The woman looks at Ted. She studies his face. "When I first met you, when you gave me the estimate for the work," she says, "I trusted you. You had an honest face. Now I see that it's a mask, it's not a face. There's nothing behind your eyes." The woman walks from the room. She carries her coat under her arm, she jingles her keys in her purse as she leaves the apartment. "I won't recommend you, you know. I won't tell anyone about you." Ted stares at the patio doors outside, into the bright sunshine, and his face registers nothing.

As a child, Ted would always tell a secret, he couldn't keep anything to himself. He found out what his brother was getting for Christmas one year and he told him. He knew about his mother's affair, that she was sleeping with that man the day his brother died, and he told his father. He cried it out when his father was trying to save his brother. His father's lips against his brother's white ones, pressing, kissing. His mother fucking the man from the next lake, riding above him like a rodeo star. That's where she was. That's why she wasn't coming to help when his father was screaming, why she had been so long at the grocery store. Fucking another man, Dad. Give it up. His brother lying lifeless on the dock. But now, as an adult, he is good at keeping things inside. He is good at not letting secrets slip. Later, when his father shot himself. Ted realized that telling the truth wasn't all it was made up to be. Sometimes things are easier if you keep them inside.

Bridget is having her nose done, her cheeks done, her lips done, her tummy tucked, her hair and eyelashes dyed, her teeth straightened, her moles removed, her breasts enlarged, her eyebrows tweezed, her nails lengthened, her cellulite removed, her skin exfoliated, her feet massaged, her bikini line and legs and armpits waxed. She is on a diet, she is exercising. The pain from the operations means Ted keeps her supplied with sleeping pills, valium, cocaine, and amphetamines. She is drinking all kinds of alcohol. She is taking lessons in diction and poise, she is doing research on the computers at the coffee shop. She is buying lipstick and eyeliner and mascara and blush and concealer and powder, practicing with the makeup. She is buying perfumes and soaps, making her smell distinct yet familiar. With each operation, each purchase, each trip to the spa, Ted is gradually losing his grasp on who his wife is. He comes upon her, covered in bandages, sore to touch, and he wonders for an instant which house he is in.

With each of her purchases, with the doctors' bills and medications and drugs, Ted's bank account dwindles. Disappears. Is almost gone. And as his money vanishes, the angrier he gets with Emma Fine, the less patience he has with the job at hand.

"Clean up when you're done," he shouts at his workers. "You better make this place sparkle. I'm sick of apologizing for your behaviour. And, Graham, stop walking through people's apartments and looking around. If you have to do it, if you have to snoop, then take your boots off."

Ted leaves the apartment and takes the elevator down to the street. The day is warm, the sky is pure blue. Ted breathes deeply. He looks at his watch. Bridget will be out of surgery in an hour. Ted should go home, be there when the cab drops her off, but instead he drives out to Emma's place and gets Maria to let him in. Emma is out of town for the week, in Mexico shooting a new movie, but Ted has been given permission to use the house.

He suits up for a swim and then, instead, walks into the movie theatre and threads the projector to watch a film. He is shivering in his swimsuit. He wraps a towel around his shoulders and sits in a plush red seat. The sound blasts out of the speakers mounted to the wall; the screen fills with the image of Emma Fine running for her life, running through streets, dodging cars, running into buildings, up stairs, over rooftops, down stairs, across a park, running wonderfully. Her body is lean and tight. Emma is wearing a tank top, pink, and black shorts. Her running shoes are black. Her legs are long and tanned. He watches her run as the credits roll overtop and the music reaches a crescendo and Emma Fine finally stops and stares straight at the camera. In her look, in the blue of her eyes, Ted sees indecision. He sees fear. He sees anger. She is barely breathing, which seems unlikely considering how far she's run. Emma Fine takes a pistol out of somewhere (her tight shorts?) and fires straight at the camera in a burst of red light and black smoke, and then she disappears and the screen turns black and lights up again with a blue sky and birds and a picnic in a park.

Ted gets up. He turns off the projector. He leaves the theatre. He walks to the pool and dives in. Coming up for air once he sees Dan staring at him from inside the kitchen. Coming up for air a second time and Dan is gone. Ted dives under the water and floats like a dead man, his arms out, his body weightless, his mind empty of every thought, emotion, fear. He wants this life so badly it hurts. He wants this for himself. Damn it, Ted thinks. Every muscle in his body aches. His brain, when he isn't in water, feels fried. Ted wants, wants, wants.

Chapter Sixteen

When Shelley arrives on the plane from Calgary, Bruce feels that the last ten years were a dream. Emma was there when they broke up. Emma is there again when Shelley comes back. Nothing makes sense and yet everything is coming together. Bruce likens it to a wedding band. An endless circle. Shelley stands in his living room next to Tyler and all Bruce is missing is Amy — get them all together, surround himself with them, and he'd go right back into real estate. His life is complicated and hard and simple and easy.

"What are you doing here?" Bruce is standing just inside the front door, his hand still on the knob, his keys dangling from his clenched teeth, holding grocery bags and washer fluid for his car.

"I took a cab. I just got here."

"That's not what I asked."

"Dad, Mom's here to visit."

"But why?"

"Put your things down. Let me help you." Shelley moves towards Bruce and their eyes meet. Bruce looks away. He puts down his bags, takes the keys out of his mouth, shuts the door behind him.

"To stay? You're going to stay here?"

"In a hotel."

"No, Mom ..."

"You can stay here. The couch. Tyler can sleep on the couch. You can use the guest room."

"If that's not too much trouble."

"No, I —"

"Did you buy cereal, Dad? He doesn't have any cereal. I've been eating toast for breakfast for days."

Bruce moves towards the living room. He is floating. In some sort of dream. Everything is absurd.

"I was worried about Tyler."

"Why?"

"His school has been calling me."

"Why?"

Shelley sits on the couch. "Don't you have anything to offer a woman to drink?"

"Woman?" Bruce moves into the kitchen and mixes up two whisky sours, Shelley's drink. The blender whirrs, the ice cubes crush. Shelley jumps from the sudden sound.

"Thanks." Shelley takes the drink. Sips it. Makes a face. "It's like pop. I was thinking a beer or something."

"You drink beer now? What else is new?"

"I've grown up," Shelley says. "But never mind. This is actually quite good. It brings back memories."

Bruce looks at his ex-wife's face, the small lines around her heavily made-up eyes, the heavy clothes she is wearing, the dyed red hair.

"Why are you dressed for winter?"

"I just got off the plane."

"They make you dress for winter on the plane? It's August."

"It's cold on the plane," Shelley says. "I just thought I'd look nice. In case the plane crashed." She smiles.

Tyler is drinking a cream soda and bustling around the kitchen, giving his parents space.

"Good thing about a gay son," Bruce whispers. "He likes to cook."

Shelley looks at her feet, stockinged, her shoes by the door. She wants to leave, to run, quickly. "The school principal has been calling," Shelley whispers. "We'll talk about it when he goes to bed."

"He doesn't go to bed until midnight," Bruce says. "We'll go out after dinner. A walk or something. Doesn't the school principal have anything else to do in the summer?"

"You walk? When did you start walking?"

"Recently. To and from church."

Shelley laughs. "Church. That's funny." She sips her whisky sour.

"How do you like your steaks?" Tyler shouts from the back porch.

"Burnt on the outside, rare in the middle," Bruce says.

"Good, because that's exactly how I'm cooking them."

Shelley smiles. An innocent smile. Her son and ex-husband have made her forget for a moment why she is here, made her not afraid of why she is here, made her not want to leave, run out the door, run down the street, catch a cab, and go straight to the airport. She'd leave on a plane in a second for Mexico or Hawaii or the Caribbean. She'd leave and never go home to Calgary, never see Bruce again in California, but her children, her goddamned children, are all split up with the men she loves. She is cut in thirds: her limbs, her heart, her children. The days of them riding her hip in the shopping centre, the days of them tagging along behind her, holding her outstretched hand. Those days are gone and now she's alone, trying to get one back, wanting to take one with her.

"Why are you really here?"

"I told you. Tyler. It has to do with Tyler." Shelley whispers so her son, rushing back and forth from the deck to the kitchen table, does not hear her. "He's in deeper trouble than I thought. I need to talk to him, to talk to you."

"What about Michael?"

"What about Michael? Michael is Michael. He isn't Tyler's dad."

"He's been with Tyler longer than I have. He's been with

Tyler since he was six years old."

"It's not the same. Blood is thicker than water, that kind of thing."

"Michael is water? I picture him more as a beer."

"You know what I mean. Don't you want to help? Don't you want to be involved in your child's life?"

"My children's lives — I have two kids, you know."

"I know. She didn't want to come. She's spending the summer studying for next year's exams. She wants to get into the enriched program in high school, wants to be with all her friends."

"You don't have to apologize."

"I'm not apologizing, Bruce. I'm not saying anything. Amy's busy, that's all. She's thirteen. She's busy. Damn it. Just damn it." Shelley is standing now, her hand on her hip.

"Calm down."

"Don't tell me to calm down." Shelley is shaking. "It's hot in here. It's hot in here. Don't you have air conditioning?"

"It would work better if you weren't wearing such warm clothes."

"I can wear what I want."

Bruce stands and moves over to Shelley. She moves away from him. "Come here," he says. He takes her hand. Their touch is electric, static in the air. She drops his hand quickly. "Go to the guest room and put something else on. Put on a summer dress or something. Surely you brought a summer dress." Bruce walks over to the front door, where Shelley's suitcase stands. He picks it up, carries it up the stairs to the guest room, and he puts it on the floor amidst Tyler's rubble. Shelley stands behind him, having followed him quietly. She shuts the door after Bruce steps out into the hall.

"I really shouldn't stay here," she says from behind the door.

"Just come down for dinner after you change," Bruce says. He walks back downstairs and fixes himself another whisky sour — this time with more whisky than sour.

"The steaks are burned," Tyler says. "And the salad is spinned and dressed."

"Good job, son," Bruce says. He winks at Tyler and then sits down at the kitchen table. "Serve up the food. Your mother will be down in a minute."

But Shelley doesn't come down for dinner and Tyler and Bruce eat quietly. They look at each other every so often, forks poised, red meat gummed in their mouths.

"I guess she's not hungry," Bruce says.

"Yeah."

"She never liked your cooking anyhow. I remember when you were five years old and you made us breakfast in bed and you served us a bowl of bread covered with chocolate milk."

"That's still one of my specialties."

"Why bread? Why not cereal?"

"I liked toast back then." Tyler laughs. "Now I'm a cereal man."

There's nothing wrong with his son, Bruce thinks. Nothing at all. This kid has brains, looks, talent, a good sense of humour. There is nothing about him that won't get him very far in life. He'll go places. He'll do things. Tyler will make it to the top. Jesus, Bruce thinks. The first goddamned gay president. That's what he'll be. Bruce chuckles and drinks the rest of the whisky sour from the blender.

Late at night Bruce watches TV in his blackened bedroom. Tyler is asleep on the living-room couch and Shelley hasn't moved from her place in the guest room. She handed Tyler out his things, told him to not make a mess and to brush his teeth, gave him a peck on the cheek, and shut the door tight behind her.

Bruce is watching an infomercial about what claims to be the greatest invention ever made. A heavy-looking belt which vibrates when the wearer has loosened his or her stomach muscles. A rat-conditioned torture belt, Bruce thinks. He can't imagine tightening his stomach twenty-four hours a day. Bruce thinks that he would just get used to the annoying vibrations. He would rather walk around vibrating all day long than holding in his stomach.

Shelley is standing in the shadows at his door. She is wearing a bathrobe. Bruce can see a long T-shirt underneath. He wonders if it's Michael's T-shirt.

"What do you think?" Bruce says. He signals towards the TV. "You think you'd go crazy and kill yourself if you had to wear one of these?"

"It's good to tighten your stomach muscles," Shelley says. "Helps with all kinds of things. Bowels, posture."

"The mother speaks," Bruce says. "You still worried about bowels?"

"What?"

"You were always worried about their shit."

"Kids' shit needs to be monitored," Shelley says and then she laughs.

Bruce laughs. "You even used to write it down. Amy — one BM, Tyler — two BMs."

"Look," Shelley begins. "Look, we need to talk about Tyler, about Amy, about everything."

"Amy? What, now you're going to tell me she's a lesbian?"

"No, it's just —"

"There's nothing wrong with our son," Bruce says. "He's fine. He's great."

"He's not fine."

"I don't know about Canada, but here it's okay to be gay. This is Los Angeles. Anything goes."

"Bruce, really, think about it."

"Okay, so it's not fine. It's not so great."

"He's a minority now. He'll always be different."

"There's nothing wrong with difference." Bruce says this but he doesn't believe it. He doesn't believe it for a second.

"Look." Shelley sits down on Bruce's bed. She sits close to

him and Bruce can see her white thigh, the birthmark near her knee. He remembers kissing that birthmark, running his tongue under her knees. He moves away from her in the bed. "Something happened to him in school. Someone did something to him. It's rumours right now, hearsay, but it seems something might have happened."

"What kind of thing?"

"Sex," Shelley says, looking down. "Rape, maybe."

Bruce breathes out quickly and the erection that began when Shelley sat on his bed begins to subside.

"The school counsellor has been suspended."

"The counsellor? He told me. He lied. He said nothing happened." Bruce gets out of bed forgetting that he is wearing only boxer shorts. He parades up and down in front of the window. "He said he was making it up."

"I don't know," Shelley says, watching her ex-husband, looking at the changes in his body. "I don't know what really happened but rumours are rumours. The counsellor has been suspended because he was making threatening gestures towards one of the school secretaries. It has nothing to do with Tyler. The principal has been calling me, wants us to get together and talk when Tyler comes back. He says there is something in the air. He says he's been hearing things. Police may be involved."

"But —"

"But I can't help wondering. Amy says that everyone was saying that Tyler screwed someone. Everyone was saying" — and here Shelley begins to cry — "that he would regularly have sex in the boys' washroom. Oh my God." Shelley puts her hands up to her face. Bruce rushes over and takes her head and pulls it close to his chest. She pushes away but he pulls harder. He hugs her. The smell coming from her is different, a spicy perfume, a mild deodorant, different from the smell he remembers.

"Don't, Bruce." Shelley is pushing away, but not hard. She

is pushing and crying and then she wraps her arms around his waist and holds her cheek flat against his belly button. To Shelley, Bruce is the same. His smell, the thin hair around his belly button leading down to the thick growth below. She hugs him and cries until she can feel movement, until she realizes he is getting hard, and then she puts her head up and looks him in the eyes. Bruce moves away. He sits back down on the bed.

"I'm sorry, I just wanted to comfort you, I'm —"

"No. Don't say anything."

"I want to kill the bastard," Bruce says.

"Who?"

"The counsellor, Tyler, I don't know. I want to kill him for ruining his life."

"He hasn't done anything, Bruce. He's just a child." Shelley wipes the tears from her eyes.

"What if it was the counsellor? How can a grown man take advantage of a kid? How could he do that?"

"We don't know if that's what was happening. Right now it's all rumours. Besides, it's men in general," Shelley whispers. "They do it every day. They take advantage of women, kids, other men. It's the way it is."

"That's not true." But Bruce knows that it is true. He knows that Shelley left him because he wasn't there for her, not in the sense she wanted him there, because he was busy spinning lies about fancy houses, busy rolling in his new-found, real-estate wealth, busy in the game behind selling. Because he was looking at other women, always looking, wondering, wanting, knowing that if he just bided his time, was careful, he could have everything. Men play the game and the goal is to acquire. He didn't appreciate Shelley the way he should have, the way he could have. He took her for granted. Bruce remembered a time, after the kids were out of diapers, when Shelley would come to bed naked and he wouldn't even look at her body. He was too concerned with the next sale. He'd turn off the light and whisper, "Good night," not realizing how much he was hurting her. When she left him she said that he always made her feel like her body was good for only one thing — bearing children. She said she wanted to be sexy again, she wanted someone to passionately love her body.

And what has he done since? He's spent countless hours fantasizing about her body, her curves, her soft breasts, and warm inner thighs. And he's simplified his life, not expanded. He has no lover right now, he gave up his realty job, sold his new car, his fancy suits. Now he's right where Shelley should want him, right back where they started as students in university. Look at me, he wants to shout, I'm carefree. Fancy-free. Unencumbered.

He needs a stomach vibrator. He needs an Abs Buster, a stat- ionary bicycle, a step machine. He needs to stop drinking cream soda, to give up his cigar habit and the occasional cigarette, to stop scratching his ass in public. Sometimes it shames him that he is a man.

Shelley is sitting quietly beside him. He looks at the scar on her knee from a roller-skating accident when she was six. He looks at the birthmark on her other knee that is the same as her aunt's.

"What do we do now?" Bruce asks. "Where do we go from here?"

Downstairs on the sofa Tyler sleeps the sleep of the dead. Nothing moves. Not his fingers, not his legs, not his eyes under the heavy lids. The blanket is pulled up to his neck, cold in the air conditioning. Tyler doesn't dream.

Chapter Seventeen

Emma usually doesn't dream but when she does the dreams come fast and furious, images of her childhood creeping back towards her. Her dreams are claustrophobic, as if she has been stuffed in a closet, locked in a casket, drowned in the bathtub. She can't breathe. She can't think. She can't remember and it's the remembering, the details, that she wants so badly. And when she wakes, screaming, Dan comes quickly to soothe her, to give her a pill, to lull her into a black sleep, a sleep without dreams. If a reporter, any reporter, was gutsy enough to ask Emma why she was addicted to drugs and alcohol, Emma thinks she would say, "Because I'm afraid to dream."

Dan finds Emma in the movie room. He finds her at three in the morning, eating popcorn and watching herself on the large screen.

"Hi," she says. "I couldn't sleep."

Dan nods. He sits beside her. He is conscious of the fact that he's wearing his boxer shorts and a T-shirt. His new girlfriend, Cheryl, just left his bed, her long legs naked under a miniskirt, her shoes off so they wouldn't click down the driveway. She tiptoed away, back to her houseboat. Ted is upstairs in Emma's bed. He is snoring slightly, twisted up in a silk sheet. He is dreaming about making love to Bridget and Emma and others. He is dreaming flashes of colour: the black of loons, the white of the stars, the green of pond water, the unnameable hue of bare skin.

Dan cups his hand under his chin and rubs. He can smell

Cheryl all over him and he wonders if Emma can too.

"I couldn't sleep either. Dreams?"

Emma shrugs. "Popcorn?"

Dan takes some from her. He scoops it in his large hand and feeds it into his mouth. He watches Emma up on the screen. She is delivering her famous speech from the Oscar-nominated movie she filmed last year, the one that starts, "You must know the reason."

Dan thought it was a silly movie about blood relations and murder and angst. He much prefers comedies and Emma is a fine comic actress. She is stealing the show in the one she is doing right now. Dan watched filming all last week. He crept into the lot after he dropped her off and watched as Emma made jokes and twisted her face into all sorts of positions. Her usually seductive body looked almost awkward on-set, long legs tripping, arms swinging. Dan couldn't stop watching. But then he's done nothing but watch Emma Fine since he came to work for her several years ago.

"Did I ever tell you," Emma says, "about the time my mom left me in a department store? Did I tell you about that?"

Dan shakes his head. "Is that what you were dreaming about?"

"No," Emma says.

They are quiet for a minute as they watch the murder scene, Emma's head thrown back, her mouth open.

"No, I was just thinking about it. She thought it was funny but I was scared shitless."

"How old were you?"

"I must have been around five years old."

Emma's father's body lying, white and pale, full screen, Emma sobbing, holding her head.

"We were shopping and I was running everywhere, getting into trouble. I was hiding between the clothes in the racks, peeking out, disappearing again."

Emma's father's funeral and the police arresting her,

leading her away from the grave.

"I like this part," Emma says. "I look so sad."

"It's an okay movie," Dan says. "I've seen you do better."

Emma looks at Dan. "Anyway," she says. "My mom paid for something at the counter and then just walked out of the store. I saw her walk away. She didn't look back. She carried her black purse and the bag of clothes she had bought and she pushed open those heavy doors and walked out into the street."

"Where were you?"

"I was watching her from between the clothes, I think. I remember feeling hidden. I remember thinking that she'd just turn around and walk back in, that the whole thing was a joke."

"So what happened?" Dan reaches into the popcorn bowl and takes some more. He watches the credits roll across the screen. He yawns.

"I stayed where I was. I sat down between the clothes until someone pulled out a dress and saw me sitting there. Some older lady. She took me to the cashier who then took me to security. They called my mother."

"She went home?"

"No, she wasn't home."

"Where was she?"

Emma shrugs. "I don't remember. That's not important. What's important is that it took hours for her to realize I was gone. It took hours for her to come back to the store and get me."

"Jesus." Dan almost laughs.

"It's not funny."

"I know. It just reminds me of that movie where they leave the kid at home and go on vacation."

The screen blacks. Dan can hear the projector clicking behind the glass partition. He gets up to stop the film.

"Wait," Emma says. She takes his arm. "Sit down."

Dan sits.

"Then she finally came back to the store. After I had been sitting in that stuffy room above the store, watching the customers come and go from behind two-way glass, eating lollipop after lollipop with the security guard, she came back in. And on her way to get me, she must have seen a good price on something. A shirt, a skirt, I don't remember. I watched as she fingered the material, as she held the outfit up to her body, measured it in her mind for size, checked the price tag. I watched from that small room above the store as she took the outfit, whatever the hell it was, to the change room, tried it on, and then — would you believe this? — bought it. With her bag in hand she climbed the stairs to security and knocked on the door. Then she shed her tears. Then she pretended that she was worried, she hugged me, clutched me, told me she'd never leave me again. She didn't realize that I had been watching from behind the two-way glass."

Dan looks at the floor. He smells the popcorn smell, the velvet seat smell, the warmth of the projector, the electric smell, Emma's smell, everything lingering in the air. He wants to reach over and touch her but he knows he can't. That's a line he can't cross right now.

Emma sighs. "Can you believe that?"

Dan shakes his head. "I can't believe the security guards let her get away with it. You'd think they would have charged her."

"She seduced them. She was so pretty."

Dan nods.

"I'm going to bed," Emma says. "Would you turn that off?"

"Yeah, no problem."

Emma stands, her bathrobe concealing her nakedness.

"Ted here?"

"Yes. Sleeping like a baby." Emma slides past Dan who stays rooted to his seat. His knee accidentally catches her bathrobe and opens it slightly. "Oops," Emma says and pulls the robe shut, but not before Dan sees a long leg, a small tuft of pubic hair, flat stomach, one full breast. She leaves the room, the door swinging shut behind her.

Dan stands stiffly. He feels like an old man. His body creaks and groans, his joints ache. He tries stretching, tries to loosen his muscles. But they won't loosen and so Dan walks, humped over, towards the projector. He stops the machine, turns it off, and then shuffles out of the room and down the hall towards the kitchen. He leaves from the kitchen door and stands out by the pool, looking into its black water. All the lights are out. Dan strips off his T-shirt and dives into the water. He swims to the other side of the pool, his muscles suddenly free from ache, and then climbs out and walks out the gate and around the house, trailing water, boxer shorts clinging to his body, shivering in the night cool air, towards his apartment over the garage. He climbs the stairs, counting them as he goes up, and then disappears into his place. His dry T-shirt lies in a heap beside the pool and the open gate swings back and forth in a sudden gust of violent wind until, forcefully, it clangs shut.

Part Six

Photo of Emma Fine at the Oscars. She is posing. Sideways stance. Face forward. Perfect Hollywood smile. A hand on her hip, the other hand holding a little gold purse. Her hair is tousled up on her head, held in place with a gold clip glittering with diamonds. Her dress is lavender in colour, simple but elegant. The back is completely bare with thin, gold bands holding everything together. A man's hand is on her naked back, down by her waist. A gold wedding band on his finger. A black tuxedo sleeve. Screaming fans line up behind Emma, their arms out, autograph books flapping, a red velvet rope keeping them away. One woman stands out from the rest. She is tall, thin, has beautiful red hair. She is standing quietly by herself, her arms wrapped around her chest. She is staring at Emma Fine, eyes glued to the actress. The woman's nose is bandaged. What is striking about the picture is how similar the two women look even though one is dressed in a $20,000 outfit and the other in sweatpants, T-shirt, and black running shoes. They are both beautiful, elegant, and long-limbed. And their eyes reveal pity, impatience, and boredom, as if each woman would much rather be doing something completely different.

Chapter Eighteen

"It is not possible," Dr. Trapser says. "It is not possible to look completely like another person. There will always be marked differences. An experienced eye, no, a perfectly normal eye, anyone for that matter, would see the dissimilarities. There would be scars, defining characteristics, birthmarks, that kind of thing. What about freckles? It wouldn't work." Dr. Trapser shakes his head and looks down at his appointment book. "What about Friday? Are you free on Friday for a consultation? We could do something close, I think, but I can't guarantee a perfect match. I could lift and tuck, move things around a bit." He looks up at his patient. He takes her face in his hands. "I could pull this back. Right here. It is amazing how much you already look like her. It may be possible to fool some people. I don't know." He thinks for a minute, his hands touching her face. "I could get sued." He laughs. "She'd take me for all I'm worth." He laughs again. "But then I do like a challenge." Dr. Trapser takes his hands away from her face. "I know her, you know. I've done things for her. A little bit here, a little bit there. Oh, yes, it's not all real." He points to his chest. "Most of them come to me for something or other. Why just last week I was doing … Well, I shouldn't give away secrets, should I?" He walks around his desk and takes her hand in his. "Thank you for coming to see me. I'll get my assistant to book you in for Friday. You're lucky someone cancelled or we wouldn't be able to see you for months. Besides, your husband — well, money does talk, doesn't it?" He leads her away from his desk and towards his door. "I think you're perfectly lovely the way you are, you know. I think that people can be improved but you're just as lovely as she is. I really shouldn't discourage you. This is, after all, my business." Here he pauses and reaches over and kisses her goodbye on the cheek before opening the door. "But you are a lovely creature. Simply lovely. All that red hair. Such a fine figure." She walks away from him, towards his assistant's desk, and he stands in the doorway and watches her move, the way her legs stretch out like a young horse, all grace and shape and muscle. He watches her back, the straight posture, the flowing red hair. Dr. Trapser rubs his hands along his jaw and he thinks how remarkable it is that God made womankind in such wonderfully complete packages.

Bruce is walking through the hot grounds outside of the church with Emma Fine. He is walking close beside her, his head down, watching each step he takes, watching her long legs under her black dress. He has been back often in the last couple of days. Emma has taken a liking to him. She's opening up. Bruce thinks she's just glad to have someone interested in her to talk with. Surely, once you have a large ego, you always have one. He watches the nuns shuffling around inside the church and he wonders what they think about other than the cosmetics of the church. They are always pointing out pews that need polishing, floors that need sweeping. It seems to Bruce as if there's nothing else they worry about. Emma Fine needs something else to think about once in a while, doesn't she? Herself. Besides, he's nothing if not persistent.

"I don't know," she says. "It was just so confusing. All the attention. All the media. Everywhere I went someone was accusing me."

"Accusing or supporting. Lots of people were supporting."

"You don't see the supporters. Your eyes are only on the accusers."

Bruce is sweating. The heat is blinding. Perspiration drips down his temples, falls from the tip of his nose. He can't remember another August so hot.

"I just can't remember," Emma whispers. "I have such a hard time remembering. And people died. Two people."

"Two?"

"Bridget and Ted."

"How do you know she's dead?"

Emma looks at Bruce. She stops walking and holds his sleeve. Stops him. "What do you mean? They found her things. They found her things covered with her blood. They found her car. She's dead."

"They never found her body ..."

"The coroner said there was no way she could have lost that much blood and still be alive. They said she was dead."

"Yes, but —"

"No, buts. She is dead." Emma continues walking. "I killed her."

"You killed her?"

"Not literally. I didn't actually kill her. But by sleeping with Ted, I guess I did kill her. Emotionally. I don't know." Emma wipes the damp from her forehead. She shields her eyes from the sun. She looks at Bruce's face. "You know, I don't want to be here any more. I thought about what you said, about telling my story. I thought about everything again and I've realized that I don't want to be here any more."

"You want to go back to Hollywood?"

"No, not that." Emma pauses. "I want to have a life. I want to get married and be normal. Two cars. A garage. I really want a garage."

Bruce laughs. "Hollywood star wants a garage. I can see the headlines."

"That's the problem," Emma whispers. "Everyone can always see the headlines."

"Why did you come here in the first place? Why didn't you

just travel to Europe. Like that director, what was his name? Jack Portia? He took off but was still able to survive in the industry."

"I didn't sleep with underage girls."

"I didn't say —"

"I guess I needed to be forgiven. I was afraid. I was tired. There was too much noise. I had to get off the drugs. And then things got comfortable. People took care of me here. A routine set in. I didn't need to think. I didn't need to talk. No one cared who I was."

They sit on a bench that is hidden behind a hedge. Bruce wishes he had known the bench was here before. It is in the shade and he is suddenly comfortable. A slight breeze picks up. He lets Emma talk. He decides not to take notes. To just sit with her and let her talk.

"There are moments that I forget," Emma says. "I remember things from my movies. Sometimes I go to the revue cinemas on Sunday nights and watch myself and try to remember. Too many drugs. Everything seems whitewashed at times."

Bruce nods.

"The trial was horrible. Everything I'd ever done in my life, everything that had been done to me. My driver talked about my childhood as if he had been there, as if my mother was the reason I was an addict. The only good thing he did was tell about how beat up I was after the party, about how drugged I was. He told a story about my mother leaving me in a department store. He told stories about my stepfathers."

"Dan Pluggs, right? He got you off, in a sense. He's the one who said the right things to get you off."

Emma nods. "We were close. I remember caring about him. But he talked too much about other things, told things he shouldn't have told. Don't get me wrong. I am grateful that he drove me home from the party."

"Do you know what happened to him?"

"I think he lives in Beverly Hills now. I think he has a wife and kids. I saw it in the paper years ago."

"He probably has a garage." Bruce laughs.

Emma smiles sadly. "Probably."

They sit quietly for a while, the air is oppressive, the cicadas are loud, an electric buzz, a constant sound.

"It's amazing," Emma says, "how quickly you can sink. How fast the boat goes down."

"Yes," Bruce says. "I know." He leans forward and puts his elbows on his knees. "But you know, usually it doesn't happen that fast. Usually there's a long period of obliviousness, a period where you just move and act and do things the same way, not realizing that everything is building up around you, that life as you know it will end just around the next corner."

Emma leans back on the bench. She closes her eyes. The bright sun shines down on her.

Chapter Nineteen

"I look nothing like her," Bridget screams. "Nothing. The nose is all wrong. The cheekbones are all wrong. Fucking Christ."

"The swelling — wait until it goes down," Dr. Trapser says. "It'll take a couple of weeks."

Bridget is holding the mirror up to her face. She is looking at herself from all angles. "It's been two weeks already. The swelling is down. Look" — here she pushes on her face — "look, there's no swelling."

"I told you I couldn't perform a miracle. I told you that you wouldn't look exactly like her."

"I look nothing like her."

"It's also temperament, it's the way she moves, it's personality —"

"Shut up. Shut the fuck up."

"Nurse."

Bridget is up out of her chair. She has swung her purse at Dr. Trapser's face, hitting him on the chin.

"I think you should leave. I think you should pay up your bill and leave." The doctor rubs at his face, backs away from her.

"I want this done right," Bridget screams. "I want you to do it again. I had my breasts done and they were done right."

"Please leave. Look, I'll give you a discount."

"You're the best in West Hollywood, damn it. Can't you do anything?"

"I think I might have to call the police."

Bridget gathers her coat and pulls her purse onto her shoulder. "You bastard," she says. "You're all talk." She storms out of the office and furiously presses the button on the elevator.

"Your payment?" Dr. Trapser calls out.

"My husband will be by to settle everything," Bridget says, suddenly calm. "He'll fix everything with you."

There is a woman in the elevator. She stares at Bridget as she walks in and pokes angrily at the button to close the doors.

"Excuse me," the woman says.

Bridget turns towards her. The woman has a notepad out, a pen.

"I hope you don't mind, but could I have your autograph? I loved you in your last movie."

Bridget smiles slightly. She takes the woman's pen and scribbles, "With love, Emma Fine," in the book. She turns back to the doors of the elevator and waits for them to open.

"I like what you've done with your hair," the woman says. "The colour."

Bridget laughs. She turns again to the woman and puts her finger up to her lips. "Shhhhh," she whispers. "It's a disguise."

Shelley is fixing lunch when Bruce comes into the town-house.

"Where's Tyler?"

"He's gone for a walk in the hills."

"Hope he watches for rattlesnakes."

"Oh my God, Bruce," Shelley puts her hand to her heart.

"I'm just kidding. It's too hot for them out there today. The only thing that will hurt him will be a little dehydration." Bruce sits down at the table. He basks in the air condition-ing. He breathes heavily. "It's so hot out there today."

"I haven't been out." Shelley is wearing a summer dress. Her hair is up in a ponytail. Bruce admires her neck.

"Thanks for the lunch."

Shelley places a salad and a sandwich down in front of Bruce. "No problem."

"It feels like old times again. Except you're sleeping in the guest room."

"Did you read that newspaper clipping?"

This morning Bruce read the clipping that was pushed under his bedroom door, about some kid in Calgary who was sexually assaulting boys. It made his stomach ache. At first he thought the kid was Tyler, then he thought that one of the victims was Tyler, then he realized that Tyler wouldn't be down here visiting if he was in any way involved in the case. He'd be up in Calgary sitting in some dark room with a lawyer who would be picking his mind about divorce, about his father and mother and stepfather and sister, with a man who would be suggesting things to his son about sex and watching to see if his son reacted in any odd way. Besides, Tyler didn't go to the school that was mentioned in the clipping.

"Yeah, I read the clipping."

"You see what is happening?"

"No, I don't see. What does that have to do with Tyler?"

Shelley sits down beside Bruce. She leans into him. "Bruce, honey." Bruce looks up from his sandwich. He hasn't been called "honey" in years. "Tyler knows that boy. Tyler went to that school last year. That boy used to come to our house after school."

"What boy? One of the victims?"

"No, the boy who committed the crimes."

Bruce puts his sandwich down. "I thought Tyler went to a school called Earl Grace."

"That's this year. He transferred to Treehorn last year for the hockey team. He wanted to play more hockey. They had a better coach."

"Why didn't you tell me?"

"I did tell you. You weren't listening."

"And then what?"

"And then his grades started to slip, he started to get all nervous and wasn't eating. He wouldn't look me in the eyes."

"Oh, Christ."

"And then we transferred him back to Earl Grace and he's been there for a year now. He has one more year to go."

"I can't believe you didn't tell me any of this."

"Bruce, I did tell you. You weren't listening. You aren't listening."

"Of course I was listening. I'm always listening." Bruce throws his hands up in the air, waves them around his head. Then he realizes how stupid his actions are and he puts his hands down by his side and stares at his sandwich. "So what are you saying, then? What are you really saying?"

"I don't know. Nothing, I guess. I'm just giving you the facts. Michael faxed me the newspaper clipping this morning. He faxed me a message telling me who the boy was. I didn't know about any of this until this morning and now I'm thinking that the facts are becoming clear."

"And they are what? What facts? How clear?"

"Lower your voice. I'm right here. Don't shout."

"The facts," Bruce whispers, "are that Tyler knew the boy. He just knew the boy, was friends with him, but then he didn't like the gruelling hockey schedule and so he went back to his old school. That's it, right? He was tired. The coach ran him too much. That would make any kid nervous."

"Yes, you are probably right."

"When did that newspaper article come out?"

"It must have been yesterday. Michael says the authorities have been phoning. They want to talk to Tyler."

"Oh."

"They want him to come back to Canada. They want to question anyone who knew the boy."

"Shelley." This is all Bruce can say. He whispers her name

again. "Shelley." Even though he's already swallowed, his sandwich feels stuck in his throat.

"I have to take him back there, Bruce. I have to take him with me." Shelley begins to cry. She puts her face in her hands and leans on the table.

Bruce takes Shelley roughly in his arms. He pulls her close, rubs her back, her head, her neck. She moans, "I don't know what to do. Should I talk to him? Should you talk to him? What should we do?"

"Shhh." Bruce touches Shelley's face. Kisses her cheeks, her nose, the tears. He kisses her lips, pulls her tight towards him, awkwardly fumbles off the chair he is sitting on, and ends up between her legs, kneeling on the floor, holding her around the waist. She is sitting. They are kissing so hard that Bruce's lips feel bruised, his mouth feels stained.

"No, Bruce," Shelley breaks free and whispers.

But Bruce keeps kissing her, stopping her words.

"No."

The front door slams shut and Tyler is standing there. He looks at his mother and father, his mother's face red, her lipstick smeared on her cheeks and neck, his father kneeling between her legs, turned towards him, his mouth open, eyes just slits. Tyler runs up the stairs to the guest bedroom.

"Oh, God. Bruce."

"I'm sorry. I'm so sorry." Bruce stays kneeling while Shelley gathers herself and moves around him and runs up the stairs after her son. "Tyler? Tyler?"

Bruce stands on unsteady legs. He touches his face, his lips. The familiar taste of his wife. His ex-wife. He begins to cry. Huge, choking sobs. He can hear Shelley and Tyler talking upstairs, Tyler saying something, then Shelley, then quiet. His lungs feel as if they are going to burst and he takes a deep breath and continues to cry. Bruce's heart aches.

Emma is so high it's like she's falling up, floating skyward.

She's off balance and shaky but she feels as if her body is one fluid movement, one motion, set forward.

"I feel good, baby," she slurs to Ted.

Dan is driving. He is manoeuvring the car around the fans and photographers lined up along Hollywood Boulevard.

"Damn traffic," Dan whispers. He is not used to driving a limousine. It seems large and obnoxious.

Ted pushes the button in the back to close the window between himself and the driver but the button is stuck and the window stays open. He leans back and takes Emma's hand in his. His tuxedo jacket is itchy and warm. He turns up the air conditioning. Emma's lavender dress is tight against her body. She is leaning back on the gold ropes which hold it together. Her hair has fallen from its clip and is loose around her shoulders.

"That was some night," Ted says.

"I like it when I haven't been nominated for anything. I like it when I can just enjoy everything. Last year I was so stressed." Emma smiles a slow smile, all drawn out and teethy. "I'm really horny," she whispers and puts her finger up to her lipsticked mouth. "Shhhh, that's a secret."

Ted laughs. "Too many pills, Emma. Too much to drink."

"Never too much." Emma leans on his shoulder. "You'll never leave me, right? You'll always be here for me?"

Ted says nothing.

"Are you married? Did I get that right? You're married aren't you? And where is the pretty lady tonight? The redhead. With her boyfriend?"

"You didn't have to introduce me as your brother, Emma," Ted says. His mouth has gone hard, his lips thin.

Emma laughs. "I thought that was funny. Especially when you had your hand on my ass."

Ted shakes his head. "Did you see the look on that guy's face?"

"That was his sister he was with, you know. It really was

his sister. Or his daughter. I can't remember which."

Dan turns the corner and leaves the traffic behind. He looks in his rear-view mirror at the couple in the back. The car speeds up along the freeway.

"I really wish we could go away for a while," Emma says. "Just me and you. No wife. No baggage. Nothing. Just me and you." She snuggles into his shoulder.

"We could go camping," Ted says. "I've talked about this before. We could buy ourselves a little tent and go camping."

"I was thinking more like a five-star hotel. I was thinking maybe Paris."

"We could go camping in Paris."

Emma laughs. "Can you cook croissants over an open fire?"

"No, seriously," Ted says. "I'd like to go away with you. Soon. We could drive into the hills, set up a little camp away from everything."

Emma thinks about it. "I could try it," she slurs, her voice heavy. "I'm always up for fun."

"I'll make it romantic," Ted says. "I'll bring things."

"What kinds of things?"

"Whips, chains, leather."

Emma laughs. "I was thinking more in the line of champagne." Her head falls against him as Dan swerves into another lane. "Or maybe some Seconal."

Ted puts his arm around Emma. She leans down and puts her head in his lap. He strokes her naked back. "You'll die when you see the sunrise up in the hills. It's the prettiest sight."

"Sunrise? I'm going to sleep in, aren't I? I'm not going to be up chopping wood at five in the morning."

Ted strokes her back all the way to the house. He helps her out of the car and up the stairs into the bedroom. He places her on the bed and he begins to undress. Emma watches him. She admires the curve of his body, the way his ribs form a ladder on his back when he bends.

"I think I'm in love with you," Emma says.

Ted winces. "Shit," he says.

"I'm sorry. I shouldn't have said that."

"No, it's just . . ." Ted moves to kiss Emma. He touches her face and her hair and her neck. "I may be in love with you too."

Emma smiles and pulls him down on top of her. "I'm so high," she says. "I hope I remember this in the morning."

One day, while Emma is shooting her new movie, Ted buys a tent, a Coleman stove, waterproof matches, a flashlight, sleeping bags that zip together, and air mattresses. He buys a cooler and stocks it with food and wine. He buys cocaine from the man on the corner. And amphetamines and crack and angel dust and some good old-fashioned pot. At the end of the day Ted walks into Bully's Hunting and Fishing Supply Store and buys a pistol from behind the velvet curtain that partitions the firearms from the rest of the store. He selects something small, light, easily concealable. He doesn't care to know the name of it, knowing it won't make any difference, but the man behind the counter, wearing a hunting vest over a T-shirt, walking shorts, and black socks in red running shoes, talks on about the qualities of a larger rifle, the accuracy of the shot, the impact of the bullet.

"Not many things you can shoot with this little one, son," he says. "Maybe just some tin cans for practice. This ain't really one of those hunting rifles."

"That's all right," Ted says. "I just want it for protection."

"Against what? Termites? Field mice?" The man continues trying to talk Ted into buying a rifle. Accuracy of shot, the man says, makes all the difference.

"Where am I going to put a rifle in the city?" Ted asks.

The man shrugs. "Just thought you might be going hunting. What with that tent sticking out of your truck." The man nods to Ted's truck which is parked near the curb in front of the store.

"Going camping."

"Um-hmm." The man busies himself behind the counter.

"With my girlfriend."

The man nods. "You registered?"

Ted shakes his head.

"Well, you've got to register yourself before you can buy from me."

"That's not what I heard," Ted says, his voice lowered. "I heard you don't go in for that."

"For what? Government policy?" The man packs the small pistol in a thick black case and puts the whole thing in a bag. He avoids Ted's eyes. "Fucking government rules and regulations?"

Ted reaches into his pocket and takes out a roll of money. He gives half to the man.

"That ain't enough," the man says, his voice lowered.

Ted pulls off more bills. "We aren't in the movies."

"I said that ain't enough."

Ted suddenly notices in the mirror behind the counter another man standing just inside the curtain. He hands over all his money.

"We got you on videotape," the man says, putting the money in one of his many vest pockets. He points up to the cameras around the store. "So don't you be doing anything stupid, okay? We have ways of editing the thing to make it look good, to make everything look legal."

Ted nods. He takes the bag away from the man and brushes past the other man as he leaves the store. The bell above the door sounds like a bullet entering glass. Ted throws the package beside him on the seat of his truck and he starts the engine and drives home.

Bridget is waiting for him. Jesus, she looks so much like Emma. The red hair is the only difference. Ted feels a pain in his side when he sees her sitting in their darkened living room, the furniture all gone, sitting on the floor with her feet up to her chest, watching the TV which casts a blue glow on the room. She is strung out.

"Hi," she says. She sniffs. She rubs her nose.

"I've got camping stuff. I've got a pistol. I've got cocaine."

Bridget smiles. "Let me try some."

"I'll need it all."

"Oh, come on, honey, let me try."

Ted takes the package of white dust out of his jacket pocket and throws it down in front of her. "Special treat," he says. "It'll fuck you up."

Bridget crawls towards the package. She opens the bag and tastes the powder. "Oh," she whispers, "this is good." The pain in her face from the plastic surgery. The pain in her breasts, in her legs, in her stomach. The itchy patches of new healed skin. She gets her small mirror, rolls up a strip of paper to snort with.

Ted leaves the room. He goes into the bathroom and turns on the shower. He strips his clothes off and gets in and washes the grime of the city off his body. Everything is coming together too smoothly.

"When you finally decide to go you've got to leave me a copy of the map," Bridget says from behind the shower curtain. "I'll need a map and a really good flashlight."

Ted continues to soap himself.

Bridget opens the curtain. "And I need something else now." She takes his shirt off, the one she's been wearing for a week, dirty and smelly and stained, and she steps naked into the shower with him. He kisses her puffy lips. He closes his eyes and imagines his wife. He opens his eyes and sees Emma Fine, red-haired Emma Fine, the resemblance is uncanny. Ted tries to touch her but he can't. His life is spinning out of control. Everything is set in motion. His stomach aches from anticipation.

"Get used to it, honey," Bridget coos. "I think I look pretty smart." She laughs.

"The voice is wrong."

Bridget takes her voice up a notch. She practises. "Me, me, me, me," she sings.

Ted turns her around in the shower, her back to him, and he soaps her shoulders, her spine, her hips, her ass. He thinks about when they got married, the way Bridget cried when she walked out of city hall, tears running freely on her face. The sun was shining and her red hair lit up to an orange, the glow of a sunset. They had bubbly white wine, salty crackers, blue cheese, in a hotel room in Toronto. Bridget got a man good with his hands, a man wanting only to build things made of wood, a man who thought structure more important than form. And now here he is, massaging Emma Fine in the shower, his wife gone and missing, disappeared, dead. Soon he's going camping with Emma Fine up in the hills. He's got his equipment, his tent, his truck, his food, and drugs, and all kinds of caviar and champagne. He'll take her in his arms and make love to her under the starry sky, and the hazy night will come to a close around them.

"Bridget," Ted whispers. "I miss you."

Her nostrils red and flared, coke high, Bridget turns to him in the shower. She wraps her arms around his shoulders and hugs hard. "It's an amazing thing, isn't it?" she says.

"What?"

"Plastic surgery."

Chapter Twenty

"What about the camping trip?" Bruce asks Emma. "What about the pistol that was found in Ted Weaver's truck?"

"I don't know. Maybe he thought we needed protection from the snakes, from the chipmunks, from the coyotes."

Bruce nods. "That's what they said at the trial. But maybe he needed protection from something bigger. Maybe it's just like you said before, maybe someone was following him. A deal gone wrong? Maybe that's why he wanted to take one of the most famous actresses in the world up into the mountains to a dingy camp and make her sleep in a tent."

"What's wrong with sleeping in a tent?"

"I just can't see you doing it."

Emma laughs. "Neither could I back then. But I've done a few things since then that I could never have seen myself doing." She pauses. They are sitting again on the bench before the church. The sky is overcast. Bruce has told Emma a bit about his life, about Shelley, the kids. He has wormed his way into hers, it was only fair he would let her into his. "I'd like to go camping," she whispers. "I guess I never really got to go." She laughs, slightly, her mouth parted gently, her lips puffing the air out. A tiny wisp of a laugh. Bruce thinks it's a sad laugh. It's the same kind of sad laugh Shelley gave him this morning when she bonked her head climbing into the airport limousine, the kind of sad smile Tyler gave him from the back seat. His boy, eyes forward, stoic, riding towards the airport, his mother perched upright and strong in the front seat. She was the picture of confidence but Bruce could see her mind twisting. Bruce could see it. As if he were looking through her skin, through her scalp, shining a bright light on the workings within.

"I guess the question is, Why did he want to go camping?"

Emma looks at Bruce. "What do you mean? Don't people just want to go camping? To get away? Why would there be an ulterior motive? Ted's the dead one. He wasn't up to anything."

"I'm not so sure about that," Bruce says.

"What do you mean?"

"I've been looking at the evidence. I've looked at everything. I've studied it."

"As did my lawyers, as did the other lawyers, the judge, the police, everyone in the world, practically."

"But —"

"And you're going to accuse a dead man, a man in a bad situation, caught in a place that maybe I should have been, a place that he wasn't supposed to be caught in, and make him look bad in front of me? Is that what you're trying to do?"

"No, I —"

"Because I don't want to hear it. Whatever it is you have to say." But instead of getting up and leaving, Emma sits still beside Bruce. She looks away from him, over towards the iron gates, towards the outside world, the cars teaming past, the people walking by.

"He was buying you drugs, right?" Bruce tries again.

Emma shrugs.

"There were drugs in his truck and everyone says he never touched them himself."

"So what? So what if he were buying me drugs. Lots of people bought me drugs."

"By all accounts he was also keeping his wife high. She was an addict."

"How did you find that out? How do you know that?"

"Seems his drug dealer was arrested a couple of years ago and he confessed to selling to Ted and a lot of other people, confessed to selling a lot of stuff to him over a long period of time. Seems he was buying a lot of very potent stuff. New kinds of drugs that could make you forget things for days on end."

"So now you're telling me a drug dealer is making up stories about Ted. You're telling me that because Ted bought me drugs, I can blame it on him. That that's why I forgot those couple of days. That it wasn't my fault? That I wasn't the one who pushed those pills in my mouth, who snorted that coke, who drank all that alcohol?" Emma shakes her head. "And if his wife was an addict, so what? Have you ever seen an addict come down? It's not pretty. Maybe Ted was just trying to avoid the bad. Maybe he just loved women who had addictive personalities."

"He just didn't seem like such an upstanding citizen." Bruce looks towards the road too, watches a woman walking her dog, the dog panting in the heat. "There is video coverage of him buying the pistol. The men that sold it to him videotaped the exchange and then collected award money for the tip to the police. Do you know that?"

"Yes, I saw it at the trial. And they weren't arrested. That wasn't fair."

"He didn't get it registered."

"So what? So what? Do you know how many people don't register their guns? You heard him in the video, said he just wanted protection, said he was taking me camping." Emma is standing now and the woman on the street walking her dog stops to look at her. Emma turns from the woman. The woman's dog lies down in the cool grass by the sidewalk, its tongue lolling. Emma speaks softly. "He got murdered, Bruce. He did. Not me. What does that tell you about him? What does that tell you about anything?" Emma keeps her face away from the woman and walks away from Bruce and up towards the church. She walks up the front steps and disappears into the dark, cool interior without so much as a wave, without turning her head.

Bruce thinks about following her, but then gets up, wipes the dirt off the back of his pants, and leaves out the front gate.

"Excuse me," the woman with the dog says.

Bruce stops.

"Do you have the time?"

Bruce tells her the time and then continues down the street, away from the woman who stands there, her mouth slightly open in the heat, her pink tongue visible, looking much like her dog. He continues towards home and he opens the front door with his key, stands in the hallway in the air conditioning, and listens to the sounds of silence all around him. The fridge humming, his computer buzzing, the toilet hissing, the kitchen sink dripping. All the sounds that constantly surround him but sound like nothing to him. Tyler has admitted that the boy sexually assaulted him, he has gone home to be questioned, he has promised to be cooperative. Shelley, locked in the guest room until the airport limousine came, has gone with him, has gone home to be with her real husband and daughter and son. Leaving Bruce right back at the beginning. Just where he started. Alone.

Part Seven

Photos from forensics file of parts of Emma Fine's body, close-ups, as she lies naked on the hospital bed. Her skin is badly bruised and cut. Cuts running up her legs. Close-up of bloody scabs. Her hair is a rat's nest around her head. Her breasts are bruised, tender looking. Several shots of side views of her breasts where the bruises are blacker. Emma has a dazed expression on her face. Cracked lip, black eye. She hardly resembles herself. The front of the photos are stamped, "Confidential," in red ink, but Bruce found them on the Internet, on a pornography site about S&M.

Postcard of the Mt. Trellis National Park Sign. Taken from Bridget McGovern's Car.

Behind the sign the background is misty, moist with fog. The trees narrow, thin, bony, like fingers sticking up from the ground. The sign is green and the script is yellow. There is a small chipmunk in the bottom right side of the postcard. It looks startled, surprised, terrified. On the back of the postcard is a map with directions to the campsite. "Less than fifty miles from Los Angeles" is written in pen just beside the map. It is addressed to Bridget McGovern:

> Take the San Rotunda 10 freeway east past the 87 freeway approximately 5 miles to the Eucre Ave. off-ramp. Go north towards the mountains to the end of Eucre Ave. Jog left around the fire station, turn right at the yield sign, and continue uphill until the road meets Mt. Trellis Road just beyond the lower San Antonio Ranger Station. Go right and continue up Mt. Trellis Road to town of Mt. Trellis. The camp store/snack bar is located on the right-hand side of the road one quarter mile beyond the lodge. The Morton Hills campground is located between the lodge and the camp store/snack bar. If you have driven past, the road hits a dead end at the Mt. Trellis ski-lift parking lot half mile beyond. There is a sign there that will notify you of this. It says, "DEAD END. TURN AROUND."

Chapter Twenty One

Bruce drives up to Mt. Trellis, gets lost at the dead end, turns, and heads back to the lodge. The front doors of the restaurant are open and several children are playing on the large front porch and in the parking lot. Bruce climbs out of his car and stretches.

Shelley and Tyler have been back in Calgary for less than a week and Tyler has already spoken to several lawyers, a judge, and three policemen. Shelley says he can't sleep at night. Bruce has begun writing what he thought would be a feature article about Emma Fine but now knows will be a book-size exposé. He sees photos throughout, cutting through the words. Pictures of everything: Emma as a child, a teenager, Emma and Ted together, the forensic photos. Bruce thinks that if he were artistic, he could put together the entire story by photographs. Start with the dead body in the pool. Move on from there.

Bruce walks up the large front steps and into the restaurant. It is early afternoon and several people are finishing off their lunches. The wait staff hover around the bar, cleaning up, preparing for the evening meal. Above the bar is a slanted roof and on the roof are dead animals and hunting trophies — a cougar, a lynx, deer bones, a ferret, a buckhorn, a deer.

The ferret moves. Bruce jumps back, startled.

"My pet," the bartender says, seeing Bruce's face as he stands at the door. "Can I get you a drink?"

Bruce nods and walks towards the bar. "Didn't expect it to move."

"Lucy's usually outside but it's so hot today that she's found the coolest place around. Surrounded by dead animals. Who'd of thought."

Bruce smiles and orders a beer. He sits at the bar. The ferret's feet scurry around overtop his head. The sound gives Bruce the shivers. Ten years ago, right after Shelley and the kids left him, Bruce used to have a recurring dream about squirrels in the roof. He used to dream about their feet tapping and digging and pulling out the insulation, ripping their teeth through the wires. He would dream about the townhouse being pulled apart by these damn red squirrels and he would lie awake, panting, and imagining he heard their nails scratching. He hasn't had that dream in a long time, he hasn't even thought about it, but the ferret's noise brings it all back.

"Listen," Bruce says. "Do you take reservations for campsites?"

"Yeah," the bartender says. He's shining the glasses behind the counter with a dry towel, just like in the movies. He has a cigarette dangling from his lip. "But you've got to book months in advance. Things fill up quickly. We're already filled up until October."

"Did you take reservations ten years ago?"

The bartender stops polishing and looks at Bruce. "Ten years ago?"

"I'm doing some research. I'm writing a book."

"Oh, yeah?" The bartender continues with the glasses. "Join the club. I'm a writer too."

"Hey, Sal," a waiter yells. "Can you fill up the salt on the tables?"

"Whatever," Sal shouts back.

"What kind of research?"

Bruce says, "I'm writing a book about Emma Fine."

"Who?"

"She was before your time."

The bartender nods.

"She was a movie star. A dead man was found in her pool. She disappeared for a couple of days."

"Oh, yeah. I remember something about that. I think I was, like, fifteen or something."

Bruce suddenly feels his age come crashing around him. He touches his hair to reassure himself that it's still there.

"I was just wondering if I could do some research, look into past reservation books, that kind of thing."

The bartender looks at Bruce. "You aren't a taxman, are you?"

Bruce laughs. "Do I look that seedy?"

The bartender smiles. "I'll get Joe to help you out. Joe runs the place." The bartender pokes his head around the door to the kitchen. He shouts, "Joe. Someone here to see you."

Bruce leans his head back and looks up for the ferret. It is gone. The other dead animals stare down at him.

An older man with grey hair and a slight limp shuffles out into the restaurant. He whispers with the bartender and then comes over to Bruce, hand out, smiling, "Hello, hello. Beautiful weather we're having here, isn't it? What can I do for you?"

Bruce takes the man's hand, explains what he has come for, and Joe stands, smiling, staring at him. The bartender disappears behind the bar and the ferret appears again on the roof.

"Well," Joe says, "we've got some books. Why don't you come into the office. We'll talk all this out." Bruce picks up his beer and follows the limping old man. "Seems I can't remember much these days but surely I'd remember if that Emma Fine woman had come up here."

"Oh, she didn't come here. She was going to come here."

"She was quite the looker. I was old even then and I still remember feeling sexy whenever I saw her on the big screen. Matter of fact, my wife wouldn't let me go to too many of her movies. Said it'd weaken my heart." Joe chuckles. "I do remember the police nosing about up here just after the incident. They took some samples and such. But nothing ever turned up."

In the office Joe points to past reservation books and Bruce sits, with a complimentary coffee, at the large desk leafing through them. Joe shuffles out of the room and leaves him to his work. Bruce finds nothing on the dates he is looking at. He glances through some old files of reservation letters and finds a photocopy of the postcard sent to Ted's wife. On the postcard is a scratched note: "Original with West Hollywood Sheriff's Station." They were thorough. Checking everything out. It amazes Bruce that they screwed up so completely at the crime scene. Bruce sits back in the chair. He thinks about police, about what they might be doing to Tyler right now, about the trial in Calgary, the young boy's parents, the other victims' parents. He thinks about Tyler there, with Michael and Shelley, surrounded by their love. And he thinks about himself here, alone. And Amy, who is studying in the summer to get into the enriched high school, wears her hair long and stringy, has big, thick glasses and protruding teeth. Bruce wishes so badly that he were there to take his children in his arms and tell them everything will be all right. But Shelley said not to come. She said that it would only make everything uncomfortable.

Joe comes back into the office with another coffee.

"Thanks," Bruce says, "but I think I'll be heading home now."

"Did you find what you're looking for?"

"No. There's nothing here. Just what I already knew."

"I was thinking," Joe says. "What you're looking for — that's about the time we had those long stretches of perfect weather. I remember that the days seemed so bright and clean and clear."

Bruce nods. He clears up his papers and puts away the reservation books. An old man's ramblings.

"I remember that because it was such a beautiful time but there was no one booked at the campsites. Or if they were booked, no one showed up. It was completely deserted here. Me, the wife, our old bartender, and two or three wait staff. There was a woman working at the camp store but she just up and left that summer. Never saw her again. That's it. And we lazed around in the pool most days and didn't do a stitch of work." Joe smiles, remembering. "It was odd, is all. No one here when it was the best weather." He shakes his head. "Me and the wife — my God, it was spring fever or something."

Bruce nods.

"She's the one," the old man says, "the one who killed that man in her pool, isn't she? Didn't she go to jail?"

"No," Bruce says. "There was no conclusive evidence. She disappeared at the time. Went on kind of a drug binge, an overdose, was found with no memory days later."

"I remember now," Joe says. "Dress all ripped up. Pictures of her in the papers. Hired some fancy lawyers to take on her case. Where is she now?"

"I don't know," Bruce says. "She disappeared again right after the trial."

Joe nods. "Listen," he says. "Take a couple pamphlets with you. Give them to your friends. We're getting less and less customers every year. No one wants to camp and hike any more. Nowhere to plug their computers in at the campsites, I guess." Joe laughs. "It took us until May this year to book up all the campsites."

Bruce takes a stack of pamphlets with him on his way out the door. He thanks Joe and walks towards his car but then sees a sign for a hiking path and decides to stretch his legs a bit before the drive back to L.A. He starts walking up the path, the trees growing over him, the forest cool and thick. He sees chipmunks and hears birds overhead. He thinks of Emma Fine up here, away from her adoring fans, with Ted Weaver and his pistol and truck and tent, and he wonders what they were up to, what made Emma fall in love with this married man, this man with no past, when she could have had anyone. Bruce knows that his book will be lacking information about Ted. There is simply nothing to report. No friends, no relatives, barely any papers. A marriage certificate on record. Bruce looked. Seems Ted's father committed suicide, his brother drowned, his mother had cancer. All gone. And his wife gone. Bridget is presumed dead. Her family in a car accident when she was in her twenties. Everyone dead. That's what it all comes down to. Two tragic pasts. You're remembered only by your family, and if they die, when they die, you might as well be dead yourself. Emma won't talk about Ted, or doesn't remember much about him, or didn't know anything. Probably didn't know anything. He seemed, to Bruce, to be a man of mystery. He seemed to be a man who liked his secrets.

Bruce thinks that since he has no family any more, maybe he's dead as well. Who will remember him when he's gone?

Bruce continues down the path. He breathes in the fresh air. It feels good to be out of the heat of the city. After Shelley and Tyler left, Bruce felt depressed again, as if they were just leaving him for the first time. But he bounced back, he feels a little better about himself now. Actually asked the tanning woman next door over for a beer. She couldn't come, had things to do, but it was obvious that she wanted to. They rescheduled.

He kissed Shelley, he felt her next to him again, and although he wanted her badly, the magic he remembered, the magic he thought he remembered, was somehow dim, washed away. Bruce's mother used to tell him he couldn't go back to the past. She used to tell him that he romanticized everything. Bruce wonders if this is the case. Shelley's lips felt good touching his, her mouth tasted the same, but it wasn't quite what Bruce thought it would be, what he imagined for ten years that it was. It was just a kiss. A passionate kiss. And now she's back home with her husband, Michael, and she's involved in a messy situation with their son.

Bruce is out of breath. He's going up the mountain now and his lungs are aching. The climb is a steady vertical slope, Bruce didn't know he was actually going up. But his breath is heavy and he hits a lookout point and sees the lodge there below him. He sits on a log to rest and admire the view. There are large birds, eagles maybe, circling overhead and the sky is clear and blue. Not a cloud visible. Bruce can see for miles. The lodge, the road, the camp store, and snack bar. There's his car. Two kids are playing soccer beside it and one kid bounces the ball off his roof. Bruce pulls the pamphlets out of his pocket. They are scrunched up there and hurting his thigh. He looks through them.

Pictures of tennis at the lodge, of swimming, hiking, the restaurant (complete with dead-animal roof, but when Bruce looks carefully he doesn't see the ferret), campers setting up at a site. He looks through them quickly, noting the changes in the dates, the changes in hairstyles and swimwear. He has pamphlets from years ago. Joe must put out an unorganized pile. The whole business here seems fairly unorganized. Ferrets in the restaurant. Bruce notes the prices ten years ago, eight years ago, five years ago. He's amazed that everything has pretty much stayed the same. As the accommodation became less classy, the prices have remained the same, meaning that with inflation everything became cheaper. A hot dog is still only a buck at the camping store and snack bar.

Suddenly Bruce looks carefully at the picture of the store in the pamphlet dated from ten years ago. There is a woman standing just in front of the saleswoman. She is long, tall, thin. A small bit of red hair is sticking out from a scarf wrapped around her head. She is wearing black running shoes, blue shorts, and an orange sweatshirt. There is a large shopping bag beside her on the floor and a purse resting up beside it. The woman is turning away from the camera so

Bruce can only see the back of her head. The saleswoman is smiling brightly, handing the woman something. She is looking straight at the camera and she is the centre of the picture. The other woman just happened to be there. Bruce looks carefully. It is a package of something, a small box of some sort. A three-bar box of soap or those waterproof stick matches or a box of macaroni and cheese. Bruce can't see. He knows the size of the box, a familiar size, hair dye or ... Jesus, hair dye?

Bruce squints up to the picture. He looks as close as he can look without bugging his eyes out. There she is, that must be her, Bridget McGovern, at the Mt. Trellis camping store, buying hair dye. If Bruce remembers correctly, those were the clothes she was wearing when she disappeared. The clothes found bloodied in the car at the Pasadena Mall.

Hair dye.

Bridget McGovern.

Bruce stands.

To make her red hair blonde.

Bridget had extensive plastic surgery.

Of course.

Bruce starts to run down the mountain. He runs heavily, out of shape, carrying the pamphlets out before him as if balancing an egg on a spoon. He runs straight for his car, pushes away the kid who is loitering alongside, and hops in. The kid falls to the ground. Bruce starts the engine and skids out of the lot, drives down the mountain towards L.A., checking his watch. He needs to find Emma Fine.

Bruce's brain is working like mad, trying to process information, trying to understand everything that is before him. Court transcripts, forensic reports, testimony, Emma's story, photographs, Maria saying, "She came waltzing straight into the house and she conned everyone, even the police and lawyers, but she didn't con me." And then Tyler and Shelley somewhere in the Calgary wasteland that is in Bruce's mind, together dealing with Tyler's sexuality, with potential rape charges, and ... Bruce drives faster and skids through a stoplight, narrowly missing a pedestrian, through the town of Mt. Trellis, back towards L.A., towards Will and his newspaper, towards Emma Fine, Emma Fine, Emma Fine. Her hand, Maria said, it was different, a mole or birthmark or freckle, Bruce can't remember which. And when he met her for the first time her voice was huskier than he remembered and her face looked so much older and shifted. Plastic surgery. Would someone with extensive plastic surgery age quickly if they weren't going back, if they had no money to go back, again and again to the doctor? Would the implants sag? The facelift fall?

At a red light Bruce looks again at the pamphlet. Bridget standing there, looking so much like the back of Emma with red hair, turning quickly from the photographer, getting caught in the image. What the hell was she doing at the campsite? Setting a trap for Emma? Kill the movie star, change identities? But then something went wrong, didn't it? Somebody killed Ted Weaver and left his body floating in Emma Fine's fabulous pool. And then the new Emma came back from the dead and fooled everyone.

But the blood? Bridget's blood everywhere, in her old car which was left under a highway off-ramp behind the Pasadena Mall, her blood soaked in the clothes she was wearing the day she disappeared. How did she do that? And then Bruce wonders for a minute if Emma herself committed the ultimate crime, if Emma Fine killed Ted Weaver, killed Bridget McGovern, pulled a fast one on everybody. And then he laughs. She is a good actor, he has to give her that, but not that good. There is the fact that many people testified to her drugged-out state the night before she disappeared. The doctor found high levels of drugs in her blood. How would you kill two people so carefully, so sneakily, in such a condition?

Maybe Bridget killed Ted and then Emma killed Bridget. There was the jealousy excuse for Bridget. Her husband was sleeping with the world's sexiest movie star. And then maybe Bridget was going to kill Emma. Take her place. Something went wrong. Maybe Emma's strong sense of self-preservation, even in a drugged state, made her attack Bridget at the campsite just after Bridget bought the hair dye and got her picture taken. But where did Bridget's body disappear to? Did Emma Fine have the wits about her to bury a dead body? Or, perhaps, the wild animals ate everything at the campsite. Is that possible? Do animals eat human bones? Or maybe, more logically it seems to Bruce, Bridget killed both Ted and the movie star. Buried Emma, drugged herself (she was an addict, Bruce reasons), and came back to life as Emma Fine. That would explain the picture of Bridget buying hair dye. But the blood in the car — there are ways of putting blood in your own car, your own blood, aren't there?

Other players: Dan, the driver? Maria, the maid? Common burglar or stalker and just bad timing? But that doesn't explain Bridget disappearing. And why would Emma Fine end up in an alley? Bruce begins to drive slower as he coasts into L.A. He gets stuck in a traffic jam and rests his head for a minute on the wheel, cars behind him beginning to beep. Move forward. Inch forward. Graze the bumper ahead. Feel a push from behind. The sky is hazy and thick with pollution. Hazy. Bruce's mind feels that way. The damn police messing up the evidence. He hits the steering wheel with his palm. The blurred identities of Bridget and Emma. They've melded into each other in his mind now. He can't separate them. Bridget playing Emma, Emma playing herself.

Bruce can't see straight through the glare of car lights, through the thick fog of pollution that has fallen over the city. He feels as if he is groping through water, something is holding him back, a hand on his shoulder, pushing him under. A knock on his head.

"God," Bruce says. He thinks it's funny, suddenly, that Emma is working at a church. An idol surrounded by idols. Is she even Catholic?

And then he thinks of Shelley and the way she tasted there before him, the smell of her on his face after she rushed upstairs to calm their son. Their son. Hers and his. A joint proposal. They worked on making Tyler together and then she went and left Bruce for another man. Sperm. Egg. Tyler is theirs, together. They are bound forever. What does Michael have to do with any of that? Bruce searches the glove compartment and his pockets for cigarettes and finds only a stray cigarillo from a woman he dated a year ago. He sniffs it, caught up at the light. It smells old but he doesn't care. He lights it and sucks in the smoke.

He should be with Tyler. Right now.

His window lowered, the hot California evening coming down upon him, the street lights flickering on. He's been driving for hours and he's still stuck in traffic. Bruce is trying to get his bearings. Shelley, when they got married, standing before the minister at the church, her eyes on Bruce, she wouldn't take her eyes off of him, and when the minister gave her the ring to place on his finger, she reached out and dropped it right on the floor before them. Bruce bent and retrieved it but he felt strange, as if fate had sealed something between the two of them before they had even begun. And Tyler, coming out of Shelley's body, all bloody and quiet, like some prehistoric creature from muck, Shelley's first words alluding only to the pain of the situation when all Bruce could think was *miracle*, miraculous, a bloody shrine. The next, Amy, came out quickly, pushed out fast, like squeezing the toothpaste for hours and then the dam breaks and the hard stuff shoots about, exploding all contents, and Shelley, again, lying tired against the pillow, her eyes scanning Bruce's eyes, looking for something within her husband that she couldn't somehow see.

"What happened?" Bruce whispers into the night air. He throws the finished cigarillo out the window.

A dead body in a pool, a famous West Hollywood movie star, a disappearance, a reappearance, drugs, alcohol, hair dye, adultery, divorce, children, rape, Calgary, murder, murder, murder — everything drowned in that pool. All at the same time. Bruce sitting on the couch in his darkened living room, three days' beard growth on his face, nursing a beer, and Shelley disappearing down the street with the children and her lover, driving up to Canada, going, going, gone. A knock on the head and Ted Weaver is floating in a pool. One minute he was wide awake, alive, planning something devious, the next minute he was dead. Emma Fine missing, coming home smashed around, damaged goods, parading back into her house with no memory, no fear. A judge throwing out all claims, turning soft evidence into hard trash, and then, oops, Emma gone again, this time for good. Blood on clothes, hair samples, fingernail cuttings, sperm, fingerprints, dirt, contents of a glass on a bedside table.

Lists. Everything comes down to lists.

Lists and all the evidence that the cops screwed up. Their footprints on the grass around the pool, their fingerprints all over the gates and tables around the pool, the doctor's faulty examination of Emma Fine's body at the hospital, the jeans under the bed moved because the cops thought the case was cut and dry. A suicide in a pool. Nothing more to it, they thought. Nothing tested properly at the beginning, nothing taken properly, nothing done well. If the cops had been doctors, everyone would be dead.

Ted Weaver is dead. Bruce wonders if he saw it coming, if he knew, for even a brief second, that his young, muscled body would soon be nothing but the shell that released his useless soul. Did he look up at the sky after being knocked on the head and think, Today is a nice day to die? Did he turn in on himself, his memories and dreams, or did the hit come too fast, Ted lying unconscious and unthinking by the side of the pool as the murderer rolled him, pushed him, dragged him, towards its depth.

Perfectly fitting, Bruce thinks, tying everything together: A man is born into the world from a sac of water, and he dies nestled again in warm, flowing liquid. What goes around comes around. *C'est la vie. Que sera, sera.*

Bruce pulls his car up onto the curb in front of the iron gates of the church and he sits there, silently, thinking. He looks towards the church, towards the glass doors of the added building on the side, towards the bench under the tree. She won't be here, he thinks. It's been almost a week since he last saw her. She's gone. He feels sure of it. The last thing he talked to Emma about was the camping trip. He knows she has disappeared. Like he knew that Shelley would drive away and never come back. There was no doubt in his mind that she wouldn't change her mind and come back to him, arms outstretched.

Chapter Twenty Two

Emma is in her bedroom painting her nails dark blue to match her tight, blue evening dress, when Ted pulls into the driveway with the camping equipment in the back of his truck.

"Let's go today," he tells her.

Emma has her hair up in a towel. She is wearing a short, silk dressing gown and furry, pink slippers that she's had since she was seventeen. She holds her fingers out in front of her and blows on them. Emma is sitting on the loveseat just under the front window. She pulls her legs up, her knees touching her ears, and she laughs. Ted sees that she isn't wearing anything under the gown.

"My nails are wet," Emma slurs. "I can't go camping now."

"You've been drinking."

"And smoking and popping and snorting. Oh, but I haven't had sex yet." She laughs again.

Ted kneels down in front of Emma. He pulls her legs down and wraps them around his waist. "Baby," he whispers, "I can make love to you in the tent all night long. If we go now, we'll make it there before dark. We'll set up our tent and roast hot dogs."

"I hate hot dogs," Emma says. "Those tofu ones aren't bad, though." She wraps her arms around Ted's shoulders, sits up straight, is careful with her nails. She blows in his ear.

Ted smells wine on her breath. He kisses her softly. He spreads open her dressing gown and begins to kiss her neck and the tops of her breasts.

"That's right," she says. "We'll do some of that and then

I've got to go to this party."

"What party?" Ted murmurs, lost in her flesh.

"Cast party. Closing party. Something like that. I don't know. Dan's taking me. He's driving me. He'll bring me home." Emma suddenly pushes Ted back. "Hey, you come. You come with me."

"I want to go camping, Emma. I want to take you away."

Emma stands. "I can't go camping," she laughs. "I might break my nails on a tent peg or something. Do tents have pegs still? I filmed a movie once where the tents had pegs. I kept tripping on them when I came out from the tent. I skinned my knee." Emma looks down at her naked knee and smiles. "It hurt like hell."

"You won't skin your knee. I promise." Ted pulls Emma down to the floor with him. He lies her underneath him and her wet hair falls out from the towel. She smells like lemon soap, strawberry shampoo, vanilla cream. Ted licks her but she tastes nothing like she smells. Creamy lotions and oils. A hint of salt. Something bitter. Something cool.

Emma holds her hands up over her head. Ted loosens her dressing gown. He continues to kiss her, lick her, touch her.

"I don't want to go camping, Ted," Emma says dreamily. "I'll book us into a little cabin my agent owns, okay? I'll book us in there for next week maybe. There's a private pool and maid service."

Ted stops kissing. "I want to go camping," he says. "I've got the whole thing planned."

"Oh, honey, don't get mad." Emma directs his head back down to her stomach. She pushes lightly on his hair and then says, "Damn," and shakes out her nails, checks to see if she smudged anything.

"I bought a tent. I bought a little stove. Waterproof matches."

"Wadder-poof matches," Emma says. She giggles. "You

can take it all back. We won't need stuff like that at the cabin. I think there's a Jacuzzi bathtub there. There might even be a sous-chef."

"Christ." Ted sits up. He looks at Emma lying there, her hands up over her head, her dressing gown flung open, her hair damp and mussed. Her eyes are bloodshot and her focus looks off. She's staring blankly at the ceiling. "What have you taken? You look like shit."

Emma stands shakily. She holds onto his shoulders. "A little of this, a little of that. I've had a bad day."

"You're going to ruin your career."

"Honey, my career was made off pills and coke. My career wouldn't even be a career if I weren't always so high." She laughs. "Do you think I can really act?" She stumbles into the bathroom. "Don't start without me."

"Start what?" Ted stands. He walks over to the bedroom door and locks it. He takes off his jeans which are damp from kneeling on Emma's towel and he kicks them under the bed. "Maybe I'll sleep," Ted says to himself. "Maybe I'll take you there in the morning."

"What?" The tap water is running in the bathroom. The hair dryer starts.

Ted takes off his T-shirt and climbs naked into bed. He curls up under the covers. The blinds are drawn in Emma's room and the late afternoon light filters through the windows. He rolls towards the bedside table and looks in at all the bottles of pills in the drawers. He shuffles them around a bit. Then Ted looks up at the mirror above the bed. He pulls his hand out from the drawer and he points it up at the mirror as if holding a gun. He takes aim and shoots, imagining the glass shattering down upon him. He cringes and ducks. The hair dryer stops. The sound of drawers opening and closing from the bathroom. The toilet flushes.

"Famous Hollywood star takes a crap," Ted says to himself. "Famous fucking star so drunk she pisses on the toilet seat."

Emma emerges from the bathroom and pulls her dressing gown off.

"I have to go soon," she says. "You'll be quick, won't you, darling?" Her dressing gown falls to the floor between the bathroom and the bedroom. Ted can see the bathroom. A mess. Makeup on the counter, a hairbrush lying next to the sink. Emma's face is perfect, though. Somehow she always manages to fill in the lines. "Who were you talking to?" she asks as she throws off the covers and straddles Ted.

"Nobody. Myself."

"Hang on," Emma says, bending from the waist, reaching into the drawer beside the bed. She takes out a bottle of pills, squints to read the label, shrugs, and then pops a couple into her mouth. She is still sitting on Ted. "I'm losing that glowing high, you know. I'm starting to feel my body again." She washes the pills down with a glass of wine that is beside the bed.

"You don't even know what you are taking," Ted says. "You can't even have sex without being high."

"Yes, I can." She moves her upper body, gyrates her hips. Reaches high above her head and then slowly caresses her shoulders, her arms, her breasts. "Did you know I used to strip?"

"One day you're going to overdose. One day you'll be dead."

"Everyone dies, baby. I'm just going to have a great time until I go." She begins to kiss Ted. To suck on his ears, his neck, his chest hairs. "Fuck me," she whispers.

And Ted complies.

Ted thinks, Anybody would want this right now.

The stove and tent and sleeping bags and cooler of food are outside in the driveway in the back of the truck covered with a blue tarp. Dan manoeuvres the BMW around the truck and into the garage. He climbs out of the car, closes the garage door, and walks around to peer in the truck.

"Dirty construction worker," Dan says. He brushes his hands off on his pants after touching the sides of the truck. He looks up at Emma's bedroom windows and sees that the blinds are closed. Dan walks up to his apartment and steps inside the cool interior. He has to get ready for tonight. He will drive Emma to the party, then he will drive her home, and then he will visit Cheryl at the yacht club. He will sleep in her houseboat, rocking through the night, he will sleep beside this honey-haired wannabe actress. He will fuck her, and while he comes, he will quietly whisper "Emma" into her ear. He will whisper this so softly that she will think he's just cooing like a baby or mewling like a cat.

Emma passes out briefly and Ted has to shake her to revive her. His fingers leave marks on her upper arms.

"My dress," Emma murmurs. "The party."

"You can't go like this."

Maria comes in to help Emma dress. She brings black coffee. An ice bag for Emma's head. "Sober up," Maria says. "This is a big night."

"It's always a big night," Emma sighs. "Everything I do is important." She laughs.

"You could do the dishes every once in a while. That would be important. Everything is crusted over. You could at least soak them."

"Do them in the morning, Maria. Go home and get some rest."

Ted stands by the window wearing a terry-cloth robe while he watches Maria help Emma into her panties, her bra. Emma is childlike, clutching onto Maria's hands as she steps into her panties, holding her hair up as Maria fastens the clasps on her bra. Ted looks down at his truck and notices that he has a clean, dry pair of work pants in the front seat. He yawns. He'll get them later.

"You can't wear this blue dress," Maria says, holding it up. "It's too tight."

"Who are you? My mother?" Emma giggles. "What do you want me to wear? This?" Emma walks to the closet and pulls out a summer sundress. Soft and green and flowing. She holds it up to her body and strokes it.

"Perfect."

"It's a closing party. This isn't fancy enough. My nails don't match. Green and blue don't match."

"Hurry up. Step into the dress and I'll button you up."

"My nails. They should be pink or white, not blue." Emma yields to Maria.

"That's pretty," Ted says. "You look like a breath of fresh air."

"I look seventeen."

"That's good, isn't it?" Maria says. "You're skinny enough to be seventeen."

"Watch yourself, Maria, or I'll start dating your son."

Maria throws up her arms in mock horror. "What would his wife say to that?"

"Aren't you coming? Get dressed." Emma goes to Ted at the window. "Come with me. We'll go to the cabin next week, okay? Come with me now."

"I'm tired. I think I'll just sleep. I'll be here when you come home."

"Oh, baby."

"Go. Have a good time."

Emma stops by her side table on the way to the bedroom door and she takes out several bottles of pills. Without looking at them she empties the bottles into her purse. Ted sees this but Maria has turned away and is straightening the bed.

"Let's go," Maria says. "Dan's got the car ready. He knows where you are going."

"He'd better know," Emma says. "I have no idea where I'm going."

Ted watches Emma get into the back of the BMW. She

is laughing at something Dan is saying. Dan looks up at the window, sees Ted looking out, and waves. Ted waves back. Dan gives Ted the thumbs-up sign. He watches Dan drive carefully around his truck and out the circular drive to the street. The brake lights flash on at the gate. The signal light flashes on and Dan turns the car and they disappear out of sight. Ted moves back to the straightened bed. In the bathrobe he climbs into bed and he closes his eyes. He falls asleep almost instantly and he sleeps the sleep of the dead. Not a single dream. Not a single movement. He sleeps still and heavily and the light darkens and soon it is as pitch-black outside as it can get in the city of Los Angeles.

Part Eight

Emma's favourite photograph is the centrepiece above the fireplace mantel in her sunken living room. It is large and has been professionally framed in silver. The photograph is nothing, really. Solid black with a small circle of white directly in the centre. Glowing white. Noticeably white because the black is so black. A giant expanse of black with a tiny hole of white. Right in the centre. Perfectly in the centre. And in that white are two shapes. Emma took the photograph when she was sixteen on the MGM lot just after shooting her three lines in the movie *Armed Conflict*. Her first camera. A present from Mr. Rice, the star of the film. After the director yelled, "That's a wrap," Emma went outside and stood up close to a black velvet curtain that was billowing in the wind outside. Her mother called, "Emma, get a move on, honey. What have you got? Rocks in your pants?" and Emma moved as close as she could to the curtain and she took the picture. She didn't know that there was a hole in the velvet until she got her film developed. Until she took a magnifying glass to the dot, Emma didn't know that behind the curtain a famous Hollywood actress was pushed up against the wall, her dress hiked up, her legs spread, her hands steady on the bricks, and her married co-star was penetrating her from behind. Emma always joked at parties that the picture summed up Hollywood for her — a huge expanse of nothingness circling a tiny dot of success, beyond which someone, usually a woman, is always getting fucked.

PSYCHIATRIC ASSESSMENT OF EMMA FINE TRIAL TRANSCRIPT:

DR. SNIDER: It was a type of dissociative amnesia. She knew certain things about herself but was missing key points, key moments in time.

Q. What key points in particular?

A. Particularly the days leading up to her disappearance and the entire time she was missing. She has no memory of that still, although she now has some memory of the days previous to her departure.

Q. Go on …

A. She had large amounts of toxins in her blood when she resurfaced. Drugs. Alcohol. The doctor has already given you a list. It has been clearly documented that alcohol can cause short-term amnesia as, say, a blow to the head might cause, or even, perhaps, witnessing some sort of traumatic event.

Q. Are you saying that Ms. Fine could have witnessed the murder and, therefore, lost memory of it?

A. No, not at all. I'm just comparing the memory loss to one that sometimes occurs during post-traumatic stress. For example, Vietnam vets often relate stories of witnessing severe incidents and then not being able to recall the incidents for days, sometimes months, sometimes years on end.

Q. Back to Ms. Fine …

A. Yes. Ms. Fine has regained some of her memory, as I said, but is still suffering from blanks. Black spots, say, blinders. She isn't making this up. She really does not remember a thing.

Q. I want to get back to this idea of post-traumatic stress. You say that people witnessing severe incidents, say a murder --

MR. WRIGHT: Objection.

JUDGE LIONS: On what grounds?

MR. WRIGHT: We aren't talking about post-traumatic stress. We have no idea what caused her memory loss, but the good doctor on the stand says it was probably due to alcohol.

JUDGE LIONS: Overruled. Because we have no idea we should explore all angles. Continue, if you please.

Chapter Twenty Three

"They never found Emma Fine's missing shoes," Dan says to Bruce.

They are sitting in front of Dan's garage on lawn chairs, eating shelled peanuts and drinking beer. The sun is setting over the mountains and the overall effect reminds Bruce of the red light he had in his bedroom in high school. The walls were painted black and the red light was somehow peaceful. Bruce feels high, the beer has gone to his head after a long day of sweating. Dan has a boom box propped on milk crates in the garage, playing Def Leppard and Pink Floyd. Bruce thinks it's odd how many people use both her names, Emma Fine, they don't just call her Emma. Her name is her title, he supposes — not just any Emma, the Fine Emma — admirable, rare, choice, expensive, delicate, elegant, excellent, refined. Or the opposite — unrefined, mean, crude, unpolished, harsh, inferior, rude, grainy.

Bruce needs another beer but doesn't want to ask.

Dan gets up from his folding chair and goes to the refrigerator in the garage. He takes out two beers, opens them, and walks back to the chairs.

"Thanks."

Dan's eight-year-old son comes barrelling out of the garage on his bicycle and disappears up the street.

"Be back by ten," Dan shouts after him.

In the kitchen window Bruce can see Dan's wife, Susie, drying dishes. She is staring out at them, her eyes unfocused and worried. She doesn't see Bruce glance her way.

"Susie's always letting him get away with murder," Dan says.

"So you've got a pretty good life now, don't you?" Bruce says.

"Yeah, not bad. Steady income driving limos for the company. Bought the house last year." Dan signals over his shoulder at the house behind them. Bruce looks again at Susie and sees that she has put down her dishtowel, has lit a cigarette, and is still staring out the window. Her hair is golden blonde, dyed blonde. It looks like she is really a brunette. Her face is pretty. Girlish. Young. Under the kitchen window, behind the counter and sink, Bruce knows that her belly swells from childbearing and her hips are wide. When he met her he noticed the varicose veins on her naked legs. The thick ankles.

Dan is short, muscular. He has a day's worth of stubble on his face and his sideburns are long and untrimmed. He rubs his face as if noticing Bruce watching him.

"I met Susie a couple years after everything," Dan says, swigging his beer. He waves at a passing neighbour. "We got married right away and had the kid." Dan flicks his head at the still-receding image of his son. "All that publicity. The trial. I could have married anyone I wanted for a while. I could have written a book about everything."

"Why didn't you?"

Dan shrugs. "I don't know. There wasn't much to say, I guess. I didn't have anything to say that hadn't been said already."

"Is that still the case?"

"What do you mean?" Dan glances at Bruce.

"I mean, is there anything you forgot to say at the trial?"

Dan says, "Those lawyers sucked me dry. Got me to confess to everything illegal I'd ever done. Wanted to get me on narcotics charges because I'd kept Emma Fine supplied with drugs. Tried for a while to nail murder on me because the bitch I was with that morning, the morning the asshole was found in the pool, she said I'd left early. I hadn't left early. I went for a swim on the beach and then went back to the boat and fucked her." Dan shakes his head. "She was so out of it on drugs she didn't even remember." He laughs. "Don't know what hurts more. To be accused of murdering someone or to have some bitch say she can't remember your fuck."

Bruce swallows his beer. "You and Emma Fine. You were close, weren't you?"

"Yeah, we did things together. We talked. We both didn't sleep much at night and so we sometimes watched her old movies together."

"So why do you think she turned against you at the trial?"

Dan shrugs. "Beats me. She wanted someone to blame, I guess. I was convenient."

"And you told the media things about her."

"She was heavily into drugs when I worked for her. Everyone knew all that shit anyway. Like I said, the lawyers got it out of me. And by the time I spilled my guts she was already accusing me of murder. Saying that I'd watch her and Ted whenever they went out. That I'd stare out my window at them or something."

"What about the pictures? The stuff in your closet?"

"Shit," Dan says, leaning back in his chair. He looks over at his wife, still hovering in the window, finishing off her cigarette. "Can't a guy have a crush on a movie star?"

"It was a shrine almost."

Dan laughs. "A shrine? It was pictures of the woman. It was a couple of candles near the pictures that I stored in the closet. It was a glove she wore to the People's Choice Awards. It wasn't a goddamn shrine. What is it with you people?"

"Us people?"

"You think a guy can't be in love with a woman he can't have without killing her lover?"

"I didn't imply …" Bruce is glad he's almost finished his beer. He wonders if this will get nasty. He wonders if he has it in him to fight back. "I just want to know what happened. I want to know the whole story."

Dan sits back.

"Did you know," Bruce says, "that Ted's wife, Bridget, was at the campsite that Ted and Emma were going to at about the time she went missing? Did you know that I have a picture of her at that campground wearing the clothes that were later found covered in blood in her car at that Pasadena mall?"

"No shit?" Dan sits up straight in his chair. Suddenly Bruce can see what must have made him attractive to women. There's a look in his eyes. Danger.

"Here, see." Bruce hands a pamphlet over to Dan.

"What do you know about that," Dan says, and then he looks closely at the picture. "Hey, that's not Bridget."

"What do you mean?"

"That's Emma, isn't it? Look. That's Emma Fine with a red wig on or something. Bridget stood differently."

"No, I think Bridget had plastic surgery to look like Emma."

"No, that's definitely not Bridget. That's the way Emma stands. That's the way she picks at her fingernails with her thumb. Look." Dan holds the photo back up to Bruce.

"No, I think that Bridget was there, that she was trying to be Emma Fine, that she had plastic surgery, was going to dye her hair blonde, went missing … missing … disappeared …" And then, in his hazy, beer-soaked, humid mind, it occurs to him that maybe Emma was acting like Bridget instead of the other way around. He shakes his head forcefully and some drops of sweat hit the pavement. It's too confusing.

Two girls growing up wanting something, wanting the world. One girl got the world by accident, the other girl gets the world on purpose. Which one?

"What are you doing?" Dan asks.

"I don't know, I just … I'm confused."

"Look, I know for a fact that that's a picture of Emma Fine. I know the way she stands. I know the way her ass curved like that, attached itself to her legs. Bridget rounded her shoulders a little as if … as if she were ashamed of her height." Dan sucks on his beer.

"What would Emma be doing at the campsite wearing Bridget's clothes? She claimed she never went up there. Why would she have red hair? And look — that's a box of hair dye on the counter."

"No, looks like tampons to me."

"What?" Bruce peers at the picture.

"Tampons come in those blue-and-green boxes. Believe me, I should know." He signals back to his wife, to the house.

Bruce turns fully around and looks at Susie in the window. She is still looking out. He feels like he's on "Candid Camera." But she isn't really looking at them, the two men in the driveway, she is looking towards them but into her own mind. She is smoking another cigarette.

"Thinks the stupid things will make her thin."

"Tampons?"

"Cigarettes," Dan says, laughing. "She's smoking them to lose weight." He snorts. "Another beer?"

"No, I —"

"Listen, I don't know what Emma Fine was doing at that campsite. And maybe it's Bridget, I don't know any more. But what I do know is that the trial is over. It's been ten fucking years. Give it a rest. Besides, Emma Fine took off and no one knows where she is."

There is silence around them, as if the mountain has suddenly sucked in all the noise a small subdivision can make. And then, from down the block, a door slams and some kids start shouting at each other.

"I know where she is," Bruce whispers.

It takes a moment for Dan to register this whisper. "You

what?" He stands up, almost knocks over his chair. "You've seen her? Where? When?"

Bruce looks at the dying sun. He looks down the road and for the first time notices that there are no trees on the side of this mountain. There are small shrubs and green lawns and flower gardens but no massive trees, no shade to keep the sun off the houses. And then he notices that every third house is the same house. As if spacing them out like this will hide the fact that they are identical. Bruce supposes the spacing did hide that fact for a while, for an hour or so, but if you look up from the hot pavement, for a minute, your mind registers the uniformity. Suddenly Bruce feels as if he's on a movie lot, he's somehow stepped into a studio and everything is unreal, plastic. Dan's son rides past them on his bicycle, a swarming group of other kid bicyclists surrounding him, and Bruce wonders if his life is nothing but a giant Hollywood concoction. Maybe all of California has been made from foam and plastic and paint and cardboard. Maybe there is no ground under his feet, no sky above his head. And then, of course, Bruce remembers a movie that dealt with this theme, a man in a bubble world not knowing that his existence was only a prime-time television show, and Bruce thinks that everything in life moves around in circles so quickly that time often feels like it's standing still.

Bruce stands from his chair. His feet are slightly swollen from the heat, from the beer. He feels hobbled. Turning, he puts his hand out to Dan who is still standing, looking confused.

"Thanks for the beer and your time," Bruce says. "I appreciate it."

"She's in town? In L.A.?"

Bruce starts to walk down the driveway to his car. He is limping slightly as he gets the feeling back in his feet, as the swelling dissipates. He feels so old suddenly. Dan follows after him.

"Where is she? You've got to tell me where she is."

"I'll be in touch, Dan," Bruce says as he gets into his car.

Dan pounds on the window but Bruce locks the door and starts the engine. He looks at Dan's face. Frayed, frantic, excited, worried. "You've got to tell me where she is," Dan mouths to Bruce. He pounds some more.

Bruce backs the car up and then drives around Dan and down the street. In his rear-view mirror he sees Dan standing there, at the foot of his driveway, a beer in his hand, his shoulders fallen. And farther off, in the distance, Bruce can see a line of small boys on bicycles, a posse of boys, riding closer to the man, closer, until they come upon him, swerve around him, and continue on. Dan stands there, unflinching. He raises his hand to Bruce's car. A weak wave. A salute. He climbs back up his driveway and sits again in his folding chair in front of his house. Bruce feels he doesn't know much. He doesn't know where Emma has gone, for example, but he does know three things for certain: that Susie is still staring out the window, that the beer is still warm, and that Pink Floyd is still loud and strong.

Chapter Twenty Four

Emma keeps putting her hand in her purse and pulling out pills. She doesn't know what she is taking and she doesn't care. The party is boring. Loud, obnoxious men surround her. Emma pushes her breasts out and stands tall but she still feels young in her flowing summer dress. She wishes she were wearing stiletto shoes and a push-up bra, at least, something that made her feel more desirable. No pain, no gain, she thinks, as she pops another pill. Why is it that the men in her life seem to like those shoes, high spiky things, and thong underwear, and underwire bras? Torture. Emma thinks that maybe she would like to go camping with Ted. Wear no makeup. Put her hair in a ponytail. Slip a loose pair of jeans on, some hiking boots, maybe not even wear a bra. But her breasts. They'd sag without support. And, Emma thinks, her lips are pale as ghosts without her red lipstick. She could go a day or two without doing her nails, but thinking about even one day without showering makes her sweat.

Emma strolls over to the bar. She orders another drink, she's had far too much, she knows, and then sees a couch in the corner and asks the bartender to bring her drink over there. He complies and soon she is sitting cozy on the blue velvet, her legs crossed, one hand inside her purse fingering the pills, the other hand holding her Manhattan. The pills feel different. The capsules are of varying lengths and thickness, they feel nothing like the drugs she normally takes. A Manhattan in L.A., she thinks. Typical. She hopes Ted hasn't bought her the wrong drugs. Or Dan. And then, suddenly, she hopes one of them did buy the wrong ones and that she's going to overdose and die. Right here at the goddamn party. A Marilyn Monroe ending to a glamorous life.

Glamour? Emma is lonely. Lonely and cold and tired. The couch is soft. She wants to lie down but here come the director and her co-star and soon she is in the middle of a conversation about whose tits are bigger, hers or Sarah's, the director's assistant. Sarah walks over and somehow Emma and Sarah are standing in the corner, their backs to the crowded room, pushing their breasts out against the fabric of their dresses. The director and co-star are nodding, pretending to measure with hands, playing at seriousness. Sarah and Emma are laughing. But Emma doesn't know why she too is laughing. Two men are comparing her breasts to another woman's breasts, both fake, she is sure, in a room full of movie stars, and her mind tells her this isn't funny but her mouth is strained and laughing.

Stripping was an addiction she solved with moviemaking. Hey, watch me. I'm up here onstage and all eyes should be on me. But moviemaking is no different from stripping, Emma thinks.

And then she moves away from the director who has acquired a noticeable bulge in his pants, who is stoned and drunk, and heads off with her co-star to the bathroom to do some coke. She came to hate her co-star during the filming of the movie, but a few shared lines of coke, she is sure, will make him seem wonderful and perfect.

"Only a line or two," Emma says, but her voice is separate from her mouth, seems to be floating somewhere to the left of her ear, seems disconnected and lower and raspy. "I've got to go camping in the morning." She laughs.

The co-star locks the private bathroom door and Emma sits on the counter and they do a line or two, or three or four, and they laugh and then he touches her thigh and moves his hand up her naked leg to her underwear and she lets him. She wants him to do it. She doesn't think of Ted at home. The star takes her underwear off gently. Emma spreads her legs and leans back so that she is sitting on the base of her spine, and the actor, the married actor, the actor with two kids, unzips his pants and pulls himself out of his fly, enters her, and they screw in the bathroom with the compact mirror still in his hands, the lines of coke balanced carefully on top. But the actor gets rough and mean suddenly and has thrown down the mirror and is squeezing Emma's breasts so hard that the ache is palpable even over all the drugs in her system. "You like that, don't you?" he hisses and she sees his hands there, grasping, pulling, bruising her breasts, she feels the squeeze, but it's as if she is looking down from a great distance. She can barely hear him. And then she passes out and the actor kneads her breasts like hard dough. He leans Emma back carefully on the counter. He stands there, cleaning himself up, and he looks at her. Then he takes a piece of glass from the floor and, very lightly, traces three small lines into her upper thighs, near her vagina. He watches the small beads of her blood and then he leaves the bathroom and enters back into the party, smiling, happy, the famous movie star. Emma, lying on the counter, stays passed out for a while and only wakes briefly.

And Emma moves in and out of consciousness. Emma's mind is somewhere far gone, away from all of this. She feels nothing but numbness, a beautiful sense of self-worth, a floating, careening, flying feeling. Warmth wraps her up and massages her. Emma's eyes open and close, but she sees only the square ceiling tiles and smells flowers and vanilla and baking cookies.

But when the cleaning staff comes in, after the party is over, there is no one in the bathroom. Just broken glass, fine white powder, and a hell of a lot of Kleenexes and cigarette stubs in the garbage cans and toilets.

Dan, helping Emma out of the party, feels like attacking

the lot of them. The smiling, fake movie stars and directors and producers, drinking champagne, eating smoked salmon and asparagus tips. All of them going about their business while Emma Fine lies on the counter of the bathroom, passed out. How could no one have helped her? How could no one have noticed she was gone? His eyes tear as he helps Emma into the back seat, as he lies her down on the leather and strokes her hair and whispers that everything will be all right.

He drives her towards home. It is two in the morning. He circles around, up the mountain, until he comes to the look-out. There he stops the car and turns to look at Emma. Her mouth is open. There is a line of drool down her chin. A small bit of blood crusted on her nose from the coke she snorted. Dan gets out of the driver's side and goes around to the back. He climbs in. He puts Emma's head on his lap and strokes her hair. There, atop the mountain, all of Los Angeles glowing beneath him, Dan begins to cry. The sound starts deep within him, the tears well and spill. He cries so hard he thinks he pulls several stomach muscles, the gut-wrenching sobs pouring out of him. Emma doesn't wake. She lies there in his lap and then she grunts and rolls towards him, her mouth inches from his penis which instantly reacts and makes Dan angry. Emma Fine's mouth. Her green dress open almost to her waist. Her naked hip jutting out. Her underwear missing, left behind in the bathroom. Her full breasts heavy upon his thigh.

This is what she is, Dan thinks. This is what she stands for. Sex. Emma Fine's body, her beauty, makes her good for nothing but sex.

He eases her mouth up against the bulge in his pants and he rubs himself up and down.

For all the times she paraded naked around him.

For all the men she's fucked when she hasn't given him the time of day.

For the skinny-dipping in the pool at night when she thinks no one is looking.

For the movies where her body is airbrushed and steamy.

Dan climbs back into the driver's side of the car and starts the engine. Emma's lips are rough from rubbing against his pants. Dan drives her up to the doorway, and with the lights out, stealthily carries her inside, lies her on the front-hall carpet. She will wake in the morning and make her way up the stairs to her bedroom. She won't know what happened, he assures himself. He will tell her that he drove her home, that she passed out at the party, that she insisted she was all right, and that she wanted to walk up the stairs alone. He will tell her that he tried to help her to bed but she refused. She told him to go away. Ted is upstairs, sleeping, and Dan doesn't want to look him in the eye. He thinks Ted will know what he has done if he looks him in the eye. Dan closes the door behind him, automatically locking it, and gets back into the car, starts the engine, and drives to his girlfriend's houseboat. He makes love to her and then leaves the houseboat. He walks out onto the pier. He looks down into the water. Cheryl sleeps in the rocking boat with a pillow up to her back. She thinks Dan is there behind her, still in the blackness of the night.

At Emma's house a sound from the street, Dan's car pulling off perhaps, wakes Ted from his deep sleep and he looks out the bedroom window and sees nothing. He tiptoes down the stairs and finds Emma passed out in the hall.

It doesn't surprise him to see her like this. After all the pills and shit she put in her purse before the party. She was drinking too. But Ted wonders why Dan didn't bring her up the stairs and then he thinks that the driver must have raped her, roughed her up, and then left. Ted thinks for a minute. He stands there, watching her, and he thinks. Then he picks her up and carries her outside by his truck. He sits her down on the pavement and brushes the hair from her face, checks her over, looks at her condition. He feels her pulse and listens to her breathing. He shakes his head. Ted opens the door of his truck and takes his cellphone out of the glove compartment. He makes a phone call. Then he sits down beside the slumped-over Emma Fine and he waits.

Ted isn't nervous. He isn't worried. He feels no guilt. He glances at the house only once and sees that the only light on is the one coming from the window in the master bedroom. It's a good time, Ted thinks. It's better this way. Ted suddenly feels a strange sense of peacefulness. He feels as if he's in church, as if beautiful hymns are washing over him, as if sunlight is streaming through stained glass and warming his soul.

A car pulls up to the gate and Ted lays Emma down on the pavement, looks at her once, and then stands and walks quickly into the house. He buzzes the gate open, using his shirt to cover his fingerprints. He waves at the driver of the car. Signals to where Emma Fine is lying. Then he shuts the door behind him, locks it, and climbs the stairs to Emma's bedroom. Outside he can hear the car in the driveway, the engine idling. He refuses to look out the window. Ted turns the light off and climbs into bed again. He thinks a bit about the morning. About the condominium buildings he has to check on before he leaves for camping. He thinks about how this may be the last goddamn time he has to set foot in one of those shelled out, poorly constructed things. The next time he's in a condo it will probably be one he owns in southern France. It will have high ceilings and curtains that billow through the glass doors in the wind. Before Ted falls asleep he thinks about how it's ironic that everything will soon be over, but then again, everything will be just starting. One phase in his life done, gone. Another about to start.

His plan has changed slightly, become easier. She didn't want to go camping. It would have been hard to persuade her. Besides, it's always easier to deal with someone passed out than someone fully awake. Nothing can go wrong, he thinks.

Ted falls asleep. The car pulls out of the driveway and drives quietly, lights off, down the darkened street.

Part Nine

Photo of Emma Fine from the paper as she is led from the courthouse by two plainclothes security officers. She is smiling at the cameras, waving at a fan standing on the corner, holding open an autograph book. The plainclothes officers are leading her towards a black limousine. The caption under the photo says, "Emma Fine in good form for closing remarks."

MR. REYNOLDS: Dr. Snider, to continue with your testimony, I am going to ask you to refer to the psychiatric report you wrote regarding Ms. Emma Fine's behaviour after she was found in the alley.

A. Yes.

Q. I'm going to ask you to turn to page two where you mention her childhood and the narcissistic attitude she displayed during your meeting.

A. Yes.

Q. Checking her lipstick, smoothing down her hair.

A. Yes. I see that in many of my more well-known clients.

Q. Yes, your curriculum vitae says that you treat many of the stars in West Hollywood.

A. They make up most of my practice.

Q. So her behaviour was not unusual?

A. Not in the real sense, no. But because she had just experienced such trauma and because she was involved in a murder --

MR. WRIGHT: Objection. The witness has implied that my client had something to do with the murder.

JUDGE LIONS: Overruled. The witness is implying no such thing. Ms. Fine was a part of the murder in that it took place in her pool. The jury is smart enough to understand the difference.

MR. REYNOLDS: Needless to say, the defendant had just gone through a traumatic experience. She had gone missing for several days and had come back in a bad condition.

A. Yes.

Q. So you thought her behaviour was ...?

A. A bit odd. She seemed wholly unconcerned with the state of her affairs. She answered questions pleasantly enough but was, on the most part, very nonchalant about everything. It was as if I was asking her about her shopping list.

Q. And what did you make of this?

A. Well, I think it relates to the fact that Ms. Fine has always been surrounded by trauma. Drugs, alcohol, for Ms. Fine, were a way out of her life, a way to avoid reality. Hence, the overdose that led to her disappearance and subsequent amnesia. Ms. Fine's way of coping with the events in her life, things she can't deal with, is by using drugs or alcohol or persistently and repeatedly forgetting horrible experiences.

Q. Are you saying that she is doing this on purpose?

A. No. She doesn't know she is doing this. She really is forgetting the events that led up to her disappearance. She is forgetting what she may or may not have seen happen in her pool --

MR. WRIGHT: Objection.

JUDGE LIONS: Sustained. It's speculation. No harm intended, I'm sure.

Q. And the narcissism?

A. Yes, well, I think that for the rest of us, all of this -- this publicity, this trial, the psychiatric assessments, and such -- would be traumatic and we would react differently. But Ms. Fine is used to this kind of thing. As a matter of fact, her life has always been full of this kind of scrutiny. So her behaviour in my office was normal. Her behaviour was normal for her.

Q. So, to sum up, you are saying that although we all think of her behaviour during questioning as inappropriate, lacking remorse, etc., she is really sticking true to her character. Acting only the way she can act, faced with the constant pressure of public scrutiny that is her daily life?

A. I, uh, I guess I'm saying that.

Q. Yes or no.

A. Yes.

Q. Thank you, Dr. Snider. That will be all.

Billboard Directly Outside the Courthouse

"You Only Have One Life To Live: Get the straight facts about drugs and alcohol."

Chapter Twenty Five

"Who killed Ted Weaver? Where is Bridget McGovern's body?"

"Now that would be a more interesting story."

"I can't understand it."

Bruce and Will are sitting on Bruce's patio, having a beer. The sun is setting over the clay tile roof of the house directly behind.

"I can't believe you've let the garden get this out of hand. It looks like shit down there."

"It is shit. Cat shit. Every cat in the neighbourhood thinks it's a litter box."

"I can see why. It looks like a large public toilet to me. Lots of privacy in among the weeds."

"Why do you think that solving the murder is a more interesting story than the fact that Emma Fine has been working as a maid for a catholic church for seven years?"

"Because no one really cares any more about Emma Fine, Bruce. And Ted was a nobody who screwed a princess and then died. Much more interesting. People like blood. If she had murdered Ted, then people would have cared. Then she would still be big news."

"I think," Bruce says, "that Bridget killed Ted Weaver. I'm pretty sure."

"Bridget? The wife?"

"Yes."

"But she's dead, isn't she? Did they ever find who killed her?"

"No, she's not dead," Bruce says.

"What? Hey, look, there is a cat shitting in your yard."

Bruce looks down from the railing and watches as a white cat squats over by his old patio furniture.

"I think Emma Fine is dead."

"What the hell are you talking about? You've been talking to her for the past couple of weeks."

"I'm starting to think that was Bridget."

"Have another beer, Bruce. You're sounding drunker than you are. At least drink more so that you sound normal."

"No, really, listen. I think I'm figuring it out. Dan said that it isn't Bridget in the pamphlet from the campsite but I'm convinced that it is. It can't have been Emma. Emma was too fucked up after that cast party. And Maria, the maid, said that a freckle was missing on her knuckle. I think Bridget came back as Emma."

"What are you, a private dick?" Will laughs at himself.

"Bridget and Ted were going to kill Emma. They had planned to kill her on the camping trip and substitute Bridget for Emma."

"Sure, whatever," Will says. "And, look, there's a UFO in the sky."

"Hear me out. The plastic surgery. The hair dye. They would come back to L.A. and no one would have been the wiser. They could have fired Dan, fired Maria, liquidated Emma's money, went into a bit of reclusive hiding, that kind of thing, until everyone forgot about Emma Fine. Until they didn't care about her any more. She would, of course, stop acting. She would say she was just going to focus on her new lover. Have a baby maybe. I don't know. By all accounts Bridget McGovern couldn't act. Emma Fine could."

"And what about the body? What about Bridget's identity? Dan knew Ted was married to Bridget. So did Maria. So did half the world after that picture in *Entertainment Weekly*."

"Yeah, well." Bruce thinks. "Maybe they burned the body

or hid it in the mountains somewhere. No one would be looking for Emma's body because she wouldn't really be dead, right? I was up at Mt. Trellis. It's a huge place. Lots of wildlife willing to eat fresh meat, I'm sure. And then Bridget? Well, maybe Ted could just claim that they got divorced and that she went to Canada or something. The only person who would be concerned about that would be Dan and they had already split up long before the murder. He wouldn't really care at all."

"Media, you moron. Everyone would want to know who this Ted Weaver was. Who was the man who finally captured the sex object? Don't you think they would dig into his past life?"

"But the police tried digging. Ted and Bridget had no past. They destroyed everything. He had no living relatives. She had no living relatives. No friends. No past lives."

"Hoboes. Riding the rails."

"Exactly. They spent years wiping themselves off the face of the earth."

"You're warped, Dermott. No one can completely change their appearance to look exactly like someone else. It wouldn't work."

"But they could alter themselves enough, maybe. Shit, things can be done. Plastic surgery is incredible. Have you ever seen the pictures, before-and-after pictures? I was looking at a picture in the paper the other day of Pamela Ackinson's stunt double. She's had herself surgically altered to look like the movie star. It's eerie."

Bruce goes into the house and grabs two more beers. His face is flushed from excitement.

"You forgot some very important things, Mr. Detective," Will says.

"Like what?"

"Well, what went wrong? Who killed the plan before it could happen? Literally. And, if you really want to get into it, if you think that was Bridget you saw, then why was Bridget found in an alley, battered and an amnesiac? Who did that? Explain that, Mr. Smart-guy."

"Yeah, well. The theory has holes right now."

"And what about all the blood you were telling me about? They found Bridget's blood, didn't they?"

"You can take blood from yourself. Store it. If this whole thing was planned."

"Yeah, I can see Bridget at night with a needle in her arm, pumping blood into little Glad sandwich bags, and then pouring it out over her clothes and stuffing them in her car in a mall parking lot."

Bruce grins. "That's perfect. That would work." He holds the beer to his lips. "Why not?"

"So who killed Ted, then?" Will says. "And where is Emma Fine's body?"

"I don't know. And if the cops' theory is right, then where is Bridget's body? Maybe Bridget just wanted it all for herself. Maybe that's why she killed Ted."

"What the hell for? If what you're saying is even remotely right, and, by the way, if pigs can fly, then they were doing it together out of some sort of psychotic love for each other. Your theory takes years and years of planning. If Bridget was a traitor, Ted would have discovered that."

"But she was an actress, right?"

"A wannabe actress. Remember those commercials she was in? The ones they ran over and over after the murder? She sucked."

"For the plan to work," Bruce says, sitting back, lightheaded, "she wouldn't get to act any more. Maybe she wanted to act. Maybe Ted said she couldn't act any more. I don't know. Maybe Ted was abusive, maybe the jealousy over Emma Fine was just too much. There are tons of reasons to kill someone you love. Hell, I've heard about people who kill people because their peas weren't salted properly or because their toast was buttered instead of plain."

Will looks at Bruce. "That's bullshit. The whole story is crazy. We live in L.A. so you make up a story that's worthy of Hollywood. What the hell are you, Bruce? A film producer? Besides, if you could come up with this scenario in a month, why the hell couldn't a thousand police come up with it in ten years? And where is the missing body then? Either Bridget's or Emma's? One thin, drugged-out woman, either Emma or Bridget, is not capable of all this alone. Not capable of killing a big man, killing another woman, getting rid of the body, knocking herself around to look dazed and overdrugged, and then coming back and faking amnesia? That's bullshit."

"She wouldn't knock herself around. If she was drugged out, there is a huge possibility someone roughed her up. She was in an alley, for God's sake. Besides, I told you I don't have it all figured out yet. The pieces almost fit."

"Ha." Will swigs back his beer. "Almost fit? It looks like a puzzle filled with holes. Look, Bruce. I've been helping you and financing you and now you've got to write something. You tell me that you've chased away our only photo opportunity and that you weren't even sure that she was really the person you thought she was. Where the hell do we go from here?"

Bruce looks again at his yard. He swigs his beer. He burps.

"Everything is falling apart around me. Two drug-addicted women. It's ironic, really. They became each other." Bruce sighs. "I just want everything to fit, you know. My family, this story."

Will stands. "This is no time to have a breakdown, Bruce. You need a vacation. You need to take some time off. You need to write something and then cut your grass and get rid of those cats."

"Yeah," Bruce says. "You're right."

Chapter Twenty Six

A day later, Bruce is placing his suitcases by the front door. Waiting for the cab to take him to the airport. The phone rings.

"Hey," Will says. "How are you doing now? Figured anything out?"

"Yeah," Bruce says. "I'm leaving."

"Where?"

"I'm going up to Canada to help out with the kids for a while. I might move there. I was thinking I should be close to them."

"Calgary?"

"Yeah, Calgary."

"Stampedes, guns, horses. The Wild West."

"Skiing," Bruce says. "Snow."

"Shit, snow. Well, write up your piece and send it down to me. Just write anything. We'll publish it, give you some money. We'll treat it as rumoured hearsay. We'll stir up some controversy."

"I was thinking of writing a book, actually. Write it all down."

"Well, Bruce, if you want some money, turn it into a quick piece. Writing a book with no plot, no proof, no tangible evidence, will get you nothing. You'll be living out there with those cats in your backyard soon enough."

Bruce nods his head. He looks out the back window. In the garden the white cat sits upon the old furniture, inches from his shit, and cleans himself. He licks his balls, his feet.

He licks his paws which he then rubs on his ears. Bruce thinks he looks a bit like a snake. The long, triangular face. The flat-back ears, the thin body. Bruce shivers.

"Stay in touch," Will says.

"I will."

Bruce hangs up the phone and stretches.

Turning to the kitchen to get a drink of water, he sees her standing in his front hallway. The door is open. Her presence is unmistakable, as if a gust of air had moved through the house. As if snow has burst through the door. Bruce would have known she was there even if he had been blind. Bruce stands still. He stares. She stares back. She is wearing a colourful summer dress and sandals, her hair full around her face.

"Can I come in?" she whispers.

"You already did. How'd you get in?"

"The door was open. Can I talk to you?"

"Yes, sure. Come outside." Bruce watches her walk towards him. He studies her. She walks past him and goes outside. She sits down.

"I thought you were gone. I assumed you had left."

"I thought I was too."

"But you came back?"

"Only for a while," she says. "Only to talk to you."

"Me? I'm flattered." Bruce sits down. He looks out at his garden. The white cat is gone.

"The church did something to me," she says.

"Taught you about fate, I guess."

"Yes, and guilt."

Bruce laughs. "Everyone knows about guilt. They just ignore it."

"I didn't know anything about guilt before," she says. Her blonde hair glows in the sunlight. Bruce looks at her left hand and sees that there is nothing on her middle finger at the knuckle. There is no freckle.

"My life was pretty much guilt-free," she says. "Everything

was done to me. I didn't do that much."

"That's not possible."

"No, really. That's how I felt, at least."

"Yeah, well ..."

"All those men. Fucking me around. Fucking me. I really hated men but I didn't know it, you know. I hated them. Everyone played with me, treated me like a toy. There was no Emma Fine, there was only a body."

"So you killed Bridget? You killed Ted?"

She looks at Bruce. She doesn't say anything. Bruce can't read her face. It's expressionless.

"Or are you Bridget?"

"I came here," she says, "to ask you not to write anything about me. To ask you to reach into your soul and take out whatever compassion you may have. To please leave my life alone. I need to be left alone and able to live in the real world now. I can't go back to the church. I have no friends. No family."

"I need to make money," Bruce says. "I have my career to think about."

"I can pay you. I haven't been entirely honest with you. I have some money."

"Of course you do," Bruce sighs. "Of course you haven't been honest. What about my career? My name. This is a big story. What about my reputation? I have kids, you know. I'd like them to look up to me. I want to write a book."

"You don't want a name, Bruce. Believe me. Stay away from this. Besides, do your children want to look up to a man who ruined another person's life? You've already messed with their lives."

"What do you mean by that?" Bruce sits forward in his chair.

"You are free to do what you want. I just want to be left alone."

"I want answers."

"I can't give you answers. I don't know the answers."

"You can. I know you can. You know what happened."

"Bruce, I won't give you answers."

"Who are you?"

"Who the hell do you think I am? I'm Emma Fine. A movie star. A maid. A woman whose lover was murdered in her pool. Take your pick."

"You're a good actor, whoever you are. I know that."

"That's all I ever wanted to be." She stands. She smoothes her dress in front of her body. Bruce looks again at her face, he studies it. It's amazing what age and stress can do to a person. All the inner beauty that was there before, that Bruce connected with when Shelley left, the inner glow that gave Bruce some sort of hope, is gone. Now the face is grey. Neutral. Awash with nothing. Bruce can't read her.

"Besides," she says. "People will believe only what they want to believe. They will believe whatever they need to believe. Just like you. You believe what people feed you. You believed for a while that my screen personality had something to do with your marriage breakup."

"Where did you get that idea?"

"It's in everything you've told me, Bruce. Everything you've said about your family, about the importance of this story, about the meaning it will give your life." She laughs. "A story about me — it will give your life meaning? That's ridiculous."

"Not meaning. It will give me a story. Something to write about, *really* write about."

She looks at him with pity in her eyes.

"I could give them the truth, you know," Bruce says. "People want the truth. What really happened that morning by your pool. Where you were."

"There is no truth. No absolute truth. You know that. You know that like you know you won't write about me. You're a decent person, Bruce. You won't ruin my life."

"Is that what you think of me? You think I'm decent? Is that why you talked to me?"

"It was nice to have someone to talk to again," she says as she turns to leave. "It's always nice to be able to say what you think."

"Say what you think? You said nothing." Bruce stands. He tries to reach for her hand but she is too far ahead.

"It's your decision," she says before she walks through the house and out the front door, out of Bruce's life forever. "You do what you think is best. Just remember. All it comes down to is this: Ted Weaver is dead. Bridget McGovern is dead. There's nothing you or I can do to change that. Just think about it. A coronor's signature on a dotted line. Dead. Everything comes down to that."

Bruce is rooted to the floor. The door closes softly behind her. She is right, he thinks. It doesn't matter.

And she is gone.

A cab pulls up outside of the townhouse. A beep of the horn. Bruce opens the door, watches Emma Fine stroll purposefully down the street. The cab driver is standing up beside his open cab door, also watching her walk away. His mouth is open, his eyes wide. Bruce waves to the driver and then takes one last look around his home. He goes to the back door, locks it, stares at the cat outside, moves once around the kitchen, living room, out through the hallway, closes the front door, and continues down the steps to the walk. The tanning woman is lying there. Bruce stops and says goodbye.

"Where are you going?" she says, rolling onto her back and squinting up at the sun.

"To see my kids," Bruce says, as he loads his suitcases into the cab. "I just need to see them right now."

"Oh." The woman adjusts her bathing suit. She closes her eyes. Her voice is lazy and warm. "It's the little things like that, kids, family, that mean the most, isn't it? We sometimes forget." She chuckles lightly. "It's so easy just to forget." She raises her hand to wave. "Have a good time now. I'll watch your house for you."

As Ted Weaver is being pushed and dragged the few inches towards the pool — the searing pain in his head, the feeling that he's been lifted high up in the air, the slumping of his body on the hard surface of the ground — he looks up and he sees her there before him. She is smiling down at him. Her legs are long. She is wearing lipstick. Almost unconscious, fading in and out, he thinks it's odd that she's wearing lipstick to kill him. He is looking at her running shoes and he is thinking that they are brand new, that he's never seen them before. He wonders where she bought them. Which one is she? The hooded sweatshirt. He can't see her hair. He knows that he is dying. He wants to think of his mother and father, his brother, Ed, who was killed in the lake in front of their cottage, his dogs, Johnny, Piper, Lucky, all hit by cars. Shouldn't he be thinking about his wedding, about making love to the women in his life? The woman above him. Her hair. He needs to see her hair. He tries to call out. He tries to open his mouth but the force of the blow has paralysed him. Shouldn't he be remembering the feeling of the hot sun on his neck, the splash and paddle of the canoe, the loon calls, the fishing? Who is pushing him into the pool? He peers up, his vision blurred. He created one of them but he can't tell them apart. The horror of the situation sinks in, moves around Ted's body. He has done this to himself. The two women have become one. Ted feels his body scrape the edge of the pool, sees her again smiling down at him. There are tears in her eyes. Are there tears in her eyes? The sun is hot and full on his face, his eyes barely open. Take two women and mix them together. It's an evil concoction, a witches' brew. And then the splash and he is in the lake again, swimming with his brother, two kids racing together to the dock. His father laughing on the shore, cheering them on. His mother calling out from the clothesline, the sheets flapping out in the wind. His mother's face becoming Bridget's face. And then Emma's face. A movie star's face, blazing with the fierceness of fame. And then Ted makes it first to the dock, climbs up, the sun bright around him, and reaches down to pull Ed up, to use his big-brother hand to take hold of the boy's little fingers, and pull him on board the raft into the sun. They lie together on the raft, side by side, their wet arms touching all the way up to their shoulders, their matching swim trunks drying in the heat. And Ted's father, from the shore, fixing the sail on his windsurfer, shouts out, "Don't look straight into the sun, boys. The bright light will damage your eyes. You could go blind with all that brilliance shining down."

Appendix

THEODORE SIMON WEAVER A-19—-156

REPORT OF POSTMORTEM EXAMINATION

A-19—-156
Made upon the body of **THEODORE SIMON WEAVER** at Hollywood Central Hospital, 224 Ridley Street, Hollywood, California, U.S.A., on the 17th day of July of 19—, about 1 day after death pronounced.

Place where death pronounced: Hollywood Central Hospital
Examination commenced: 16.35 hrs.
Required by Coroner: Dr. Hugo L. Vago

IDENTIFICATION
The body was identified to me by:
2 ID tags one attached to body bag and the other attached to body's R great toe, both read:
Tag number: 36952
Name: Theodore Simon Weaver
Birthdate: August 28, 19—
Date of arrival: July 16, 19—
Identified by: Mrs. Maria Candalas, maid
Time and date of identification: July 16, 19—, 13.05 hrs.
Signed by: Dr. Hugo L. Vago
Witnesses: Detective Joe Maclean, badge No. 841, in the presence of Mr. Rudy Pick, morgue technician.

EXTERNAL EXAMINATION
Length: 6'1"
Weight: 190 lbs.
Sex: Male.
Temperature: Not measured.
Age: Consistent with documented age of 35 years.
Hair: Brown.
Eyes: Colour of irises: blue.
Sclerae: unremarkable.
Pupils: round, equal, each 5mm in diameter.
How nourished: Average, muscular.
Skin: "Washerwoman" appearance of hands and soles.
Widespread "goose flesh". No scars.
Rigor Mortis: Present.
Postmortem Staining: Dependent lividity on posterior areas mainly.
Decomposition: None noted.
Clothing and effects: Clothes: white tee-shirt, green work pants, black

belt, white socks, no shoes, red boxer-shorts. Valuables: Rolex watch, gold coloured on L wrist, wedding band, Gold coloured on L 4th finger.

EVIDENCE OF THERAPY: None.

EVIDENCE OF INJURY:
Head — R forehead: hematoma, 4.2 x 3.8 cm with underlying subcutaneous hematoma, 6.5 x 5.7 cm

INTERNAL EXAMINATION:
Chest:
Diaphragm: Intact.
Pleural Cavities: No significant effusions or adhesions. No metastatic disease.
Pericardium: No significant effusions or adhesions.
Mediastinum: No tumours or lymphadenopathy.

Face and Neck:
Mouth: Natural teeth. No mucosal abnormalities noted. Thick mucous hemorrhagic froth in mouth and at lips.
Nose: No evidence of fracture. Thick mucous hemorrhagic froth in nostrils.
Pharynx: Contains thick mucous hemorrhagic froth.
Tongue: No lacerations, hemorrhage or other evidence of injury.
Hyoid Bone: No evidence of fracture or hemorrhage.
Thymus: Not identified.
Thyroid: Unremarkable.

Respiratory System:
Larynx: See pharynx. Otherwise within normal limits.
Trachea: See pharynx. Otherwise within normal limits.
Bronchi: See pharynx. Otherwise within normal limits.
Pulmonary pleura: Few scattered petechiae. Otherwise unremarkable.
Pulmonary vessels: No evidence of thromboemboli.
Right lung: 850 gms. Large and bulky with evidence of pulmonary edema. No localized areas of pathology.
Left lung: 880 gms. Large and bulky with evidence of pulmonary edema. No localized areas of pathology.
Circulatory System:
Heart: 380 gms. Usual anatomic arrangement of chambers and great vessels noted.
Atria: No evidence of dilatation or hypertrophy.

Ventricles: No evidence of dilatation or hypertrophy.
Tricuspid valve: No vegetations or other significant abnormalities noted.
Pulmonary valve: No vegetations or other significant abnormalities noted.
Aortic valve: No vegetations or other significant abnormalities noted.
Mitral valve: No vegetations or other significant abnormalities noted.
Myocardium: No gross evidence of necrosis, scars or other localized lesions.
Coronary Vessels: No significant atherosclerosis or other gross pathology.
Aorta and large Vessels: No significant atheromatous change or other gross pathology.
Character of blood: Predominantly fluid.

Gastrointestinal system:
Esophagus: No mucosal abnormality noted.
Stomach and contents: No mucosal abnormality noted. Contains about 330 cc water mixed with semidigested paste-like food.
Intestine: Within normal limits. The appendix is unremarkable.
Liver: 1530 gms. Unremarkable cut surfaces. No localized lesions noted.
Gall Bladder: Present. No stones or other gross pathology.
Spleen: 320 gms. Unremarkable.
Pancreas: Unremarkable.
Mesenteric Lymph: No enlargement noted.

Nodes:
Peritoneal Space: No ascitic fluid, adhesions, hemorrhage or metastatic lesions noted.
Genito-Urinary system:
Adrenals: Unremarkable.
Urinary Bladder: No mucosal abnormalities. About 20cc of clear urine noted.
Kidneys and Ureters: No evidence of obstruction. The ureters are normal calibre.
Right: No significant nephrosclerosis. No localized lesions.
Left: No significant nephrosclerosis. No localized lesions.
Prostrate: Within normal limits.
Testes: Not examined.
Vagina and Vulva: Not applicable.
Uterus: Not applicable.
Tubes and Ovaries: Not applicable.

Head Skull and Osseus System:
Scalp: Hematoma, please see at evidence of injury. Otherwise unremarkable.
Meninges and Blood: No aneurysms, meningeal exudate or subarachnoid hemorrhage noted.

Vessels:
Skull: No fractures identified.
Middle ears and Sinuses: Not examined.
Remainder of Osseus System: Normal to palpation. No joint deformity noted.

Nervous System:
Brain: 1850 gms. Swollen with flattening of the gyri. Usual Anatomic arrangement noted. No recent or remote hemorrhage or infarction noted.
Hemispheres: Symmetrical with no localized lesions.
Ventricles: Unremarkable.
Pons: No hemorrhages or other localized lesions.
Cerebellum: No hemorrhages or other localized lesions.
Medulla: No hemorrhages or other localized lesions.
Pituitary body: Not examined.
Spinal cord: Not examined.
Remainder of Nervous System: Not specifically examined.

MICROSCOPY AND LABORATORY FINDINGS:
SIGNIFICANT MICROSCOPIC FINDINGS:
Heart — contraction bands
Lungs — pulmonary edema
Brain — edema, ischemic neurons and Purkinje cells
Kidneys, liver, spleen, adrenal and thyroid glands — no significant pathology

TOXICOLOGY:
The following postmortem specimens were taken:
— Two containers of blood: 1 W 35912 and 1 W 65821
— One container of urine: 1 W 32896
— One container of liver tissue: 1 W 32956
— One container of stomach contents: 1 W 12834
— One container of vitreous humour: 1 W 56921
— R femur: 1 W 23864

Neither the blood nor the urine showed significant ethyl alcohol concentration. General drug screen of blood was negative.

The diatoms of the femur were identical to those found in the swimming pool the body was recovered from.

SUMMARY OF ABNORMAL FINDINGS:

Head — skin, R forehead — hematoma 4.2 x 3.8 cm with underlying subcutaneous hematoma 6.5 x 5.7 cm.
Brain — congestion with ischemic neurons and Purkinje cells.
Heart — contraction bands.
Upper airways — froth, thick, mucous, hemorrhagic
Pleura, visceral — petechial hemorrhage
Lungs — pulmonary edema, R 850 gms, L 880 gms.
Skin — "washerwoman" appearance, hands and soles, "goose flesh" appearance, widespread.
Femur — diatoms, identical to diatoms of the swimming pool deceased found.

CAUSE OF DEATH:

This is to certify that I have examined the body, have opened and examined the above noted cavities and organs as indicated and that in my opinion the cause of death was:

ASPHYXIA SECONDARY TO DROWNING

Dated: July 16, 19—.

SIGNED:
Dr. Hugo L. Vago
Chief Forensic Pathologist
Hollywood Central Hospital
224 Ridley Street
Hollywood, California
U.S.A.